I0592627

THE WISH GIVER

THE TRUE MAGIC IS WHEN IT ALL COMES TOGETHER.

KAREN WEAVER

Copyright © 2018 Karen McDermott.
Editor Teena Raffa-Mulligan

All rights reserved. No part of this book may be used or reproduced by any means, graphic, electronic, or mechanical, including photocopying, recording, taping or by any information storage retrieval system without the written permission of the publisher except in the case of brief quotations embodied in critical articles and reviews.

This is a work of fiction. All of the characters, names, incidents, organizations and dialogue in this novel are either the products of the author's imagination or are used fictitiously.

Making Magic Happen Academy books may be ordered through booksellers or by contacting:
Making Magic Happen Academy
www.makingmagichappenacademy.com

Because of the dynamic nature of the Internet, any web addresses or links contained in this book may have changed since publication and may no longer be valid. The views expressed in this work are solely those of the author and do not necessarily reflect the views of the publisher and the publisher hereby disclaims any responsibility for them.

The intent of the author is only to offer information of a general nature to help you in your quest for emotional and spiritual well-being. In the event you use any of the information in this book for yourself, which is your constitutional right, the author and the publisher assume no responsibility for your actions.

ISBN: 978-0-6484525-7-7 (sc)
ISBN: 978-0-6484525-6-0 (e)
Printed in Australia

DEDICATION

To Mum and Dad.

I dedicate this book to you, in love and gratitude

for you both having dedicated most of your lives to me.

PREFACE

When the idea for this book found me, I had already started writing *The Memory Taker*. The knowing that there was a book to come before it was overwhelming and so I complied with the notion and *The Wish Giver* was born.

I have enjoyed the process immensely and discovered so much about myself as a writer. It was not quite the emotional rollercoaster of writing *The Visitor*, but it has a message all the same.

I wrote the first half of this story during the 2011 NaNoWriMo challenge and then put it aside to grow in my mind. When it was time to dust it off and get writing again it flowed without stopping. I worked on the principle of one thousand words a day for a few weeks and discovered this is the right balance for me as a busy mum.

I have come to realise that when I wish for something hard enough it will always make its way to me; but I have learned that life always creates balance.

Have you ever wondered what happens when you wish for something? Maybe by reading *The Wish Giver* you will understand that to allow something new to enter your life, something else has to make way for it.

ACKNOWLEDGEMENTS

I would like to express my gratitude to all of my family and friends for without your unwavering support and belief I would not be living my writing dream.

To all of my children – Dylan, Eithen, Kiera, Saoirse, Eimear and Mary – you are my inspiration and passion. Thank you.x

To Kieran, I am grateful for you, thank you for all of the learning.

Mum and Dad, I dedicate this book to you. You are very special people indeed. I am very blessed to have you guide me through my life.

To my brothers and sisters, thank you for your belief and your unwavering support.

My beautiful friends, Donna, Sascha and Jen. You are all so special to me; the positive energy we create is magical. Thank you for always being there. I am blessed.

To my forever friend, Tesha. Thank you for reading my manuscript and for keeping me motivated to keep going.

To Bill and Bev, thank you for continuing to be such a positive in our lives. We were truly sent a gift the day we met you.x

Finally, to Mildred, thank you for being so enlightening we hope that you are resting well with Bill in heaven.

CONTENTS

PROLOGUE

It all happens here in *The Waiting Zone*. Messengers are distributed to all corners of the universe to help needy souls move forward in life. There will be a time for everyone to encounter a messenger of some kind during their physical presence; some may even be lucky enough to encounter one after their evolution. One thing is for certain: these messengers leave their mark on the lives of the chosen few. It is often a bumpy ride but there will always be a changing point, one from which Spirituality can manifest. Advancement along the spectrum of being is easier because of the lessons learned.

Without us, the world would be a different place; we bring magic and sometimes tears. True happiness is what we all look for and in the pursuit of that happiness we may need to realign our thinking in order to achieve our highest potential.

The Boss holds the key that unlocks the well of enlightenment. It is through this source that wisdom is distributed. Wisdom is power and because he is the key holder, he is all knowing. Messengers are gifted enlightenment when they need it most and guided through their missions. As they assist others to connect with their inner self they become all knowing themselves. This is a true gift.

It is now time for *The Wish Giver* to make her presence felt. It may not appear like it for some but when the wishes are received with the right intention, the magic follows. '*Be careful what you wish for because you might just get it*' is a reminder to be conscious of our thoughts and the process that may occur to make way for those desires to manifest.

The true magic is when it all comes together.

CHAPTER ONE

Perspective

I have never ceased to be amazed by the selfish desires of others and the sacrifices they will make to have them fulfilled. Don't get me wrong; there are many who choose not to jeopardise what they have already had in abundance. They honestly request meaningful heartfelt wishes, of helping others and in the interests of genuinely bettering themselves without putting others' happiness in jeopardy. These people will be touched by the magic that is my coming. The others will be given the opportunity to listen to the signs I send their way indicating that what they desire may not be worth the sacrifice. Harsh that may be; however, there must be some sort of balance in humanity or selfishness will consume the human race. This would lead to a severe lack of enlightened souls reaching their inner potential to experience divine beauty beyond imaginable proportions.

True happiness comes from finding the treasure chest of abundance that is within us all. Sometimes we must reach a low point and that will guide us inward. Unless you have allowed yourself to discover your Aladdin's cave you will not understand my words. But when you find this treasure, it far overcomes any temporary high given by external materialistic pleasures. It is like receiving the true gift of life. Fulfilling happiness comes from self-discovery and that is why I stand in glory, when the opportunity finds me, to shine a beacon from the inner depths of humanity. It is an honour to be The Wish Giver in this instance; I know that if I had a wish I would use it to gift myself this way.

I can say that now because my being has turned full circle, but for many years I was The Wish Giver and still had a piece of my puzzle missing. However, I never gave up hope that I would one day reach completion; where I could let go of all past hurts and live wholly in the happiness of the now. The excitement of what each day may bring my way is a purposeful meaning that completes me. I am now in the knowing that I have reached my destination and can set up residence and enjoy what I have been sent. Some people may never reach this destination in a physical form or in afterlife. I count myself blessed to have opened myself to receiving this gift. It came only with the sacrifice of letting go of all past hurts and freeing myself to be content for all eternity.

Standing here in my heavenly sanctuary, I cannot help but smile as I look around at my surroundings and feel the life that grows within me. Yes, I have received a gift and it is not one that I have given myself. As The Wish Giver, I do not have the power to satisfy my own desires as and when I wish. No, this gift was sent to me as a wedding gift from my husband Rupert. He is now the Boss of the Waiting Zone, the place we have both called home for so long. We have served here hand in hand and now we have the opportunity to stand united to help so many others to serve and be rewarded accordingly. Many who find themselves here do so unknowingly. They are here with the intention of earning a place in Heaven, biding their time because they have arrived too early. But that is not our case; we are here to stay.

Until recently I used to think about worst case scenarios but since things have turned around for me, I know that beauty is here for us all to behold, no matter where we are in the spectrum of the universe. These lucky few that I will encounter have the opportunity to also turn things around for themselves. If what they wish for is what is meant for them on their spiritual path, then it is my pleasure to be forthcoming. However, if the desire is motivated by greed or selfishness it is my duty as The Wish Giver to offer an alternative choice. I will do my utmost to bring about a realisation and navigate each individual towards the serenity that is there for each and every being in the universe, should they choose to embrace it. Our minds and hearts are powerful beyond comprehension when they work in unison. Even those most fortunate will be rewarded with the opportunity of a partner with equal qualities and that will further enhance the power of this strength, creating divine supremacy beyond the realm of most intellectual capacity.

I am relaxing on my bouncy beanie, a gift from my devoted husband to assist me in getting comfortable as I progress through my pregnancy. How considerate he is! At times it is as if he is inside my mind, but I know he would not impose himself on my precious thoughts. It is a prime example that we are in unison and he knows my needs well. I sit here pondering the undertaking before me. I have now been honoured with the authority to grant wishes as I see fit. Being in unison with The Boss has its advantages; he is my right-hand man and I his left-hand woman, and we trust completely in each other's ability. This undivided trust is immeasurable in the advancement of all the missions commissioned by the Waiting Zone. We specialise in those proceedings that allow for advancement towards enlightenment, not pleasant at times, but sometimes what is worth having is not easily obtained.

As I am going to be out of service for some time when our special gift comes to join us, and the wishes still need to be distributed, I shall choose a successor. That will allow me to use my energies wholly to focus on supporting my husband and raising our daughter. Our gift will be like no other in the universe because she will be born here, and I have been informed this has never happened before. Our gift created from the most amazing circumstances will shine brightly, as it will be the first and only unique special descendant and have extraordinary supremacy throughout every domain. I shall not think too much about that now as I want our baby to be 'normal' even though she will not be born into a 'normal' situation.

I look around in gratitude and try my best to let go of any procrastination that at times overwhelms me. But I can't help wondering how I have been so lucky to be in receipt of such beauty and abundance in all areas of my life. I have this wonderful home that more than fulfils all of my needs and desires. I have a wonderful husband who completes me, and our hearts beat as one; and I am expecting the child that not even in my wildest dreams I ever thought possible.

Beep... Beep... Beep... Beep... My messenger lets me know it is time to prepare myself for the meeting.

I must get a move on or I will not be ready in time. The special meeting will begin soon, and I do not want to let Rupert down. He works so hard to keep things working efficiently in this realm.

My thoughts are interrupted by the ringing of my phone and I answer it.

"Hello, Sydney speaking."

"Hello, Syd, my precious, is everything running all right for you? I can set the meeting back if you need a little more time."

"No, Rupert, I'll be there on time. I promise, honey, I won't let you down."

"That's wonderful, precious, but don't be rushing now. I will wait for you."

"Okay, Roo, but I must go now or I will be late."

"Calm down, precious. We don't want to upset your body when you are incubating something so special."

"Oh, Roo, I know you mean well, honey, but please stop fussing. Everything will be fine; you know that as well as anyone . . . Okay, hanging up now. I'll see you soon."

"Are you sure you don't want me to . . ."

I hang up the phone.

I have never thought of Roo as the over protective type but since we found each other he has treated me like a porcelain doll. All very nice at the start but after a while, constant attention and shielding from any possible harm can get pretty intense. I know it all stems from love and possibly his previous experience of pregnancy, so I shouldn't be so tough on him. Maybe I should be more compassionate because we may never have the opportunity again to have another.

I get ready super-fast. Today I choose to wear something special: a full-length peach dress that I must admit complements my figure and shows my ever so slight yet ever so loved emerging bump. I got Dana to make it especially for me, and Rupert doesn't know about it, or the surprise dinner at Dave's place that I have arranged for his Entrance Day (the anniversary of his arrival here). We have known each other for thirty-five years and been united for one, so cause to celebrate.

I sit at my elegant vanity table. The cushioned seat is the most comfortable place imaginable to sit, and it hugs my bottom. The mirror frames my outline perfectly and seems to enhance my good features. It is as if it was made especially for me. Come to think of it, it probably was as the Boss before Rupert did not have his wife with him. He left here to join her at the gates to Heaven. Oh, this is a beautiful realisation. I top up my ruby red lipstick and indulge in one more squirt of the floral mist that I adore. I check my watch to ensure I am on time and am surprised to discover I am early, so decide to fix the little blonde curl that doesn't look right.

I hook in the curler again; it won't take long as I was using it not so long ago. See, looking better already. Oh no! I can't get it out. It's stuck. Okay, think, think, think... Breathe, think calm thoughts. My hair is burning so switch off the curling tongs. I try to prise my singed locks from the device but to no avail. I check my watch. I am now late. What am I going to do? I can't arrive with this stuck to my head, although I doubt that Roo would be surprised. Oh, why does this always happen to me?

Knock. Knock. Someone is at the door.

"Who is it?" I ask as I am unable to distinguish who it is through the peep hole.

"It's Joyce, Rupert asked me to make sure you got to the meeting safely and when I see that you . . ."

I open the door and pull her straight in.

Immediately she grabs the tongs and fiddles with them a little and *voila!* My hair is released.

"How did you do that?"

"Let's just say it is my job to help when I can."

I give her the biggest hug. "Oh, thank you, Joyce, you are amazing."

I quickly grab my shawl and we leave together. I am now chaperoned to the meeting so that I cannot fail to arrive.

"My pleasure, Sydney, I am all too happy to help. I must say you are looking amazing today. Are you not a little dressed up for a meeting?"

"Well, I'm going to surprise Roo. I have a special lunch planned as it is his Entrance Day. He didn't mention anything to you, did he?"

"No. Nothing, and don't worry. I will make sure to reschedule all of his appointments for the rest of the day."

"Oh Joyce, that would be wonderful. It will be perfect to spend the whole day together before I dispatch tomorrow."

Just then the doors of the elevator open and sure enough Roo is there awaiting me. I feel like a celebrity with all of the special treatment I have been getting lately.

"Precious," he says with open arms and a loving embrace. Then he holds my hands so gently and takes a step backwards to admire every inch of me. I see true love in his eyes and I feel it energise my core.

"You look sublime."

"Roo, I am sorry that I'm late."

"Oh, don't worry about that. I have to confess that I told you an earlier time than the actual meeting start . . . not that I thought you were going to be late. I just didn't want you rushing."

"You know me better than I know myself at times, Roo, don't you?"

"Well, I wouldn't go as far as to say that, but I know you well enough by now," he says with a snicker.

He is clearly wondering why I am all dressed up, so I enlighten him.

"I have organised for us to have a special lunch today as it is your Entrance Day and Joyce has offered to defer your meetings for the rest of the day so that we can spend it together, is that okay?"

"Okay? That's wonderful, what a surprise!" he says joyfully.

I am relieved as I know he takes his job seriously. He has to because he is responsible for the wellbeing of so many and with all my heart I support him. I believe this break will be good for him and those he assists afterwards.

CHAPTER TWO
Initial Encounters

The others begin to arrive for the meeting, so we all start making our way into the boardroom. It has recently been decorated as the previous Boss had a humorous decor and seating arrangement, so Roo decided on a dramatic alternative, not bland but not as comfortable as the fluffy white chairs we previously encountered.

There is a more formal atmosphere in this zone and I understand that there must be. We are dealing with serious events that will change the life course of the chosen few; thus we must focus accordingly.

I look at the folder before me. It is quite a chunky file. I assume much will be revealed to me about those I will encounter. The one feature I never take for granted when being introduced to my assignments is the uniqueness of each situation. Each set of circumstances from which a wish arises is exclusive to the person who has requested it and the desire of enhancement may be materialistic, emotional or spiritual. Anything and everything can be requested and is. I am sent to a select few who have been chosen for advancement along their paths; maybe they have gone off track or have become a little stuck for some reason. I will soon find out who it is my energies will be channelled towards for the immediate future. A flutter engulfs my tummy and my abdomen; what a strange yet fulfilling feeling flushes my cheeks! Roo look at me with concern and I smile to let him know that all is well.

Rupert stands up at the top of the room. He is not a big man, but he now has a captivating presence. He captured my heart the first time I saw him and even though it took him thirty-four years to realise his feelings for me, he is certainly making up for it now. He fills my life with joy in every moment, even when we are not together. I still smile because of the loving residue he has left me with. Such love is special.

"Hi, everyone. Thank you for coming."

"Hi, Boss," we all reply.

"Well, as you know today we are all gathered because it is time for the Wish Giver to prepare for her mission. We have always and will always support any messenger as they embark on their journeys to enlighten those who are lost or in peril. It is of utmost importance that we are all informed of each assignment in case of an emergency intervention from any other messenger."

Everyone nods in agreement.

"Now obviously today we are viewing the file of the Wish Giver. When you look inside you need to look at each case individually and with fresh eyes. You can never bring previous experiences or judgements to any new case as even though some assignments may have similar characteristics, it is important to remember that the journey each has travelled thus far has not been the same as another's. Every file must be opened with a clear mind and heart. Does everyone understand?"

"Yes, Boss," everyone answers.

"You may open your files and any questions can be directed to the room in fifteen minutes."

Everyone reaches forward to lift up the golden files set before them. I am so intrigued to learn of those I will come across on this, my final mission. It is quite poignant when I think of it like that and a tear comes to my eye. Oh, I must be hormonal.

Opening the file, I see that my first case is a young woman. Her name is Jade, and she is in her late twenties. Her long chocolate brown hair is professionally styled, and she shines with a healthy glow. She is heavily tanned, and her dress style is modern and complimentary to her toned physique. It is her eyes that I am drawn to though, as there seems to be a lot of pain that has been covered over. A deep sadness fills this young beautiful soul. I read on to discover that she is a caring person as her focus is on helping others. She not only lends a hand to anyone in need, she also assists her family to overcome any challenges they may face.

She does, however, have self-esteem issues and has a problem believing she is worthy of true happiness. This is evident from the many relationship issues she has had, and her heart has been broken many times. She craves love because she believes this is where fulfilment lies. It is so troubling to see someone so young with such issues.

She needs to realise that in order for true love to find her she needs to truly love herself. Not in the arrogant way, but loving yourself faults and all, as they are only faults if you believe them to be. I shall tread carefully with this case for until I make my initial physical encounter I do not entertain any presumptions. However, I know from these notes that her wish may not be what will bring her true happiness or steer her onto her path. I hope to shine beauty onto this beautiful life.

The next file takes me aback, not because of the words but because of the strong intense loving energy I am receiving from it. I must compose myself before I go further, so I stand up and get myself a glass of water.

Once I have re-aligned myself, I am ready to discover the hidden details. Opening the file again I see the picture of a woman who has mid-length curly auburn hair. Her name is Melody; she is in her early fifties and has a caring appearance. She now dedicates all of her time to sharing love and kindness to others because she believes that in spreading these values the peace we get can be more far reaching. She has a special bond with young children and she brings much needed love to those that are needy. Everything flourishes through love.

But looking into her eyes, I see pain, wounds that have not healed properly and forgiveness that has not yet been gifted. Forgiveness is the special ingredient in the enlightenment of a soul as it frees the spirit. Forgiveness of another is not a gift to them for their wrongdoing; it is a gift to oneself. Forgiveness of ourselves allows us to discover self-love. When this happens, wisdom follows and a well of endless divine love is accessed for all who encounter it. I will surely recharge my energies when I encounter this lady as do many others.

I hope it doesn't all become too draining for her. I feel she may already be suffering physically. This tends to happen when the beautiful people who are on their path try to share their love with others. I am guessing she has not yet found her true calling. To me it is obvious, and it is my job to help her unearth her powers. I am also interested to discover what her wish is as I do not have an inkling of what it could be. I decide not to ponder further. I will move onto the next case.

The lady looks unwell. She wears a head scarf and to me it is obvious what her wish is going to be. Her name is Irene. She is forty-two years old and she has two children, both boys. She has been diagnosed with bone cancer and is trying hard to find a matching bone marrow donor. There is sadness in her eyes, not sadness for herself but for her two boys sitting beside her; sadness because they have to go through this heartache and she may not be there to help them along their path of life.

This I find harsh. Earth is surely the school of hard knocks. It doesn't matter who you are; you can be knocked over at any time. The strong pick themselves up again and implement the emotional changes that have occurred during this time, but others don't. This disease is touching the lives of so many now because everyone is in contact on this planet in an instant. Negative energies can flow more efficiently, forcing their way into the bodies of unsuspecting individuals and not surfacing until a later date when it is hard to detect where it came from. This cannot define this lady. I feel she has a lot more to her and I look forward to being able to observe what makes her tick. I shall prepare myself for an emotional encounter.

I open the fourth file to see a happy face beaming at me. Her name is Joy. She is twenty-two years old and has blonde, shoulder-length hair. She certainly lives up to her name as she appears so joyful. Her motto is "Happiness is something we all aspire to, Joy is ever present." She is focusing a lot of her energies trying to set up joy groups all over the world so that fear can be eradicated. If there were more people like this in the world, it would be more like a heaven than an earth.

Joy is present in hers at all times, she spreads the word in any way she can and in doing so she is also fulfilling her desire to entertain. She seems to have her head screwed on and is undeniably a big thinker; I feel she is one of those people who have the potential to make a difference. She listens to her inspiration and acts accordingly. She has masses of energy. I feel positive energy bursting from her picture; it is contagious. How does she fuel this fire?

The contrasting differences among people never cease to amaze me. There are some who are unmotivated or selfish and, on the other hand, there are those who are super charged and magnanimous. It is certainly a contrasting domain of extremes.

My final case is a fifteen-year-old girl called Lucy. She has hazel eyes and blonde hair. Her profile states that she is not content at home. She hasn't experienced genuine love from her parents and has lost the sense of belonging she craves, and which keeps her in line. She has started to associate herself with unsavoury characters, but her heart is true, so she must be salvaged from the rubbish heap as she does not fit in. It is a cry for help, wanting to get attention. She is very talented with any type of musical instrument, it comes naturally to her. It is a gift sent uniquely to her, so it must not be wasted. I am keen for more to be revealed and I wait in anticipation of discovering what she has to reveal to me. She is very young to stray off her true path but sometimes to have the desire to walk the path set out for us we must experience following another's tracks to understand that it doesn't suit us.

Right, there it is. I have now been introduced to my assignments. These five females are going to feel my entity surround them. They will progress from where they are now. They will no longer stand still; it is time for the effect of their wishes to take hold. They will now encounter the Wish Giver.

"Have we all had time to scan the cases?" Roo enquires.

"Yes, Boss," we all answer.

"And does anyone have any concerns or issues to raise at this point?"

Everyone is silent.

"Has anyone any words of wisdom or suggestions they feel will assist Sydney in any way shape or form?"

"I think that I might, Boss," a timid voice comes from the back and a hand is raised to offer support. It is Claire. We are all amazed that she has spoken up because she so rarely does. We call her 'the silent messenger' because she seldom talks, but shyly observes. She has been in training for some time because it is not known which area is best suited to her talents.

"Claire, please enlighten us."

Roo gestures for her to come to the top of the room and address us all. My heart skips a beat as I contemplate how nervous she must be feeling. To my amazement she gets up and walks confidently to the top of the room. She has such a tiny frame and mousey blonde hair that drably hangs half way down her back. She always presents herself in order to not stand out. It is as if she wants to blend into the background and could quite easily be overlooked.

"Hello, everyone," she says while looking at her tiny feet.

"Hello, Claire," we respond.

Rupert intervenes. "Claire, we are all friends here. We are all here because we departed our physical form too early. I hope you can relax and feel comfortable with us all as you are as much a part of this team as anyone else and we value your thoughts greatly."

Claire smiles at him and turns to face us all with her head raised.

"I just wanted to say that I have a deep belief that each of these wishes is true of heart. I know there are many who wish selfishly but for each of these I feel this is not the case. I have been learning to listen to my intuition and it is telling me this loud and clear. I also feel that Jade may not be on the right thought track; she may wish for something thinking it is what she needs to make her happy, but I feel that she may need guidance towards what is best for her.

"Often people are too close to their own selves to realise the best choices for them to make. I believe that she has made many wrong choices and has gone against her intuition on many occasions thus far. I also believe that most people pursue happiness, through everything they do. Many don't realise that they have it already and just need to open the door to it. Err . . . thank you." She smiles slightly and puts her head down again and starts to make her way to her seat.

We all rise to our feet to clap and continue clapping. She immediately responds by lifting her head, blushing and smiling. I don't think she has ever had recognition for any of her words before and so had decided within to stop trying. Hopefully this is exactly what she needs to open herself up to a new way of expressing herself. How ground-breaking, and how totally unexpected!

"Claire, we want you to know that your words of wisdom have enlightened us all. Your contribution to this meeting has been amazing and we hope you feel you are able to contribute in such an inspirational way at any time, without any pressure of course, but because you want to," Rupert encourages her.

"Thank you. I will," she confidently responds.

"Just a thought, but maybe you and Sydney could get together before she dispatches tomorrow," he suggests.

It would be fabulous to get together with Claire to further listen to her thoughts. I smile in her direction and she smiles back. I will leave it for her to approach me as I don't want her to feel pressured. She has just undergone an amazing transformation in front of my eyes. Such characteristic alterations are depicted in earthly superhero movies. It is quite powerful to witness it first hand, and I am sure this will be a topic of conversation for some time to come.

"All right, well, I think that this was a very successful meeting. I must ask if anyone else has anything to contribute before I call it to a close."

Rupert scans the room and we are all shaking our heads. Well, who could follow Claire's personal leap forward? I am going to feel great all day after that. Oh yes, and I have a lunch date. I'd almost forgotten.

"Then I formally call this meeting to a close," he concludes.

I feel the need to compose myself, so I gesture to Rupert that I need to use the bathroom. He winks to let me know he understands.

CHAPTER THREE

Wine Dine and Preparation

We arrive at Dave's place. It is our heavenly sanctuary and today we are the special guests. An exclusive area has been sectioned off especially for us so that we can have a little privacy. I feel like a VIP and I suppose in a way I am.

Rupert can't take his eyes off me; I feel his thoughts and his divine love projecting onto me, nourishing me and our little creation. Then all of a sudden there it is again, the fluttering feeling I had earlier.

"What's wrong, Syd? You have gone all flushed."

"Nothing is wrong, Roo. Something is very right. I can feel the baby moving. It is such a beautiful sensation that I can only describe as something tiny tickling my insides."

He looks adoringly at me and then gets up from his seat and kneels beside me. He places his hand on my tummy in a bid to feel something, but it is not strong enough for him to experience yet. I did notice that when he placed his hand on my tummy it calmed right down. He is such a calming presence that even our child is responding to it. Again, I feel so eternally fortunate for this perfection to have found me. I am a true example of how you will receive if you believe.

Taking his seat again across the table and cupping my hands in his he says, "So, Syd, please share with me why you did not go for the big hooray that you usually surprise me with each year?"

"You mean you knew I had arranged something? Who told you?"

"Whoa, Syd, no one mentioned anything, honest. It is just that you are usually extravagant. Not that it is a bad thing of course."

"I just thought it would be nice for us to spend some quiet time together before I depart tomorrow. We don't often get alone time now as you have so much to do as Boss, so I thought that intimacy was what we needed this year."

He jumps up, lifts me off my chair like a baby cradled in his arms and swings me around. "This is perfection in the highest degree, Syd. What did I ever do to deserve such inner joy?"

"I think the same, Roo. I have concluded that we both desired the same thing and then it all clicked into place. We opened ourselves up to true joy and it came to us in abundance. This is our little heaven, isn't it?"

"It sure is, precious." He kisses me in the most caring, loving way possible.

Just then we hear an "Ahem" as the waiter tries to attract our attention.

Rupert gently places me back into my chair and pushes it into position. Then he takes his own seat and we pick up our menus in unison.

"Hello, Mr and Mrs Boss, are you ready to order?"

"Yes, of course. Well let's see, shall we? Can we have a bottle of your finest sparkling . . .?"

Roo looks at me inquisitively wondering what to order, as we would usually order wine, and so I say, "Grape juice, please."

He smiles at me, happy that we are in a position to make these compromises.

"We will have Number One entree, Number Nine main and a plate of heavenly delights to finish. Is that okay with you, Sydney?"

"Perfect, Roo." To be honest I don't care what I eat, and I believe that Rupert doesn't either. Love tends to fill you like that. It is as if love is providing us with all of our needs.

"So how are you feeling about the mission?" he enquires, sounding a little concerned.

"I'm feeling good about it, Roo. You know I love what I do."

"Yes, Syd, but I was hoping to talk to you about your role in the Waiting Zone."

I knew this would come up at some point and I have already decided this is my last mission as I want to focus on our little creation. I haven't told Rupert yet though. I didn't want to commit until I had found my replacement. I think, however, that my replacement has now found me because I opened myself to the possibility. I love the way the laws of the universe work. They never seem to fail me.

"Go on, Roo, I'm keen to hear your thoughts."

"Okay, well, I know you are the best Wish Giver ever and that no one could take your place, but I was hoping you might consider stepping down and focusing on being my right-hand person, so to speak, and on our new arrival when it delights us with its presence. I hope I'm not out of line with my request, but I do feel strongly that it is a reasonable one."

"Oh, you do, do you?"

"Yes, Syd, I do," he cautiously replies.

"I must let you in on my little secret then. I have been thinking about this for some time myself. Recently I opened myself up to the possibility of not being the Wish Giver and the idea sat well with me. So, I decided that this is going to be my last mission. I know the perfect person to replace me must be found, but I think she has found us."

"Oh, Syd, you don't know how much of a relief it is to hear you say that!"

"So...your right-hand woman? That sounds like fun," I teasingly reply.

"Yes of course, well, you already are but this will be more formal."

"Do you want to know who I believe to be my perfect replacement? As your right-hand woman surely, I will have a say in who my predecessor is."

"You really have thought this through, haven't you?" he says, amused.

"Well, do you want to know or not?"

"I sure do, please share your thoughts."

"Claire."

"Claire?" he answers, confused. Then his expression shows him opening up to the idea. "Do you know what, Syd, I think you may be onto something there. Have I ever told you just how wonderful you are?"

"Well, not in the last few hours, no."

"This will be fabulous. I have never seen Claire respond in the way she did today. She obviously feels a connection to the concept of wish giving already. She will be perfect."

"I think we should wait to see if she approaches either of us in the meantime. We don't want her to feel pressured. What do you think, Roo?"

"Hey, get out of my head," he laughs. "We seem to be on the same thought frequency. I opened the door for her to approach you and if she is really committed to wish giving, well then, she will find her way to you. Isn't the universe wonderful in how it sends us the answers to problems before they are problems?"

"Now you are in my head, as I was thinking exactly that earlier. Shall we eat before the rest of the guests arrive?"

"What? Hey, I thought it was just us."

"Roo, you know me well enough to know that there has to be a little gathering. You are very much loved and admired by many. So, enjoy."

"And here I was thinking that you had turned over a new leaf," he smirks.

"Doesn't this entree look delicious? Suddenly I am famished." I ignore his comment and start on lunch.

With a smile of agreement, he tucks in too.

***

A few more than expected have joined us for the celebration. It has become quite a tradition that every year I organise a get together on Rupert's Entrance Day. The mood is joyous, and I am grateful that so many have made the effort to come, but I must start making my way back to our quarters because I need to prepare for tomorrow and I am feeling a little drained. My energies are lower than usual. Rupert seems to be enjoying himself, so I decide not to disturb him. I will leave a message with Dave to let him know where I am.

It takes me a while but finally I get to make my way past everyone to the peace of the realm beyond the door. As I walk away

I hear my name being called and recognise Rupert's voice. I stop and turn around to see him galloping towards me, a sight to behold.

"Sydney, are you all right? Dave just gave me your message and I was worried. I'm so glad to have caught you," he said, panting slightly.

"I'm fine; I just need to rest because I'm feeling a little drained. It's to be expected in my condition."

"Right, well I am coming with you, so just hold on a moment until I pop back and thank everyone."

"Rupert, please don't worry. You are enjoying yourself and everyone has made such an effort that you can't abandon them. I'm going to take a little rest, clear my head and scan over my files again. We will have the rest of the evening together."

"Okay, but I am going to start saying goodbyes and finishing up here, so I won't be long." He gives me a kiss and heads back to the gathering.

Oh, what a wonderful feeling it is to get into our beautiful home and kick off my inconvenient shoes. As I sink into the cosiest chair I have ever experienced, a feeling of celestial pleasure spreads through my body. Strange how on other occasions doing this has not been as heavenly an experience, but right now it is just so blissful.

There is a knock on the door.

"Oh, do I have to get up?" I say aloud.

It is probably Rupert. I knew he wouldn't be long behind me. Reluctantly I rise from the luxury of my chair and make my way to the door. I look out through the peep hole but see nothing and assume that the mystery caller has departed due to the time it took me to answer the door. But then there are three timid knocks.

I open the door to see Claire standing there. Her tiny frame looks child-like in comparison to my tall, broad appearance. Her visit takes me by surprise as she had left my thoughts when the party began.

"Hello, Mrs Boss, sorry to annoy you," she says in a low shy voice.

"Claire, how lovely of you to call, please come in." I give her a hug and gesture for her to enter.

"Can I get you something to drink? I was going to have a fluffy white creamer. Would you like to join me?"

"Well, if you don't mind, Mrs Boss, I would love one."

"Wonderful," I respond as I make my way to the kitchen." Then I pause and turn to say, "Claire, please call me Syd."

"Okay, Mrs . . . Syd, thank you."

When we are settled with cups in hands I ask, "So Claire, I have to say that your contribution to the meeting this morning was exceptional. How are you feeling since?"

"I have to be honest and say that I don't know what came over me. I had a moment of thrilling passion rushing through my body and it felt so right to get up and share my thoughts. I am feeling good but a bit lost." She lowers her head.

"I hope you don't mind me saying that you are here for an important reason. You have so much to give to others and I hope you find that passion for life that you so confidently expressed earlier. That Claire is in there and if she makes you feel good then let her come to the surface."

"Do you know what it did to make me feel good, Syd? I have never felt that way before. Will you help me?"

"Of course I will. I will be happy to help you discover your true potential. But only if you promise to let me know if it feels as though I am pushing you out of your comfort zone. I want your natural abilities to come out from hiding and I don't want to influence you in any way. What you have inside already is a wonderful well of wisdom that you can gift to so many."

"I will tell you, Mrs . . . Syd. Can I say that you look beautiful today?"

"Oh, thank you, Claire. I made a special effort for Rupert's Entrance Day. We have always celebrated it. Did you not want to join the fun in Dave's place?"

"Well, I was going to, but I didn't want to intrude."

"Intrude? You would never be intruding, the more the merrier . . . Hold on a moment while I change into something a little more comfortable and I will bring you there."

"Oh, you don't have to do that, Mrs . . . sorry, Syd."

"It is my pleasure. Rupert will be happy to see me back and I feel revitalised after our little chat. I'm so glad you called."

"So am I."

CHAPTER FOUR

Surprise Preparation

This morning I lie here trying to figure out whether what I feel happened yesterday evening actually did happen or was just a dream.

Rupert, who is lying beside me, says sincerely, "I am sorry. I should not have interfered in your assignment."

"So, it did happen."

What I had hoped and planned to be the perfect day and evening didn't transpire that way.

When Claire and I left to return to the party, my intentions were genuine, and she was keen. We had made some progress and she was embracing the changes that were coming her way.

In my cosies, we strolled and chatted, and she really came out of herself. It was like watching a flower blossom. She is beautiful and pure of thought. She started to droop a little when we got closer to Dave's place, so I caught hold of her hand and she looked at me and smiled.

Everyone was in good spirits when we arrived, especially Rupert. I hadn't seen him so chilled out, relaxed and happy in some time because with his new role in the Waiting Zone he must maintain dominance in order to maintain respect. It's just the way it is.

When he saw us and realised that we had arrived together he came rushing over.

"Well hello, Claire, it is so wonderful to have you join us here this evening."

"Thank you, Mr Boss."

"So, what have you both been up to?" he probed.

"Claire came to visit me this afternoon, so we thought it might be nice for her to join the gathering."

"That's great. I'm so happy that you did."

Claire smiled shyly again.

"So, did you decide if you are going to train to be the next Wish Giver?"

I couldn't believe my ears. Surely Rupert didn't say that.

Claire looked at me, then him. I could see what she was thinking. She thought we were conspiring to entrap her, that we had this planned when of course that was not the case. All of the groundwork that I had just completed with her was gone in an instant. She stepped back, lowered her head and shoulders and quickly left.

I gave Rupert a '*What you have done now?*' look and he responded by asking that question.

For someone who is so heavenly wise all of the time, he had surely had a lapse of reasoning.

"Rupert, I was making real progress with Claire. She came to me and we had struck up a real connection. She trusted me and was coming out of her shell and now with your comment she has put her head back into her safe little haven and may not come out."

"I don't understand what I said wrong."

"You sounded as if we had been planning to trap her. I lost her trust at that moment and she lost in an instant the confidence she had just discovered. All of the connection I had built beforehand was gone in a flash."

"I'm sorry, Syd. I do realise how inconsiderate of her feelings and situation I was, but I was just trying to push things along a bit for you. You are dispatching in the morning, you know."

"Oh Roo, we already discussed that we were not going to push her, that we were going to wait until she came to us and it was happening until you scared her off."

"I do understand your concerns, Syd. Don't lose faith though, for I have a feeling it will all turn out fine.

"I do hope so, Roo. Do you think I should go after her?"

"I think it is best to leave her with her thoughts now. We may make things worse. Hopefully she will see through the mist."

"Yes, there is always hope . . . Now how is this party going?" I said, changing the subject.

Rupert put his arms around my waist. "It has been great. I miss interacting with everyone this way. Thank you for the opportunity to realise that."

"You're very welcome; it's my pleasure."

He caressed my cheek. "I think things are going to wrap up here now as Dave has an evening sitting to prepare for. Do you fancy taking an extremely slow walk with me followed by a relaxing restful shoulder massage when we get back home?"

"Sounds divine, Roo. I'm ready when you are."

We said our goodbyes, then strolled along the Lagoon of Serenity. I love to view the white doves that make their homes there, a sight you would never think existed here until you witness it yourself. Everything is white and before us lay a blanket of different shades of white. It is like a winter wonderland without the coldness.

I felt my core being recharged; nature tends to do that for me. The energy we can absorb from the natural energy which surrounds us is ever so nourishing for our inner core. I believe it is just as important to feed our souls as it is to feed our bodies.

We didn't talk much; we didn't need to. Being together was more than enough. It is wonderful that when you find the one meant for you there is no pressure to make idle conversation. Our energies have combined on the same frequency and are liaising without us having to do anything else. It is such a magnificent feeling to experience!

We saw a shadow in the distance so picked up a bit of pace and soon realised that it was Claire, huddled into a ball-like position and staring out into the distance. She must have been in deep contemplation because she didn't even hear us approaching.

"Claire, are you all right?" I cautiously enquired.

She didn't answer. I knew we couldn't just leave her, so I asked Roo to take off his cardigan and went over and put it around her. I helped her to her feet and we all made our way back to our place. She never spoke along the way; simply stared ahead and allowed us to steer her. Perhaps we had pushed her too far when she wasn't ready, I thought.

When we arrived home, we sat Claire comfortably into a chair. She was still not responsive, so I felt it best not to offer her a drink yet. A few hours passed and there was no change. Just as we began to think we might need some outside assistance, her finger moved, then one foot. Relieved, we waited.

Once she became more responsive, I asked, "Claire, love, are you okay?"

"Yes, thank you," she politely replied.

"Would you like a drink? Something refreshing maybe?" Rupert asked.

"Oh please. I am fine. You don't need to worry about me. I can get myself a drink."

"We will get you one; you sit where you are for a moment." I gestured to Rupert to go ahead and get her the drink.

I sat beside her and took her tiny hand into mine. "Do you know what just happened to you, Claire?"

"Oh yes," she replied, unconcerned. "I often drift off to another realm; sometimes I am called but at other times I choose to go there myself."

I was taken aback. What a gift she has! I wondered if Rupert knew of this special inner power of Claire's.

"Were you called, or did you choose to go on this occasion?" I asked.

"I chose to go, Syd, to visit those on the wish receiving list to help me make my decision."

"Really, Claire? You can do that?"

"Yes, and I have made my decision. I feel a real connection to wish giving so would you mind me joining you on your mission?"

I gave her a big squeezy hug. "That's wonderful news, Claire."

"I must go." She stood up. "I want to check over the files before starting in the morning. What time do you need me to be ready?"

"You are so sweet, Claire. It would be good to meet here in the morning before dispatch so that we are in sync. Is seven good for you?"

"Seven it is. Thank you, Syd. I won't let you down," she promised and scurried like a little mouse towards the door.

We said our goodbyes and she left. Rupert didn't even have enough time to return from the kitchen with her drink as it all happened so fast. As I stood with my head and back propped up against our door he came into the room and asked, "Where's Claire?"

As I explained, I could hardly believe what had happened.

And lying here 6.30 am I still don't believe it. This mission just keeps getting stranger. Luckily, I adapt easily to changes and believe in going with the flow of things as they come, otherwise I would be feeling quite overcome.

Today will flow beautifully though, I know it. That indisputable feeling of certainty engulfs my very being and I am excited about the quest I have before me.

I was awakened in the most beautiful way. Roo had his loving arms wrapped around me and when I finally fully awoke he expressed his true love to me.

Now he is making me breakfast before my big day. I will miss him terribly when I am away, but his energies will always be with me every step of the way as I navigate my way through this assignment. I never feel alone because I have him to call upon any time I am in need.

"Mmm," I say as the smell of breakfast is helping me rise to this new day.

It doesn't take me long to get ready and move to the kitchen. Our kitchen is so heavenly; everything seems to flow perfectly in it and there is lots of room for anything we desire. We both like things to be simple but cosy, so we are always happy with each other's choices.

"Roo, this smells yum, thank you."

"You are very welcome, my precious," he says as he bends down and puts some food onto my plate and gives me a gentle loving kiss on my lips. It makes me blush and I don't know why. Strange but in a good way.

We are just about to make a start when there is a gentle knock on the door.

"Oh, that will be Claire."

I attempt to rise but Rupert says, "You rest yourself. I will let her in." I don't argue. I resume my delicious feast.

The table is already set for three, so Rupert is on top of things as always.

He and Claire come into the kitchen and I gladly greet her. "Good morning, Claire."

"It certainly is. Oh, you are going to have breakfast. Please don't let me disturb you. I'll wait over here."

"No, please join us. We have a place set for you already," Roo says as he directs her to the chair.

"Well, if you insist. I must say it all looks very tasty indeed. You have been busy this morning, Syd."

"I can't take the credit, I'm afraid. You can thank Rupert."

"Oh right. Thank you, Mr eh . . . Rupert," she says warily.

"You are very welcome, Claire." He pauses briefly, then continues. "Well, I have a lot to do this morning to prepare for dispatch, so I will leave you two ladies to do what you need to do." He gives me a quick kiss on the cheek. "I will see you before you leave, my lovely." Then he disappears.

"So Claire, do you have any idea about the process of dispatch here?" I asked.

"I have heard stories but nothing that I would call believable. Could you please fill me in?"

"I sure can. I'll start at the beginning. Our dispatch time is scheduled for 11am and the process takes on average one hour, so we will need to be in the dispatch area no later than 10am or we will be out of our scheduled time slot. Everything is precise when it comes to time management in dispatch, otherwise it won't work effectively. Dispatch is down in the lowest platform of this realm and you will need a special pass to gain access. Rupert will be sorting all of that out for us, so we don't need to worry."

She smiled shyly. "I hope you don't mind me saying that you two make a perfect couple. You glow when you are together. It is lovely to watch."

"Ah thank you, Claire. That is so nice of you to say. It took some time for us to get together but it was certainly worth the wait. I'm very lucky."

"Yes, I can feel that from you. It is so refreshing. I am happy that you have found this love."

"Well, maybe someday you will find it too, Claire."

"Yes, maybe...You were saying about dispatch?" The quick change of subject leads me to I suspect there is more to discover from her on the subject of love.

"Oh yes, sorry. I got off track there. Once in dispatch we will go to the distribution department to collect the Twinkles. They are the entities in which the wishes are transported. They keep them safe and are the most magical looking objects I have ever laid eyes on. I shall never cease being mesmerised by their sheer beauty."

"They surely do sound outstanding."

"Well, you'll soon find out for yourself just how outstanding they are. Anyway, after we pick them up we make our way down the long corridor. This brings us to the dispatch area where Heavenly Harry will take us through the process and to the Vortex. How do you feel about all of that, Claire?"

"It all sounds very exciting. I have never done anything as adventurous as this."

"Sure you have. Haven't you visited other realms in your subconscious mind on many occasions? That's what I call exciting."

"I suppose it is a little different, isn't it?"

"A little different! It's a wonderful gift to have."

She smiles confidently as she realises that within herself she has such a powerful gift that is unique to her. I think she has perceived it as a negative thing until now.

"So how does it work for you, Claire?" I ask.

She frowned thoughtfully for a moment. "I can only explain it as; my energy penetrates different dimensions. I liken it to Quantum jumping. I don't physically see with my eyes, but I do physically feel with every molecule of my being. My energy encounters the energies of those I focus on and I can interpret things from them. Does that make any sense?"

"More sense than you can imagine. I hope that you can show me more on our mission."

"Yes of course."

"Great. So, we will get cracking and go through the assignments before we leave. I'm keen to hear what you experienced last night. Let's start with Jade, shall we?"

"Well when I visited Jade's zone I was shocked to discover that her daughter knew I was there. She started talking to me; such a friendly little girl. I sent her some loving energy which she acknowledged by saying, 'Thank you, lady'. Such an aware little soul that I do hope she maintains this awareness throughout her life. I drew myself closer to Jade; her energy was one of deep sadness and pain. She needs intervention as she feels that she is losing grip of her sanity. Even when I think of her now I can physically feel the pain pressing on my chest. Syd, I have never felt anything to this intensity before. I will have to move on," Claire explains as she leans forward.

"Yes, do move on, Claire, quickly before it gets any worse. Here, take a drink."

She takes a little breather before sharing what she experienced with Melody. This information is priceless in helping me determine the authenticity of each of the wishes.

"Melody's energy is more controlled. She surrounds herself with peace-promoting activities like meditation, Pilates and painting. She does this as and when she can and her inner essence flourishes because of it. She has scars from past hurts but is learning to forgive. Her energy is one of peace and goodwill and a pleasure to encounter. It calmed me because I was a little on edge after the first encounter."

I nodded in understanding. "Energy is something that we all encompass and if you don't protect your energy and leave it open to being intruded by others' energies it can have a draining effect. On the other hand, when we encounter a vibrant super- charged energy, we can all gain so much from that. Being aware of our own energies and that of others can help us avoid unnecessary energy bumps."

"You explain it so well, Syd. Do you use your energies in the same way?"

"Unfortunately, I have not been gifted the way you are; however, I have a deep awareness of energies and am always on guard with my own personal inbuilt energy radar. I can pick up on energies and danger and other frequencies. It has taken me a while, but I think I have got it functioning fully. Now, what about Irene?"

"Yes, I was a little confused by this because her energy and Lucy's kept getting overlapped so that it was hard to determine the difference between them. I did get a sense of sadness and some hope, which I took to be promising. I'm sorry I couldn't be more help in these two cases."

"What you have picked up is still wonderful as it gives me some insight that I would not have had if I were preparing on my own for this mission."

"I'm happy to report that Joy is exactly that, joyful. She has an energy that is vibrant, powerful and really strong."

"Yes," I say excitedly. "I imagined her energy to be so super charged that it could run the whole world if they plugged into her."

"That's exactly how it would be, Syd. You explain it so well."

"I'm looking forward to encountering her wondrous energy. If only more people in the world were like this beautiful lady, it would be a heavenly place to be!"

We both ponder this thought for a moment.

"Shall we go help these ladies move on to their next level?" I ask.

Claire nods and smiles. "I'm ready, Syd."

"Okay, it's almost time for dispatch, so we'd better get moving."

CHAPTER FIVE

Dispatch

As we arrive at the dispatch lounge we are first greeted by Rupert who is there making sure we have a super smooth departure. He knows I don't need any stresses right now, so he offers support whenever he can. The departure lounge is in keeping with the rest of the realm; white is the dominant theme. If you look up there is the illusion that it goes on forever and the walls give the impression they are more expansive than they are. The floor is a like a glass sheet. When I first saw it, I was amazed that it was possible but when I became more accustomed to this realm I learned to accept things the way they are, allow my eyes and mind to adjust and not to ask silly questions.

We approach the distribution desk, so we can sign out the *Twinkles* from the Waiting Zone for a time. Julie greets us. She is quite new here even though she is in her late sixties; I am afraid she will not be with us for much longer. That will be a pity because she has such a warm and welcoming presence. Claire is smiling; it is as if this is the biggest adventure she has ever experienced.

"If you just sign here, Claire," Julie indicates.

Then it is my turn and when I am done, she asks, "So how are you feeling with that little one growing inside you? Tired I bet. I remember when I was having my children. I was so tired all the time when I was carrying them."

"I am a little more tired than usual I guess, but it is still early days and so not too bad. Just looking forward to the arrival."

"How far are you on now, dear?"

"We have just passed the three-month mark," I say, slipping my hand into Rupert's.

"Well, I wish you the best of luck for the safe arrival of your firstborn."

"Thank you, Julie. We appreciate your kind thoughts," Rupert replies.

We move on with our treasured Twinkles secure in the golden encrusted box. There are four of these mesmerising entities in all and five potential receivers to visit. One wish will not materialise. Instead hope will be left in its place.

We enter the corridor before the dispatch room and this is where Rupert must leave us. I feel quite emotional and I am not good at that. Luckily Rupert is aware of this and when I give him a swift hug and a brief kiss before making my way through the big white doors he smiles at me. I had peered over my shoulder to see his reaction and I knew that he understood. The doors open automatically as we walk towards them. They give an illusion of openness, and it is as if we are being drawn into a whirlpool. When we enter there is a lengthy corridor before us. It is quite plain, with white walls and seems to go on forever. In the distance there is a large doorway and that is the dispatch area.

Claire seems to be a little dazed. "So, what do you think?" I ask her.

"It's so, so long," she replies.

"It is, isn't it? We better get moving or we will be late. Harry likes things to flow easily."

We set out on the long walk we have before us. I often wonder why it is so long and I have concluded that it is, so we are encouraged to contemplate the task ahead. As there is not much else to stimulate us, that can lead to thoughtful realisations which will help us on our way. By listening to the guidance from within we become distracted by the continuous flow that consumes our moments.

Claire is trying to look closer at the white walls and I know she is seeing the doorways that blend into the vastness. I still don't know why they exist, and I have never asked Rupert because I feel that he would tell me if I needed to know.

"I don't know why they are there either," I inform her.

"Oh, thank goodness. I thought I was seeing things," she replies.

We are making progress and although we have been walking for some time we have not said much. We don't need to as our energies liaise just fine without us having to utter a word. This is a calming feeling as on occasion I have felt the pressure of expectation to maintain continuous conversation. In this bond it is not the case and that fills me with peace.

"Yay, we are there," I say in celebration.

Harry has sensed our presence and comes to welcome us into his domain.

"Good morning, ladies. I thought you would never get here. You did take your time toddling down the corridor."

"And it is lovely to see you again, Harry."

"This young lady is new?" He extends his hand for Claire to shake.

"Hello, I'm Claire," she says softly.

"It is nice to meet you, little lady." He greets her warmly and she responds with a smile.

"Now if you follow me to the light adjustment area I can prepare you for dispatch. Are you dispatching together or separately?"

"I have been meaning to ask you about the best way to dispatch as I am now expecting a baby and I want to ensure that I'm not taking any risks."

"Sydney, my lovely, would I ever let anything happen to you? Or your precious little gem?"

"I appreciate you safeguarding our wellbeing, Harry."

"I wouldn't have it any other way. Right this way, ladies."

We follow him into a cosy area where warm yellows and textures are prominent.

"So, ladies, I will leave you both here for a few minutes enabling your eyes to adjust to the new light glows you will be experiencing from this point on. If you could just imitate me and do a few of these eye exercises it would be beneficial for you."

He starts doing wiggly eye movements that make me and Claire giggle.

"You are funny, Harry. How many times do you do that in a day?"

"More than I care to remember, Sydney dear. Yes, I do suppose it looks rather funny," he remarks with his dry humour that makes us giggle some more.

"I shall go and prepare the Vortex for dispatch and I will be back to check the progress of your eyes shortly."

"Thanks, Harry," I say gratefully.

When he is gone we both take a look around the room. It is filled with little knick-knacks that are so interesting to look at and seem to originate from many different dimensions of the universe.

It is a relief to the mind to see such fascinating artefacts in this realm. I sit in a cosy chair that hugs my body and I feel so relaxed. Claire looks at me and starts wriggling her eyes about, making me laugh. She has a sense of humour too. I am warmed to know that she is feeling more comfortable in my presence.

It is not long before Harry is back with his eye-monitoring device. He checks if our eyes have adjusted from the brightness of the Waiting Zone to the warmness of the Earth dimension.

"It seems you are both ready to progress to the Vortex," he announces. "Are you ready to take the next step?"

"As ready as I will ever be," I reply.

Harry looks to Claire who seems a little nervous.

"Are you all right, love?" he asks.

She is unresponsive, and it is as if she is absent from her vessel. I am in receipt of some sort of message. I am being told to bring her with me as her energy has already departed. Oh boy, how am I going to explain this one to Harry?

"Harry, this is Claire's first departure from the Waiting Zone and she is very nervous; this is how she deals with her nerves. I will take her with me now and then at least the Vortex experience won't shock her any further."

"Well, I suppose it is a rather daunting experience for many and it may be best for this young lady to travel when she is in a more dream-like state."

"Right, well, I'm ready when you are, Harry," I say after positioning myself and Claire in the correct location for departure.

"Righto, ladies, a successful mission awaits you," he declares and at that we have dispatched.

***

Travelling through the Vortex has become second nature for me; I no longer feel the effects. When I first began projecting, it took me some time to rebalance when I arrived. This time I do not have only myself to worry about; there is Claire and she still looks quite vacant, so I assume that her energy has not returned yet. This could end up being a problem, but before my thoughts run away with me I will catch a hold of them and rein them back. This is a skill that Rupert has taught me, and it is really assisting me with the 'worst case scenario' thought process that I used to embrace.

"The answer to every problem is always close by if you are patient and allow it to find you," he would say.

So here I am with a problem and I am going to remain calm and wait for the solution to this predicament to find me.

As I sit I come to the realisation that Claire is not quite the person we have all been imagining. All along her energy has been departing her body and she has been like some sort of superhero going around curing the essence of those energies in need of healing. Now here I am at the vortex porthole with her vessel and she is nowhere to be seen. I look everywhere but I cannot find her. I can only hope my messages were correct and that I haven't left her behind. Then I remember to connect with her, but I cannot do that by seeing or shouting. I must feel her energy. My energy must summon hers. I close my eyes and vibrate my energy like a beacon so that she can home in on it. In no time at all she is back with me.

"Sorry, Sydney, my energy was summoned."

"Do you know what, Claire? I totally understand, and I am in awe of you. Should it happen again I shall ensure that your vessel is safe. You need not explain any further if you do not feel the need," I say in a bid to offer her some support.

The power of every individual's energy never ceases to amaze me. So many are unaware of its capabilities and people choose to simply ignore it because it cannot be seen physically. But they are the ones who are losing out as it is those who are aware of their energy frequency and the vibrations they are putting out into the universe who will receive their hearts' desire. I feel much richer for this increased awareness. This is a poignant moment in my existence and I feel that I have evolved because of what I have just become conscious of.

It is now time to get down to business, so united we stand and forth we travel.

CHAPTER SIX

Jade

We have been drawn to the location where Jade resides. It is a two-storey town house, in a cul-de-sac setting. Her number is 22 and it immediately registers with me that it is a spiritual home. The energy around the area feels a little intrusive indicating that with all good intentions at heart, people are ignorantly imposing themselves into other people's lives. However, on the whole, a sense of community seems to be paramount, so balance between the two is maintained. I observe the comings and goings for some time and Claire takes notes. Finally, I enter.

The atmosphere is one of emptiness. I would never have expected this. It is as if there is no hope and a cloud of accepting things as they are, has overshadowed this home. Where is the passion? Pictures I see on the wall: family photos of a lady who I believe to be Jade and two children, two girls with a considerable age gap and not too many similarities in appearance. I cannot feel the energy though; where is it? There must be some dynamics in this home or it can't function properly.

I look to Claire and she points upstairs. We have both agreed that for the duration of this assignment, when we are assessing cases, we will communicate telepathically as the frequencies from our vocal communications can be picked up on. This happened to me on one occasion before and it caused a right stir. Priests were called for exorcisms and ghost hunters engulfed the quiet little street, not to mention the paparazzi.

That is another story altogether, so it is time to focus on the task in hand. I hear someone upstairs, so I ascend to that floor. There is a woman, who I believe to be Jade, with a bath towel wrapped around her tanned body and a matching one on her head covering her long brown locks. She moves towards a unit where a stereo sits and switches on the music. Finally, I feel some emotional energy flowing. She is buzzing because her favourite song has just come on and she is now dancing around the room with her hair brush in her hand; it seems she really knows how to connect with the sensation that music can bring. We watch her bop around her bedroom in her underwear, singing loudly and giving it her all. Then her mobile phone flashes and she stops everything. It is as if she is pinning a lot of hope on one momentary act of contact.

Suddenly she drops the phone, turns off the music and hops under the covers. Whatever that message was she had anticipated a more jovial sentiment than she received. I move to the area on the floor where the phone now lies and can clearly see a message:

not be able to call meeting friends. chat soon ☺

Poor thing. Her heart is broken. When we pin so many expectations on another we are running the risk of disappointment. Unfortunately, it is our own ego that manifests expectations and therefore we are the ones who can control the severity of the emotions we subsequently experience. As humanity exists on emotional connections at all levels on the spectrum it can be difficult to determine how each person will react to any given situation. It is especially so in the present day where people no longer have to exert themselves to make the effort to visit someone face to face to deliver a message. In doing so the message is conveyed with emotion and therefore the reaction is also taken into consideration. Message devices have their place I am sure, but when it comes to emotional connection something can easily be misinterpreted when conveyed digitally.

The pain that Jade is feeling now could have been avoided should there have been consideration.

I shall leave her momentarily and use some of her twinkle's energy to get a sense of where this pain has come from.

I hold this beautiful creation in my hand. It shines so brightly that I am forced to close my eyes. I am then drawn to a happier Jade. She is with her family. They are in a clothes shop and she is posing for a camera man. (It never mentioned anything about being a model on her profile.) She is smiling and quite at home in front of the camera as she changes into another ensemble. I feel nervous excitement about her. She seems to get excited about looking and feeling good in her clothes. She looks great though and the shoes, well, they are in a league of their own.

"How do I look, Sophie?" she asks a young girl who resembles her and whom I recognise from a picture in Jade's home to be her daughter.

"You look great, Mum," Sophie answers with a smile.

Jade continues with the photo shoot. Happiness beams all around her. If only she only knew that she could shine like this all of the time if she focused her thoughts on the good things in life that satisfy her and over which she has influence! I should like to see more of Jade in this type of mood, so I shall move on now to the time of great importance, the wish.

I am catapulted to a family home where I see a younger Jade with others in pictures on the wall. There is a party atmosphere. Drinks and food are in abundance and Jade is the centre of attention. She is dressed in a figure-hugging dress and stand-out shoes; in fact, she clearly stands out in comparison to anyone else in the home and there must be at least twenty others. This is strange. How did she go from this confidently vibrant woman to someone who is as distraught as the one we saw climbing under the covers of her bed in a bid to shield herself from further pain?

Oh, here comes a cake and everyone starts singing. She smiles and loves the attention she is receiving.

"Happy birthday to you, happy birthday to you. Happy birthday, dear Jade, happy birthday to you. For she's a jolly good fellow, for she's a jolly good fellow, for she's a jolly good fellow and so say all of us. Hip! Hip! Hooray!" They all sing in unison.

"Go on, Jade, make a wish," someone shouts.

She closes her eyes. She thinks really hard and she takes a long moment to project her wish to the right source. Her heart beams as she puts so much passion into this wish. Then she blows with all of her might and all thirty-one candles are blown out in one mighty breath.

I hone in my wish giving senses to pick up on the vibration of thought that she has put out there and hear a whisper: "I wish to find true love."

She has obviously never felt fulfilled by love and yet she is surrounded by it. She has the biggest desire to be unconditionally loved. I suspect her idea of love is expectation and not in the truest of forms. Love is not just an emotion. It is a gift. It is not something that can be taken lightly but it can create miracles when we open ourselves up to it. To receive true love from another we must first truly love ourselves as like attracts like. Loving ourselves is being in contact with our heart central, accepting ourselves for all that we are and forgiving ourselves and others for mistakes that have been made. I feel that my job in this case is to help her through the external darkness into the lightness she has within. Until then I will not be able to grant her wish as it would be negligent of me to do so as it would only create further despair.

I shall start by returning to the Jade I have first encountered on this journey. Her energy needs comforting to save her from destructive despair. I absorb a little of the beautiful energy from the twinkle before placing it back into its compartment to recharge.

Standing looking at the quivering lump hidden under the radiant duvet cover that is wrapped around her slim frame, I move closer, to the side of the bed. I lie beside her and wrap my arms around her and then I project. I open up my heart chakra. The loving healing energy that I am instilling into Jade's core will help her feel some relief for a time. I am finding it virtually impossible to unlock her heart chakra; it is sealed so tightly, and I think it has been sometime since it has been opened. I feel that there is a scar from a past hurt that is carved deep inside it.

For healing to be successful, she must restrain her urge to keep her love locked away and she must free the pain from the past. It is the past and must be left there. Claire then lies on the other side of her body and the loving energy we both create has instigated some tears, some release. Suddenly, Jade hops up, catching us off guard and we both tumble to the floor. She grabs her pillows and starts screaming and punching those pillows as if they were the pain that hurts her heart. Then she lies back down and covers herself over and begins the healing process.

We have done all that we can for now; she will go through a process of healing if she listens to her inner self and she will be stronger if she allows herself to be. I do hope so. Claire and I take up position in the corner of the room. We must not talk as our voices may be picked up on a frequency that will jeopardise our actions.

We observe for a few moments more to see if our energies have taken effect and for self-love to shine through, but there is no further movement. Then suddenly Jade throws back the covers again – less aggressively this time. She sits at the side of the bed.

She says, "Okay, Jade, pull yourself together, get ready and do something else."

She stands up and walks towards her full-length mirror and looks at herself for a few moments. I feel her projecting some love onto herself as she gazes at her reflection in a caring way.

She then picks up her mobile phone from the floor and telephones someone.

"Hi, Cheryl, are you free tonight? You are? Great. Do you fancy having a girlie night out? Don't worry about money, my shout. Great. See you in The Stable Bar at seven."

She then makes her way over to her gigantic wardrobe and starts pulling out dresses and shoes of all shapes and colours.

"Oh, now what to wear?"

This I expect will make her feel good. She will make herself look a million dollars and by the sounds of it paint the town red with her friend. I do hope there are no repercussions. I shall leave her to it now and revisit again in a while. My energy level is quite low as that took a lot out of me and I need to replenish it in order to visit the others.

When love is gifted to us and our hearts beat as one it is then that we truly understand the highest potential that love has to give; magic comes from this source and much healing in the world comes from the energy created. So, the more people take the time to allow the love that is meant for them to find them, the better the world will be. It may happen in younger years or in old age, but the one thing that is definite is that even if it passes you by in the first time around or the second or third, it will find you when you open yourself to it.

CHAPTER SEVEN
Melody

Revitalised by Claire, my personal energy reviver, I am now able to move on. We arrive at a quiet wilderness location. The atmosphere is tranquil and the exact place I would have pictured Melody residing. I am happy to know that her surroundings complement her personality.

I stand at the bottom of her driveway which leads through some mature but perfectly pruned trees. Her cottage-like home is serene with flower beds arranged in such a way that you are guided to an emerald green door that seems to invite you in for tea. The door opens, and Melody emerges with a mat, a bottle of water and some earphones. She strolls over to the little wooden gate that leads to a meadow, heads right to the middle of the vastness and spreads her mat. The sun is shining and when she sits down with her legs folded in front of her she stretches backwards. It is as if she is allowing her body to consume as much of the sun's energy as it can hold. She looks very radiant.

Claire and I exchange glances. She also looks relieved at what she is able to witness here. I know the energy of our thoughts is combining and she is constantly connected with me during these encounters.

Sitting upright, Melody takes a meditation position. She is clearly focused, and her earphones are relaying a guided meditation. I watch her closely for some time as she goes within. The energy that her oneness with her mind, body and spirit is creating is cleansing her soul and connecting her to her spirituality where she has found true peace and happiness. This intensity does not happen for everyone. Melody is on the perfect path for her and she is open to all that comes to her.

She also understands that we are all a magnetic field attracting certain experiences to us. For instance, if we feel love we project love and then we will receive love in return. If we feel fear, we will then project fear and something to be fearful about will come our way. This is increased awareness of the laws of attraction that were created from the beginning of time. If only Jade knew a little of what Melody does! She is on her own journey though, and she may take time out from the hustle and bustle of life to pick up on the opportunity to connect with herself and her inner wisdom.

Melody's energy is peaceful, and I am relieved to say that this is an easier introduction. She opens her eyes, takes a deep breath and rises. Suddenly, she drops everything she is holding and quickly makes her way towards a lone dandelion that is standing tall and filled with seedlings ready to float away with a single gust of wind. I have a feeling this is going to be a moment of wishing, so I prepare myself to capture the wish as it floats by. That enables me to have full control over it.

Picking the dandelion, she closes her eyes and concentrates. The wish comes rushing towards me and I prepare myself to catch the seedling as it floats past. I listen closely to the request coming from this precious embryo of Mother Nature; it whispers, "I wish for the ability to heal the hearts and bodies of those in need." A tear comes into my eye as I think of the unselfish beauty that is this gorgeous lady. The beautiful seedling that carries this peaceful aspiration is so full of life. I shall keep it with me and plant it close to her home where it will flourish and always be close by. It is obviously my job to help her recognise that by emitting the energies she possesses, she is already spreading peace and happiness to others.

She must, however, have crossed many bridges in life to have reached this pinnacle. I feel we need an insight to a part of the Melody that we have the joy of experiencing today. Claire and I hold hands. With our thoughts combined and the twinkle to guide us, we are projected back to a time when Melody was a young girl. She looks about fourteen and is standing outside a home similar to the one she lives in now. Oh, my goodness, it is the same one. Is it any wonder she is so grounded? She has had the one home base to flourish from all of her life.

She is outside and walks in the direction of the gate that leads to the meadow. At the top of the hill there is a big tree and it has a homemade swing attached to it. This is the cherry on top of the cake of this picturesque idyllic family home. It truly is the dream that many people aspire to and it leads me to further understand why it is that peace and happiness are fundamental values for Melody.

We follow her to her hilltop retreat. The views are breathtaking as we can see all around us. Even the nearby town is visible because the roof tops of the houses peek above the treetops and the church steeples give an indication of the town's perimeter. I see that Melody has a tree house in the branches that she accesses by using wedges of branch stumps that have been left over after pruning. As she sits there swinging her legs something catches her eye. A young bird in a neighbouring nest is preparing to take flight. It holds on to the edge of the nest clearly fearful of the prospect of flying but, like every species in life, we all must learn to leave the nest, and this is the first big step for a young bird. After spending some time struggling with the challenge it finally jumps from the nest. To our horror we are not the only ones watching. A big tom cat is also watching on a lower branch and just as the baby bird takes its plunge the cat pounces. It swings at the bird and knocks it zooming in another direction.

Instinctively Melody hops right out of her tree house and shields the bird from any further harm from the cat by firmly saying, "No, Tiger, no, go home." It turns around defeated and retreats back to the house.

She immediately lifts the little bird into her hands. It is hurt and may not survive this ordeal. The shock would be enough to kill such a vulnerable little thing. Clasping it gently in her hands she holds it close to her heart and closes her eyes. She is projecting healing love to the bird. We can see it flow straight from her and into the little mite. After a few moments she opens her hands and there is a little bird cheeping away, sitting as if nothing had happened. She smiles and puts him back up into his nest. I cannot believe what I have just witnessed. This is a little miracle all on its own. This girl is filled with so much pure loving energy that it is obvious she can heal life-threatening ailments. I am almost certain that Melody still holds this gift within. I shall have to consider further the possibilities of such a modern-day healer.

We are back to the present and Melody has started walking up the hill to the very tree we have visited though it is now many years later. She sits on the same homemade swing and looks out at the view before her. There are a few more rooftops and high-rise buildings and the two steeples are still there. The next thing that happens will be imprinted in my mind for eternity. A bird flies down from the tree and rests on her shoulder chirping away in her ear as if she understands what it is saying. I have not seen such a peaceful interaction between a person and an animal before. I have come across cases where people are controlling an animal but, in this case, it is as if they are equal and coexist in this world close to each other. She truly has so much to give and a desire to share it. But why is she not already?

This little world she has created for herself is a little heaven on earth. This is the vision that His Almighty has envisioned for us all, so that we are at peace with each other even through species. Is it any wonder Melody feels compelled to share peace with others? She lives in constant peace within and outside her core. Should she be a selfish person she would spend all of her days here and not want to share her pleasures with anyone. But that is the thing about human nature; each human is different, it is how the world goes around. Should we all be the same, think the same way and want the same things it would be mundane. Instinctively people want to learn new things and challenge themselves physically and through thought.

Quite unexpectedly Melody's twinkle starts beaming. I peer in to see that it is trying to show me something. I allow it to shine and it brings us to a place far from the tranquil setting of the sanctuary Melody usually surrounds herself with. Melody is there. She is dressed differently, and she is hugging a baby. There are numerous children around, many of them babies. There is a lot of crying and the language they speak is different. Melody is playing with some children and they are giggling. When she moves to another area they follow her like little ducklings after the mother duck. Melody seems very happy. She is sharing so much loving energy with these children and they are absorbing it like little sponges as they must have rarely experienced such raw, true love before. I realise it is an orphanage. The foreign lady, who seems to be in charge of the babies, smiles and thanks Melody continuously. She is humble and grateful for the help she is receiving. I can see that Melody is feeling quite fulfilled here. She is happy that her love is being gratefully received.

I continue to observe as she says her goodbyes for the day. It is quite emotional for the babies and she is putting on a brave face. She leaves and when she gets out of the gates she runs as fast as she can to a nearby stream. It smells a bit and the water is quite polluted, but Melody doesn't seem to mind as she creates a little stream all on her own with the tears that fall from her eyes. She feels so much pain as though holding the babies isn't enough. She wants to provide a peaceful and loving place for them all to grow. Love is a vital ingredient for anything to flourish beautifully. When something is grown and nurtured with love it lasts longer and is a love giver in return.

I am drawn to another time when Melody is younger, and she seems to be in a doctor's surgery. She is sitting with an older woman who I assume is her mother and she is holding her hand tightly. The doctor looks up from the screen and starts talking.

"Mrs Harrington, you and Melody have come to receive the results of the scan that we have all been eagerly awaiting?"

"Yes, we have, Doctor." She gives Melody a hug.

"I am sorry to have to inform you that Melody is unable to have children."

At this revelation they both start to cry.

The doctor looks at Melody and says in a sympathetic tone, "I understand that this is a very hard thing to come to terms with, especially for a sixteen-year-old who has her whole future ahead of her."

"I wanted to have children and now you say that will never happen." Her voice is a whisper.

The Doctor tries to offer reassurance. "Try to remember that you are young and at least you have discovered this before you settled down and started trying for a family. And with all of the advancements in the medical profession, well, you never know what may become available in the future."

"I'm sorry, but that doesn't make me feel any better."

"Of course not, and I am sorry too. I would like to refer you to our practising counsellor. She is very good, and I feel that she will assist you in coming to terms with this shocking news."

"I don't think a shrink will give her back a functioning womb, Doctor."

"Mrs Harrington, you are not helping your daughter in her vulnerable time."

"Melody is not the only one who is vulnerable. Try having to accept that you have borne a daughter who will never have any children. It is like having just discovered that your child is disabled, because it is a disability."

"Mrs Harrington, that is very . . ."

The doctor tries to express his disgust at her outburst, but she quickly follows by saying, "However, we are a close family and we will support each other through this. We are both going to have to come to terms with this together. Should her younger sister Joan get tested?"

"Joan is thirteen?"

"Yes, Doctor."

"And has she begun menstruating?"

"Yes, a few months ago."

"Well that would indicate that she is producing eggs whereas Melody doesn't."

"Oh well, that's something at least," she sighs.

"Mrs Harrington, I would like to recommend that you see our family counsellor."

"Not on your Nelly, Doctor. We are not having everyone saying that we are crazy as well. One label is enough, thank you," she abruptly says as they stand up to leave.

"I will have Mavis give you a call and see how you feel over the next few days," he calls after them.

We quickly return to the scene where Melody is swinging on the swing and now there are some rabbits and squirrels joining her also. I understand why she went inward to seek enlightenment.

Claire and I exchange a look. We have so many aspects of Melody to piece together; her patchwork cloth of life is beautiful with a few bumps. I think it is time to leave her in this magical scene.

CHAPTER EIGHT
Irene

We first encounter Irene at a hospital. I get the impression that she is unwell. She is wearing a purple headscarf with the expression "Don't pity me, smile" written on it and sure enough anyone I see who has looked at her has smiled at her lovingly. She responds with a smile, the best one she can muster up with the energy levels that she is trying so hard to maintain.

I see an older lady with her; she has silver hair and is dressed in a quite distinguished manner. They have two children with them, twin boys who I estimate to be around two years old.

"I could have minded the boys at home, Irene," her mum reminds her.

"Oh Mum, stop fussing. It is fine that they are here. I just have a check-up and you know I don't like to be parted from them for too long."

"I know, Irene, and I'm sorry. It's just that hospitals – well, you know."

"Yes, Mum, of course I know. How do you think I feel about them? But they are doing what they can to save my life so that these gorgeous boys have a mum to guide them through life."

"Of course you are right, love. I am being selfish . . . I think I shall take a walk to the kiosk. Would you like a tea? I'm going to have one."

"Maybe a sparkling water, if you don't mind."

"Won't be long. Come on, boys." The boys excitedly grab both of her hands and obediently walk beside her, giggling at the prospect of what treats they may be going to receive.

I am saddened by this and feel quite emotional, maybe because of the little one growing inside me. How would I feel if my life was hanging in the balance and I was facing the prospect of not watching my beautiful gift grow up? I don't think I can bear it. I glance at Irene as she sits in the waiting room watching her boys walk away. I can imagine what thoughts she is having and so I ask Claire to send some comforting, reassuring energy into her energy field in the hope she will immediately feel it.

Some time passes, and she is called into a consultation room where a dark-skinned doctor welcomes her, and a nurse directs her to a chair.

"Hello, Mrs Dobson. How are you feeling today?" the doctor greets her.

"Yes fine, Doctor, a little tired but that's all."

"Good, good," he says as he goes through her notes.

"Well, Mrs Dobson."

"Please call me Irene," she nervously requests.

"Irene, sure, no problem . . . Well, Irene, we have been monitoring your progression through chemo and unfortunately we have not had the success we had hoped for."

She puts her head in her hands and sobs. "Does that mean that I am going to die and leave my boys?"

The nurse puts her arm around her shoulder to comfort her as the tears flood out of her eyes. She hands her a tissue and after Irene blows her nose the doctor continues.

"Don't lose faith, Irene. We are not giving up on you yet."

Irene smiles at the doctor in relief.

"However, we are going to have to put you through a more aggressive program. Are you up for that?"

"Yes, Doctor, whatever it takes."

"It is not going to be easy and you are going to need some extra help, Irene. You will need to focus on yourself right now and not on others; it is very important."

"Whatever it takes, Doctor. I'm not ready to give up yet."

"I will see you here in a few days. The nurse will arrange your appointment and we will get things underway fairly quickly. If in the next few days you have any problems please contact your local GP straight away."

She rushes out the door to where her mum sits with the two boys.

"Well, what did he say? Are you in recovery?"

"Not yet, Mum, not yet," she replies gloomily while trying to put on a happy face for her boys.

"Oh, your poor boys," her mum says, tears welling in her eyes but kept hidden from the boys who are merrily eating candy from a little toy dispenser.

"Mum, it's a long shot but I have to find her. This is the universe telling me that I need to contact her. It's time."

Her mother, looking around to make sure that no one has overheard her daughter's declaration, says, "Irene, you know you cannot do that. She has a new life and you can't go wading in and turn it upside down. You need to focus on these two. You barely have enough energy for them right now. Never mind dealing with the topsy turvy emotions of a teenager. She might not want to know you anyway and it would all be for nothing."

"No, Mum, it won't be for nothing. I need to get to know her and she deserves to know that I exist and that I do love her. We have been kept apart for long enough."

"Irene, you are not thinking rationally right now, and I want you to consider this carefully before you jump right in."

"I will, Mum. In fact, I have thought about nothing else for the past sixteen years. I think we should go now and talk about this another time."

Irene's twinkler starts to beam, and I know it is time to find out what this is all about. Our energies are directed to an earlier time. Irene is a teenager, about sixteen because she looks like neither a girl nor a woman. She is heavily pregnant and bored with what she is doing, which seems to be polishing all the ornaments in a big glass cabinet.

"Are you nearly finished, Irene?" a firm voice rises from the kitchen.

"Yes, nearly done, Mum," she answers, rolling her eyes.

"Great, when you are finished there will you come and dry these dishes as I have some washing to hang out?"

"Ah Mum, can I not have a break? I am pregnant you know in case you haven't noticed?"

"I have certainly noticed that you are pregnant, but that doesn't make you an invalid and it should definitely not make you a lazy young lady," her mum firmly replies. "Oh yes, and that young couple who are going to adopt your baby are calling around today."

"What? No way, Mum," she says defiantly.

"Yes, Irene, and don't you take that tone with me," her mum snaps back.

"Mum, please, I don't want to give away the baby. Is there no way I can keep it?"

Her mum realises that she was being a bit tough and so more caringly she gives Irene a hug and says, "Irene, dear, we have talked about this and the decision has been made and we cannot go back on it now. Of course you are going to feel a little uneasy. That is just normal for someone in your position to feel this way. It is because of your hormones, love. This is best for everyone all round; the baby will have a mum and dad that can afford to take care of it and you can get on with your life. Everybody will be happy."

"It just doesn't feel right, Mum," Irene responds.

"Ah how do we know what is the right way to feel with something like this, dear? But aren't they a really nice couple that we have chosen?"

"Yes, I suppose," she says reluctantly.

"Well then, let's wipe away these tears and get ourselves ready. All of this palaver will be over in a few weeks and you can get back to school and see your friends again. Then you will be okay."

I have seen enough here now. We shall return to visit her in the present. She is at a park with a tall man who I consider to be her husband as he is carrying the two boys and is wearing a wedding ring. They now seem to be having a lot of family fun, as they run about playing football. Irene is lovingly setting out the picnic mat and places a feast on it for them all to eat. Each morsel has been lovingly prepared by her for her family that she cherishes so dearly. She gazes at them having fun and her handsome husband, the love of her life, showing the boys some ball skills. The loving energy that is glowing from her right now is blinding. She starts to cry but keeps sorting things for her family. Her husband sees her crying and gives the boys some tricks to keep practicing while he runs to her side.

"What's wrong, love? Are you okay?" he asks, concerned.

"I just love you all so much, Brad, that I don't want to leave my beautiful family."

Hugging her tightly he says, "Oh love, you're not going to leave us. It will all be okay. We will find a donor; I believe it."

She pushes herself away and takes a moment before saying, "Brad, I have something I need to tell you."

"What is it?" he asks, confused about her changed tone.

"You are going to have to prepare yourself for a bit of a shock."

"Please just tell me, Irene, will you? You're killing me here."

"Well, many years ago, sixteen years ago in fact, I had a baby."

"What? Why did you not tell me this before?"

"I don't really know if I am to be honest. I suppose I didn't want you thinking any less of me."

"Tell me what happened. Where is your baby?"

"Well, Mum arranged for her to be adopted. I was expected to forget all about her and move on with my life."

"That's a bit harsh."

"Yeah, I thought so too but Mum was quite adamant that this was the best thing all around. She was already a single parent to me and she wanted me to go to university and everything. Well, the rest is history, I suppose. The thing is, now I feel that I need to try my best to find my daughter, to have a relationship with her. What do you think about that?"

"I am happy for you to pursue this love, once you are sure that it is what you want. She is part of you and so I am happy to embrace it all, whatever happens."

"Oh, Brad, you're the best husband ever. Thank you. I called her Hope you know, and I think that she is going to give me hope back in return."

"That is a beautiful name, love, and if it helps you get better, it is so worth it."

They lovingly embrace, and she evidently feels freer having disclosed her great secret to her husband. That is evident on her face and in the dramatic change in her aura.

"Now what about this picnic? We are starving," he says as he runs and picks up his two boys and swings them around.

I so hope that this works out for them all. It pains me to feel the sadness that surrounds the whole ordeal they are going through. It is time for us to move on to witness her wish as her twinkler has been summoning us.

We are brought back to a time when Irene is younger. She is not much older than the last time we encountered her while she was expecting. She has not got a bump now and looks quite slim. There is no happy glow shining from her and that indicates that she is experiencing sorrow. I suspect she has been finding it difficult to deal with the emotions involved with getting separated from her newborn. She is in a backyard. It has a large grassed lawn and a patio area at the back of the yard. She is sitting there drawing illustrations for a picture book that she is putting together called 'Hope's Big Day Out'. I feel that this keeps her connected to the baby she was made to give away.

As she sits there under a mature tree I see a bird above her working away, fixing its nest and cleaning itself. Such a busy little bird it is too and with such beautiful white feathers, the whitest white that I have ever seen. Then as if by magic a feather drops from the nest right onto Irene's drawing. It takes her by surprise and she picks it up, smiling.

She looks up and says to the bird, "Little bird, have you given me a wish? Should I wish for it, do you think? I know when a feather finds you like this it is a gift for sure. Aah well, it will do no harm to wish it anyway."

She closes her eyes and wishes with all of her might. She then holds up the feather and blows it away. I summon it my way and it responds by obeying my command. I gently hold it to my ear and hear the whisper.

"I wish that I get to be a mum to my little Hope when it is the right time for us both."

Well, it must now be time for this long-awaited wish to manifest or I would not be here. It is how the wish will come about that may test personal boundaries. However, this is seldom the case when a wish comes straight from the heart and for a greater good. How unselfish this girl is that she wants her reunion with her daughter to happen at the best time for her also. There is a lot going on with Irene and her wish. It is a matter of life and death. We will leave her for now with some peaceful healing energy that will comfort her for a time.

CHAPTER NINE
Joy

Our next case is one that I have been anticipating since we arrived. Joy is a thirty-two-year-old, five feet two inches of sheer energy. Her energy radiates around her and to everyone she meets she is like an energy beacon that they are free to feed upon should they need to. A smile is ever present on her small happy face.

We visit her while she is in her garden. The sun is shining down upon the rainbow sea of flowers that covers her quaint backyard. She is singing while she waters and prunes her plants. This makes her happy. I watch as she absorbs the vibrant energy from the nature she has nurtured. The love she has put into her garden is returned to her tenfold. I can plainly see that she is joyous on this occasion but as the twinkle is calling I decide to experience what it has to reveal to me.

When I open the holding vessel I am bedazzled by the splendour that is the twinkle and which I have the pleasure of witnessing first hand. I readjust my perspective and discover that the setting Joy is in seems to be a university as there is a very grand, grey building as a backdrop behind her. There are many people gathered around her and her voice is continuously chit chatting away and there is no shortage of listeners around, willing to absorb what she is saying.

"So, what does everyone think about being part of the new show that I am trying to put together?" she asks.

"I think it will be great, Joy. Who is the starring act?" enquires a tall blonde who would not look out of place in a cheerleading role.

"Hey, me of course. No one else will get a word in." Everyone giggles, and she continues, "I am actually thinking of just hiring a load of manikins so that I don't have to share any stage time."

Everyone laughs at her humour.

"Where is it going to be held and when are the auditions?" asks a lad of Oriental origin.

"Auditions are tomorrow at lunch time and it is being held in the grand hall," Joy quickly responds.

"Lunchtime – does that mean there will be food?" enquires a quite obese fellow who has ginger hair and an Irish accent.

"Only if you bring some. Are you offering to cater?"

"Yeah, catering would draw in a crowd for sure, Joy," the dark-skinned youth exclaims as the other guy is shaking his head wishing he had not shared his opinion.

"I must get moving or I will be late for my next class. I will put a poster on the notice board. Check it out. See you, guys."

"Bye, Joy," they say in unison.

I knew she would be popular. She has that sort of presence about her. No inhibitions. In situations where others would think twice and talk themselves out of it, she doesn't. She lets her instinct be her guide. It is such a shame that there are not more people like her in this world, more people who are so in tune with their inner voice that they don't question it and trust it to guide them to where they need to go. That is why it exists, isn't it? To cater for our best interest in the pursuit of our own personal goals.

Her twinkler gleams and I am tempted not to go there yet as I feel I need to experience more of her here before I see any further. But alas, when the twinkler beckons I must answer, or the powerful insight may be lost in the cosmos.

We are drawn to a time that doesn't seem too long ago. In fact, there is a school newspaper on a bench, dated the previous year. As I look closer I see that Joy's face is the dominant one on the front page. I am drawn to a toilet block and so I enter. To my horror I witness Joy being pushed up against a wall and being terrorised by two bigger girls.

Another girl is on look out and cheering the girls on.

"So little Miss Joyful, how does it feel to be not feeling so joyous for a change?"

Joy, with her head forced against the wall replies, "Hey, who said I am not joyous? I embrace all of the experiences life throws my way."

"Oh, just hit her, Francine, she makes me sick," the girl at the door shouts.

"You are just pushing me, aren't you?" The girl pushes her harder.

"No, I am sad that you feel the need to do this to me. I know you really don't want to harm me, but you feel pressured to do this by those girls."

"Don't you pity me," the girl screams.

And at that the girl at the door yells "Bob!" which I assume to be a code word for 'teacher'. The girl gives Joy one last push, saying, "We're not finished with you yet, happy girl."

They all run away, and Joy quickly pulls herself together. A tear is in her eye that she refuses to release. She looks at herself in the mirror and smiles her bright beaming smile but still cannot hide the sadness that is in her heart. She may be small in frame, but she is big in character. This is what intimidates the bully girls who have picked on her. She is bigger than them in personality and they will realise in later years that in order to change they must relive and forgive themselves for their misdeeds. They themselves will feel a stronger challenge than the one they imposed on Joy.

It is time for us to venture further into the past for Joy. This time we are in a large backyard. There is a heavily catered and massively crowded table. The atmosphere is a fun-filled family one.

Everyone seems at ease with each other and there are children running around playing games, teasing one another as they run around the legs of the adults. The sausages on the barbeque are sizzling. It is a warm and sunny day, laughter fills the air and then someone clinks a glass. Everyone responds by going quiet.

A tall man stands up and says, "Hello everybody, I know you are all keen to know why we have invited you all here today."

"Yeah, Bruce, please share with us your news."

"Okay, Phil, give me a chance," says Bruce in a sarcastic tone and continues, "Well, Anna and I have asked you here today to share with us the wonderful news that Joy does not need a heart transplant. She just needs to have a minor surgery to replace a valve and she should be able to live a happy, healthy normal life like any other child does."

"Oh Bruce, that is wonderful news," a stumpy woman exclaims as she gives them a big hug and Joy beams with delight at the prospect that she has made everyone happy.

"You all have been our rock through this challenging time for our little family and we want you all to know how much we value all that you have sacrificed and donated to us. We could not have gotten through it all so successfully if it had not been for your generosity and love. From our hearts, we love you all."

Some of the ladies are crying and Bruce continues to speak.

"And that is not the only reason why we decided to ask you all here today."

"There's more?" the stumpy lady queries.

"Anna, would you like to share this one?" Bruce asks his wife to step up and address everyone.

Everyone is waiting in anticipation for this beautiful lady with blonde hair and a slim figure to speak. "Okay, well, we wanted to let you all in on a secret that we have been keeping hidden for a few weeks and won't be able to keep hidden for much longer."

The stumpy lady asks, "Is this true? I am getting another grandchild?"

"Yes, Mum, you are."

"Oh, you little gems. So, Joy, are you happy to be getting a little brother or sister?"

"Yes, Nana," Joy excitedly replies from the embrace of her doting father's arms.

I can see that Joy comes from a strong supportive background. This is essential for any child to flourish in life. I now also have an understanding about how she wants the world to experience joy and how she has evolved to a point of wisdom and enlightenment so early in life. This is because she had a brush with death herself and was subsequently grateful for her very existence. This is something that many take for granted.

It is now time to encounter Joy's wish because my heart radiates with love as I connect with the way she has been brought up and want that for my own child. What beautiful parents she had to give her the gift of gratitude in such a way that she rejoices from it every day of her life and wants everyone to experience it also.

Her twinkler finally starts to gleam. It gave me a moment to embrace those values. We arrive at a location which is quite dark. It seems to be a festival of some kind as I see people dressed up and from their attire I suspect that the occasion being celebrated is Halloween. Ghosts, ghouls and witches are running around as free as buzzy bees. I strain to see where Joy is. Is she a child dressed up or an adult? I don't know, and then as if by magic a little girl aged around ten comes walking towards me. I know that it is Joy as soon as I set eyes on her. She is wearing a fairy costume that is rainbow coloured and stands out amongst the scary and dark clothing of all the other children.

It is time for the fireworks and everyone gathers and watches in amazement at the beautiful display that is being painted across the sky. All different colours and noises and shapes. All that can be heard from the crowd are "Ah's" and "Oh's" every time one goes off.

Joy is on her dad's shoulders and her mum is close by with a little boy who must be the new addition we learned of in our previous encounter. When the display comes to an end Joy just keeps looking in amazement at the sky.

"Hey, Dad, don't the stars look especially beautiful tonight?"

"They certainly are very beautiful tonight, Joy."

"Oh Daddy, look at that star. It is moving so fast."

"Joy, it's a shooting star," he says excitedly. "You can make a wish on that star; would you like to?"

"Oh yes, Daddy. What do I do?"

"Okay, first you say a rhyme. So, say after me, 'Star light, star bright...'"

"Star light, star bright."

"Shooting star that I see tonight," Dad says.

"Shooting star that I see tonight," Joy repeats.

"I wish I may, I wish I might," Dad says.

"I wish I may, I wish I might," Joy repeats.

"Have the wish I wish tonight," Dad says.

"Have the wish I wish tonight," Joy repeats.

"Then you close your eyes and wish as hard as you can for something that you want more than anything else in the world."

Joy innocently closes her eyes and wishes as hard as she can. I prepare myself to catch it as it shoots from her energy field. Never have I felt so strong a wish. I listen carefully to the wish: "I wish that I can help people's hearts be filled with joy."

I am overwhelmed with the unselfish nature and desires of this beautiful girl. Most girls this age would request a pony or a new doll but not this jovial treasure. I expect that she will lead a life of tiring but rewarding fulfilment. Of course, there will be many challenges to overcome on this path but to know that you have brought joy into the heart of another is a gift straight from Heaven.

Returning to the present, we find ourselves with Joy and a man who is quite handsome and not much taller than she is. He has blonde hair and a lot of love in his heart also. They are walking along a promenade which has a beautiful backdrop of the bluest sea I have ever seen. This lady is surrounded in beauty and that is because she only lets beauty into her life. Being this selective ensures that joy and sheer fulfilment are maintained at all times. I am privileged to encounter this lady. It is, however, time to move on to our final assignment.

CHAPTER TEN
Lucy

Our final introduction is to Lucy. The setting is a manor house. It is exquisite, and a lake flows right by. It is a temporary home to houseboats and speed boats alike. The perfectly manicured driveway swerves into an S bend directly up to the grand residence at the top. Lucy seems to be with her parents. She is wearing a floral print traditional dress that looks very stylish. They are all standing outside, and she is looking as though she does not want to be there. Her mum and dad are chatting with her.

"Lucy, please put a smile on your face; we are out in public and you look so sad."

"Well, maybe that is because I am sad; you know that I didn't want to come today. There is no reason in the world why I could not have stayed with Aunty Gina."

"We are your parents, Lucy, and it means we are family. Today is a family occasion. I am sorry that you feel you don't want to be part of that, but you have to try to enjoy yourself when you are here. Do you hear me, young lady?"

She turns her head and looks away disrespectfully. Others in the group are looking over to see what is going on. Her dad looks as if he is going to blow a head gasket and her mum as if she has just swallowed a wasp.

"I said do you hear me?" he asks loudly.

"Yeah, of course. How could I not? You don't need to shout. You know what, you're making a scene," she cheekily says without a care in the world.

Her father doesn't know what to do, so he gets up and storms inside and heads to the bar.

"Look at what you have done to your poor dad. He hasn't drunk a drop in twenty years and you have managed to drive him to it in a matter of seconds," complains her mother.

"Well, Mother, he made me come here and so I made him go there. It's tit for tat, isn't it? Maybe next time you will let me stay at home."

"You have gotten to be a cheeky little missy, Lucy. Where has my beautiful princess gone?"

"I am not a display doll that you just take everywhere for people to look at, Mum. And do you know what else? It's not just me who is always unreasonable. You know you and Dad are impossible to talk to at times as well."

"That is enough of that, young lady. Just get yourself into that hotel so that we can finally get the shine off us and back onto that gorgeous baby over there."

"Oh yes, the baby. Well that baby isn't yours you know and don't think that I don't know that you would rather have a baby than me."

"What are you talking about, Lucy? We are your parents and we love you."

"No, you don't!" she shouts at her mum as she runs away.

"Lucy, get back here!" her mum cries loudly after her.

Lucy doesn't stop running and there is no hope of her mum catching her, so she decides to join her husband.

"Wow, Claire, this girl holds a lot of resentment towards her parents. I wonder where it stems from," I say.

"Her energy is so intensely shadowed for someone of such a young age. I am sensing at this moment that she is releasing some tension sobbing away."

Just at that point her twinkler starts to beckon, so I believe that even though she has had only such a short existence she has still got some issues to work out. I trust the twinkler to bring us to a place of significance for Lucy.

The location is a two-storey house situated on a large block. There is a children's section and a swimming pool in the backyard and some nice cars parked in the driveway at the front. I suspect that this family is quite well off financially.

Hearing some voices from around the back of the house I venture to their location. Lucy, who is a few years younger, is sitting with her parents. They all seem to be having a lot of fun if the smiles and laughter are anything to go by. I wonder what has happened to turn things around so much for Lucy.

There are a number of people there. Lucy is bouncing on a trampoline doing star jumps.

"Look at me!" she yells.

"Well done, Lucy. You are doing so well that you will be an Olympic competitor next," says a lady that I don't recognise."

"Really?" asks Lucy excitedly.

"Don't encourage her too much, Gina. Our Lucy is already a true dreamer," says her mum.

"We all have to dream, sis. If we don't, life would be so miserable."

"Maybe so, but we don't want her encouraged too much or she will end up living her life in the clouds."

"We shouldn't try to control every trait of our children's, sis. They are all different and will all grow up differently if they are allowed to grow with guidance and love," Gina remarks.

"Gina, I think that you should leave," Lucy's mum says abruptly.

"What? Why? What did I say?" she asks, confused.

"Please go. We can't have you coming here and judging our parenting techniques. It will just confuse Lucy. She needs our guidance, or she will never amount to anything."

Gina picks up her bag and starts to depart when Lucy hops off her trampoline and runs over to see what is happening.

"Where are you going, Aunty Gina?" she asks innocently.

Bending down to Lucy's level she says, "Lucy, princess, you keep bouncing and dreaming, beautiful girl. I have to go now, and I hope to see you soon."

She gives her a big hug and then leaves.

"I don't want Aunty Gina to go," Lucy tells her mum.

"Well, Aunty Gina is gone, and she won't be back, so you are going to have to expect that you will not be seeing her for a while."

"No!" screams Lucy as she tries to run after her beloved aunt.

"Get back here, young lady." Her mother catches her and restrains her.

"I hate you, Mum. Why did you tell Aunty Gina to go away? I love her."

With that her mum strikes out and slaps her across the face. Shocked, Lucy places her hand on her face and runs off to her room where she lies sobbing on the bed.

I now have a clearer picture about the point where things changed for Lucy. This poor little girl obviously feels genuine, pure love from her Aunty, the kind that every child craves. It is through love and guidance that children grow up to being beautiful adults.

Returning to the initial scene at the stately mansion, I see that Lucy has arrived at a quaint little setting. A wishing well is a centrepiece to this area of the garden. Many coins lie at the base of the well and magic fills the air as I feel the energy of past wishes floating around. Some are beautiful and genuine while others are selfish and ugly.

Lucy checks the pockets of her dress for a coin. She finds a button and says to herself, "This will have to do." She closes her eyes, thinks for a moment and then quietly says, "I wish that my mum and dad were out of my life for good." I quickly catch the wish as it floats into the air before the other energies have any time to penetrate it.

So, Lucy is looking for some freedom to grow. I am amazed at how much she is being controlled whereas it is plain that she just needs praise and loving encouragements to grow. I think she gets this from her Aunty Gina and that is why she wants to be with her. Lucy's Mum's jealousy is ugly and is making her act negatively. It is also obvious that both Lucy's mum and dad fear losing her, and it enrages them when they feel a loss of control. If they only could see that by supporting Lucy and letting her grow naturally they could easily draw her closer to them. It is no wonder Lucy is pushed towards being rebellious in order to free herself from the shackles of control.

We are about to leave when the twinkler beams and gets my attention. I see a woman coming towards Lucy. Through her tears she can't clearly make out who it is but as she gets closer she soon realises.

"Aunty Gina," she calls, relieved and happy.

They both run to each other and wrap themselves in each other's embrace.

"Everything will be okay, Lucy; you don't need to worry. I am here now."

"How did you know I was here?"

"Let's just say that your mum and dad aren't all heartless."

"Oh, I am so happy to see you. I have missed you."

"I have missed you more," says Gina and they both laugh.

"So, do you want to fill me in with what has been going on for you?" Gina asks.

I shall leave them now. I have enough information to base my further understanding. Each of these cases is so different and must be dealt with accordingly. Sometimes I think at such moments, *'what would Rupert do right now?'* There I always tend to find my answer. So, I have decided it will be good to have a break while we visit here. It will be good for Claire too as we have been working hard since we arrived.

CHAPTER ELEVEN
REVISIT

But alas, unexpectedly Jade's twinkle starts to glimmer, so something attached to her wish is occurring and we need to witness it in our evaluation. We are drawn to a bar. There is a warm atmosphere and the smell of alcohol is strong. People are happy in the merriment of the jovial surroundings they are visiting.

Groups of people of various ages are gathered in different seating arrangements. There are others meeting at the bar who order their next round of drinks. Energy is buzzing all around. The clock that hangs behind the bar shows that it is ten o'clock.

There is a band playing music that has enticed some people from their seats to swing each other around the dance floor. They are in competition yet smiling at each other as they spin around the floor. It is quite amusing to watch. I glance at Claire and smile to see she is jiggling to-and-fro slightly to the music. She stops when she sees me. That's a pity.

I decide to try and locate Jade. It seems to be mostly older people up this end of the long wooden bar, so we move around the corner and make our way to the other end. There are people playing pool and the music is more up to date here. Even I am swaying to-and-fro to the beat. Claire smiles and I continue, even jigging it up a bit.

Finally, we locate Jade in one of the booths. She doesn't look like the same Jade we were first introduced to and her energy is on fire. She rises from her sitting position and stands at the entrance to the booth after squeezing herself out past some of its occupants, one of whom nips her on the bottom as she slides over him to get past. She lets out a little squeal.

"Don't do that, Sean, that was sore," she says as she places her hand on her bottom in disgust. She is wearing a red micro dress with the most stand-out pair of shoes. She has the figure any model would be proud of. Her locks are styled, and she is heavily made up.

She makes her way to the bar. Her friend follows.

"What are we going to have this time, Cheryl?" she asks. "It's my round."

"Whatever you're having."

"Okay, sunshine slammers it is then." They both giggle.

"Hey is Sean really into you this evening?"

"No, he's not, Cheryl, and anyway I'm spoken for. Why don't you sit next to him when we get back? I know you like him," Jade replies teasingly.

"No, I couldn't, could I?"

"Sure you can."

After a time, the last orders have been drunk and carry outs are being purchased.

"Party in mine," Jade declares. "Every one's invited."

A convoy of people follows her down the street. They sing most of the way to her house and I see many curtains twitch.

Around ten people fill up the cosy living room and Jade puts on some music. The drinks are passed around and the house party begins. I cringe at some of the soul-destroying moments I witness. Alcohol can be a relaxant, an elixir to be utilised for celebration, but when it is abused in this way regrettable moments are sure to occur.

Jade leaves the room and makes her way clumsily up the stairs to her room. She is proceeding to get changed into something cosier when the guy from the bar – Sean – walks in.

"Hey, Sean, get out," she says.

"Ah Jade, I have just come to chat. It's a bit loud down there."

Jade doesn't answer. She proceeds to change into silky, red and grey striped pyjamas and a black camisole top.

"Ah Jade, you look very nice."

"You think so?" she says while checking herself out in her long mirror in an ultra-confident way. I suspect that the alcohol she has consumed has something to do with her confidence levels and has unusually increased her attraction to Sean.

Suddenly Sean has grabbed her and is kissing her passionately. At first, she tries to push him away but in her inebriated state she kisses him back. They fall onto the bed. He continues to kiss her in a sensual way. She groans with pleasure at the kiss. Responding immediately by pulling her camisole down to reveal her naked bosom, he slowly caresses her breasts with his hand. With his other hand he grasps her bottom, slowly gliding his fingers between her cheeks, briefly touching her g-spot, which creates an arousing response from her. He starts to kiss her breasts and she closes her eyes to feel the passion of the tender and utterly arousing touch. The sparks of desire shoot around the room and for this moment they are both in a harmonised state. Their energies are tangled in a web of pleasure. I would never have guessed this was possible from her reaction towards him earlier.

He continues to slowly make his way down, confidently pulling her camisole off first and then her silk pyjama bottoms slip smoothly off the bed and onto the floor. He oozes passion and adoration for her as he cherishes every part of her body. Kissing tenderly, he pulls her red lacy pants down, to reveal her perfectly groomed garden. He holds her pants in his hands. He lifts them and inhales her womanly scent. This fires him up and he pulls her to him. She straddles him, and he enters her. The satisfying groans of pleasure follow from both of them. They speed up and then he slows down, as if he never wants it to end. In a moment of awkwardness, they change position and he slowly slides himself in and out of her. Jade is enjoying every moment of this pleasure. How would she not? This is true love making in action. This is the type of natural ecstasy that platonic love is built upon. Once he knows that she has climaxed he allows himself to release. Sparks fly and they both feel the tingle which is evident in their reactions.

I am familiar with this moment and as I look around at Claire I am surprised to see that Jayden is standing there. I can't believe that this was going to happen. I didn't know about it. Jade is obviously the receiver of a gem. Being visited twice by two messengers at the same point in time is going to be challenging for her. I hope she is strong enough to endure the toll that this may take of her emotional stability because if she does she will see herself coming out the other side of it all victorious. Her inner strength will become impenetrable; but, on the other hand, if she can't find the strength to ride the storm then it may bring her to her knees.

Sean puts his arms around her and she falls asleep in his strong embrace, none the wiser that she has just become the receiver of a gem.

I am quickly drawn to a disturbance outside the room. Muffled voices can be heard from the other side of the door. All of a sudden, the door flings open and in storms a guy who is in a rage when he beholds the sight before his eyes. He shouts, "You whore!" at Jade and goes to have a go at Sean.

"Justin, wait!" Jade shouts, holding the duvet around her to cover her chest.

He charges out the door shouting, "Don't even think of contacting me again, we are so over."

The front door slams and he can be heard kicking posts outside and shouting absurdities as he makes his way up the street.

Jade puts her head in her pillow and covers herself in her duvet again. Sean tries to comfort her, but she abruptly tells him to go away. Reluctantly he gets dressed and leaves but before he goes he says, "You know what, Jade? There is someone who genuinely does really like you standing right here, if only that was enough for you."

This poor girl has hard lessons to endure. She experienced natural sensual passion with Sean that I sensed she had not allowed herself to experience in some time if ever. I trust that this has happened for a reason and that all will be revealed in time.

CHAPTER TWELVE
Absorption

We have, much to consider and I feel that a little break to absorb it all is exactly what we need. I choose to visit a place of extreme beauty and wonder where the energy of Mother Nature is present in abundance for us all to absorb when we open ourselves up to it. Each individual twinkle will need re-energising also in order for us to give the best to the receivers.

"Claire, I was thinking that our energies are what drive us along and the twinkles are looking quite dim. Will you take our energies on a tour of some of the natural beauties the world has to offer?" I ask.

"It would be my pleasure, Syd."

We stand in silence and hold hands. Our entities entwine, and we begin our journey. Arriving at Niagara Falls I am taken aback.

The powerful magnificent energy of this place is one of the many reenergising natural sources that Earth has to offer. Its energy is dynamic and revitalising. I watch in silence as the water cascades down over the cliff and collides with the peaceful pool waiting below. The impact creates energy so dynamic that it encapsulates all of the senses. The noise is thunderous in a calm refreshing way. I watch others witnessing the scale of magnificence for the first time. Their faces are blank in sheer amazement of the wonder they behold. I can see the organic energy entering their bodies and I know these people will not only take the beautiful memories of their experiences away with them but the golden energies they have unknowingly consumed have healed them within. This is one of those places of healing that have been gifted to the world to help alleviate some of its anguishes.

We sit for a time watching, hearing, smelling, touching and even tasting the uniqueness of the waterfall. I love how Claire and I never feel the need to constantly connect verbally; we are fine just being in each other's company witnessing things on the same level. It is so refreshingly special to share this encounter with Claire. This image is tattooed in my spirit now so that I shall always be able to connect with this energy should I ever need to. We move on to our next source of energetic magnificence.

We arrive at the Great Barrier Reef. It is beauty of another dimension. Its vibrancy is beauty at its best and will restore our hearts to their highest potential. I look to Claire and she smiles from ear to ear. We both absorb the unspoilt natural buoyancy of every part of this reef. It is vast, and it is beauty beyond imagination. The colours gleam to the extreme and the fresh fragrance fills the air. We both swim in and around the corals that effortlessly sway to-and-fro with the flow of the ecological splendour.

We spend some time swimming amongst the exquisite array of fish that call the reef their home. They are free from the damaging toxins that have been absorbed into the waters far and wide. Our essences are rejuvenated because of this invigorating experience. Yet another energy source to remember and feel its instant benefits. I could freely flow here forever but we must depart and explore some of the other natural energy sources Earth has to offer.

We are brought to a location that is barren in its vast dryness. The sand is a super charged orange and a large rock dominates the landscape. We just stand and watch this rock that is mesmerising. The spiritual powers that we are absorbing are unexplainable. I feel my soul being warmed, my wisdom being increased and my love for everything being increased. I feel a magnetic connection to this huge rock. Claire and I hold hands. We stand and watch it for hours. Amazingly it changes colour before our eyes; it is at one with the sun that transcends its energy to this absorbing powerful beacon. This is a special place and its isolation ensures it is visited only by those who have the intention of experiencing its great mystery. Spending time here has been so rewarding that I shall access the comfort of this wonder on many occasions. I feel spiritually richer because of this experience.

We observe the others who come to experience it; some are on a mission to conquer it. Many capture its magnificence on camera. My thoughts are drawn to the fact that its beauty may be captured on a photo but the energy it creates cannot. You cannot experience this healing energy unless you are here although I believe the benefits of its existence are felt worldwide as it works like a positive energy beacon. It is interesting to witness the reactions of others. Some do not stop long enough to allow their internal power supply to be recharged, only feeling the benefits for a fraction of the time that is possible. It is interesting to see the different interactions. Alas, we must move forward.

I am, however, not disappointed. The scenery I am now witnessing is captivating. I blink as the grass is the greenest green I have ever seen. I am drawn towards the mountains that dominate the landscape before me. They are like twins in their similarity, but each stands separately.

As we approach I feel myself being drawn between the two peaks as if some super charge is pulling me there. Before I know it, I have entered a valley, a valley created by the two magnificent mountains on either side of us.

"Oh Claire, this is eerily energising."

"It surely is, Syd. Isn't it wonderful?"

We are not alone. There are others here absorbing the energy that charges through this gap. I watch as strong horses bring tourists from one end of the valley to the other. They must be well trained to do so. However, there is one horse that has a novice rider on it galloping away to the horror of the mounted rider. She squeals and screeches, fearing for her life in that moment to the amusement of her group of friends. The wayward horse comes to a sudden halt at a large puddle of water, much to the relief of the shaken rider, who quickly dismounts and proceeds on foot as she ignores her friends in preference to completing the rest of the journey in isolation. Maybe she will gain the most from this experience if she is on her own anyway. I like the feisty energy of this girl and so I indicate to Claire that we should join her for the walk through the rest of the passage. I gift her with some forgiving energy and see her shoulders relax as she allows herself to take in the surrounding beauty and energy. I too am in awe of it all. It is as if energy pours straight down each mountain side and fills this valley to the brim. I feel immersed in sheer superlative energy.

A little physically tired but emotionally recharged, we reach the end of the valley. Waiting for us right there is the most vibrant rainbow I have ever seen. It seems so close that if I reached high enough I might touch it. To me it signifies the end of the journey through the valley, but the beginning of a brighter future filled with the golden gift we have been lucky enough to receive.

What a colourful way to end our whistle stop tour of some of the earth's most energising natural resources! Our journey may have come to an end, but the vivid images and memories are engraved deeply in my spirit. I certainly feel reenergised. Unconditional healing love comes from these sources.

It is now time to return to the mission in hand with renewed energy and focus.

CHAPTER THIRTEEN
Past Influences

Joy

We were a presence before we were all created. All of our past bodily experiences are stored deep down in our psyche. If we allow ourselves to dig deep, we will discover elements to our make-up that we never knew were there. A lot of people don't know why they do something a certain way, even when no one in their family during their upbringing had those traits to pass on. It is because part of us is defined by our past lives. They influence the person we are now. My energy has been influenced by past lives just as each one of these ladies.

To enable me to achieve a better understanding of each individual, it will be beneficial to delve further and visit the spirits that have gone before them as they have influenced the person I am experiencing in the now. I often wonder what my past influences have been and maybe I will visit them some day. I don't know why

I haven't done so. I feel some fear around thoughts of about visiting my past lives.

I find other people's past lives interesting. I await the call of a twinkler. One starts to dazzle; it is Joy's. I focus on it and it draws me in.

Claire and I are in an old Western town. It doesn't seem too busy as I see no one around. Suddenly I hear gun shots. They catch me by surprise and I drop to the floor. Then I realise that I am just an entity and cannot be pierced by any bullets, unlike the unfortunate guy who is lying in a heap on the dusty road before us.

"Johnny, you got him. Well, I'll be darned. I'd never have thought it in a million years," says a guy dressed in brown suede and a buckled belt with lots of guns on it.

"Oh, ye of little faith. Don't you know that these rootin' tootin' guns are the fastest in the west?"

"I do now buddy; you can watch my back anytime."

"Sorry, I can't say the same to you, my learned friend." Everyone in the crowd of men that have gathered around laughs.

Just then the saloon doors open wide and a well-dressed man with a moustache and a pocket watch in his hand shouts, "That's enough of that, boys. Come on in for a drink and some girls."

The cheers from the men are loud as they steam forward like a pack of wolves past the man at the door who I presume to be the owner of this establishment. Well, all of them except for Johnny. He wanders over, taking his time, and as he is passing the man at the door, he says, "Hey Francis, is there any entertainment of the comical variety around here tonight?"

"Comedy, young man? These men want girls to entertain them, not comedians."

"Do you want to place a bet on that?" challenges Johnny.

"Your darn right I do. I bet you a warm bed, dinner and all the ale you can stomach if you can get these guys to take their eyes off these girls for one minute to watch your comedy show."

"You're on." Johnny quickly grasps the chance to perform.

Making his way to the small but prominent stage he composes himself and urges a few of the girls who were dancing provocatively to leave the stage, thus sending them to the lion's den as the guys try to grab them. Girlie squeaks can be heard every time someone nips their bottom.

Johnny starts talking. Initially he has the guys' attention, but they soon lose interest and their focus is again on the girls and their ale. Francis, the saloon owner, gives Johnny a triumphant smile to show that he is winning the bet so far. But Johnny isn't finished yet; he goes and whispers something into the ears of two of the girls. They nod and giggle at his proposition. He then starts again. For thirty full minutes he entertains the men. They laugh and almost cry at times. He has brought comedy to the Wild West. Francis reluctantly hands over the keys to room five and Johnny responds by saying, "Thank you, a good night's sleep I shall have. I will have my dinner in my room if you don't mind, and as for all the ale I can drink, well, you can share that out between the men." He turns and shouts, 'Have a drink on me!"

Leaving the barman perplexed, he climbs the wooden staircase that leads up to the rooms.

The men have all found their way to the bar and they are demanding their free ale.

I have seen enough here to determine that Johnny is Joy's past influence. He is strong of mind, not easily influenced by the temptations in life that others desire. A comedy element is there, and he utilises it to spread fun and laughter to deter people away from the abundance of temptation that was rampant throughout the Wild West. A lot can be learned about this strength of character and I shall revisit my findings in my assessment.

Melody

Another twinkle begins to shine. This time it is Melody's. The setting is a very poor environment. A city of little shacks dominates this barren landscape. Dark-skinned ladies walk around with their young children strapped to their backs with cloth as they carry water to their makeshift homes and do other life-sustaining tasks.

I am drawn towards a lady. She is in a white cloth tent that is taller than the others and has a red cross above the door. She is carrying a baby and the vision brings memories back to me of when I visited Melody in the orphanage. This lady is wearing a white head dress that covers her hair and a grey dress with a white apron attached to the front.

"Sister Mary, over here, she has just collapsed," a young man calls.

She brings the child she is carrying back to his makeshift cot and rushes to tend to a woman who is lying on the floor in a malnourished and dehydrated state.

"We must get some fluids into her straight away. Let's get her up on to the bed," she instructs.

When they get her up on the bed it is obvious that this lady has a bump.

"This lady is with child," she notes.

She quickly rushes off and brings back her bag of medical supplies. She takes out a little device that resembles an egg cup, but I understand it to be a hearing device of some sort for she puts it to the lady's tummy.

"The baby is in distress and must be delivered immediately. Please prepare for surgery," she says as she checks the lady's vital signs. Seeing that her patient is conscious and staring at her, in a moment of pure intimacy she strokes the lady's head and says something in a different language. I translate it as, "I shall save your baby for you." The woman nods, knowing she can trust this angel with her life and the life of her child.

It is an intense few minutes as she prepares for this life-altering undertaking. Finally, she is getting the baby out and when it appears into the world things are not looking good for the little mite. All of his vital signs are failing, and she is working on him as best she can but to no avail. Then she does something I have never seen anyone do before. She cradles him in her hands –he is so small that he fits perfectly – and closes her eyes and it is as if a beam comes from her heart chakra. She draws the newborn to her heart and holds him there for a moment. The mother of the child is calling for her baby as she knows that she has not heard him cry yet and fears the worst.

Then in what I can only describe as a moment of miraculous proportions the infant starts to cry. Everyone stands for a moment in amazement as they absorb exactly what they have just witnessed. Even the baby that had been crying continuously since she placed it in the cot to tend the patient has also quietened. I too am amazed as I have never witnessed so natural a display of what healing love can actually do.

Sister Mary, however, does not bat an eyelid as she carries on with her duties and delivers the baby to his mother who is full of tears and gratitude. She keeps repeating, "Thank you, angel, thank you, angel," as Sister Mary places the child on the woman's naked bosom. The child begins to feed straight away.

Sister Mary sits by the side of the lady's bed and takes a moment to soak up some of the loving goodness that comes from watching something so natural. She then rises and smiles at the woman who in turn smiles back and then looks to her child with love in her tired eyes. Sister Mary walks outside and takes a deep breath. About fifteen children aged from five to twelve come running towards her calling for her to join them in a game of football.

She asks teasingly, "You want me to play?" to which they all giggle and scream, "Yes!"

"Okay, let's go then," she says as they all run around with the ball. It is a sight to behold. This lady is amazing. I am not surprised to know that Melody's past existence was this astonishing. It gives me a clearer insight into the potential that Melody has within, and about which avenue is best for her to grow in. I am excited for her future and I hope she embraces it instead of being fearful of her gift and restraining herself from sharing it with others.

Lucy

My next twinkle starts to gleam; it is Lucy's. The setting we are brought to this time is what I deem to be a concert. It is a free love concert and people are all quite happy sharing their love with one another. The atmosphere is one of peace and love and the location is a big field. From where I am situated I can see thousands of people all coming together. I also see many campervans with VW encrypted on the front of them. They are in all of the colours of the rainbow and with all sorts of patterns painted onto them.

I am drawn to a person who is sitting on stage with a guitar and a microphone singing his heart out in a chilled-out kind of way.

He is wearing baggy jeans and a rainbow-coloured t-shirt and has a band of some description tied around his forehead holding in place his shoulder-length brown hair. We stand and listen for a while and I pick up that his songs are all heartfelt and deep in meaning. He is very aware and is using his vocal and physical talents to spread goodness into this world.

He finishes his set and thanks everyone for listening and they all cheer as loudly as they can and shout for more so that he takes his seat again and says into the microphone, "This is one I wrote for all of you light workers out there. It is called 'Our changing world'. Let us make a difference together."

The crowd keeps cheering and clapping and shouting, "We love you, Peace buddy."

He starts strumming on his guitar and they all go quiet.

"We must, we must be the change we want to see in the world. When our hearts sing, it is a magical thing. We must be the change, no matter how strange. We must be the change we want to see in the world tonight. Sharing the joy from your heart, it is a great way to start. It will shine like a star and reach everyone afar. We must be the change we want to see in the world. This love is all healing, oh what a beautiful feeling. We all have the right to endure, so don't let yourself be so unsure, be the change you need to be in the world. We must be the change we want to see in the world. If we start from today, we are one step closer to being okay. Let's heal the world with our joyous love, let it shine far like a peaceful dove. Let's be the change we want to see in the world."

He stands up to the loudest applause ever and takes a bow. He then heads out through the back of the stage where waiting for him are some of his family members and a woman who I assume is his girlfriend. She is wearing a full-length maxi dress which has an array of patterns and colours in it. Her hair is long, blonde and beautiful and her eyes are the bluest of blues.

"Loved your set, bro," says a man who has to be his brother as they look similar.

"Peace, bro," he responds.

Fruit punch seems to be shared around and his girlfriend approaches and gives him a kiss and stands close to him while he chats to all of his mates and family.

"It has been organised for a meet and greet, if you don't mind, PB?"

"Sure. Cool, of course. I don't mind. Bring them in."

Three people appear from around the corner, one an excitable teenager, another a cool cat somewhat similar to PB, and the third a lady in her fifties who is wearing a t-shirt with a big peace sign on it. She seems to be acting strangely as she can't take her eyes off him and a glow is surrounding her that I am sure will be detected by the others in the group.

"Hi guys, I'm PB. It's nice to meet you all."

"I am so happy to meet you. I am your biggest fan," says the excited teenager.

"Is that so, young lady? Well, that is cool. Make sure you don't leave without a signed t-shirt and my latest album, will you?" he responds in a bid to meet her expectations of their encounter. She seems to be happy with the special treatment and will tell her friends who will tell their friends and it will snowball into everyone knowing how cool he is.

Next to meet PB is the cool cat. He puts out his hand and says, "Hey man, I'm TJ. If you ever need some back up in the drum department, I'm your man."

I sense an instant commotion as their energies entangle with each other. "You may be on to something, man. Will you have a chat with my main man cool Joe over there and leave your details? You could be cruising with us soon, my man."

I always find it wonderful when people's energies dance in front of me. I have a feeling these guys will make great music together.

It is the lady's turn to meet him and for some reason he is not as forthcoming but yet still polite. Maybe he feels a little uncomfortable to have a fan in this age bracket. She is quite well dressed, so I presume that she leads an abundant life. Their energies have a familiar connection though.

"Hello, PB, I'm so very happy to finally meet you," she says.

"Yes, sure, it's nice to meet you too, lady. Have you heard my latest album?"

"Your latest album? Well no, not yet, but I will be investing in a copy today."

"Cool . . . You can help yourself to drinks and eats. It was nice to meet you," he says as he walks away feeling a little uncomfortable.

Anxiously the lady calls, "Paul, please don't walk away."

"Hey, lady, how did you know my name?" he asks, walking back towards her in a slow shimmy type of way.

"Can we talk somewhere in private? I really need to talk to you."

"Hey, lady, you are hotting up the mood here and we like it cool."

"Please, I will only speak for one minute and if you still want me to leave then I will go straight away."

"You will?"

"Yes, you have my word on it."

He starts to stroll over to an enclosed space and she follows him.

"Okay, lady, you got one minute."

"Oh, how am I going to put this?" she says out loud to herself.

"I expect you just say it because time is ticking."

"Paul, you are my son and I want to get to know you if you would like to."

Looking a little startled he replies, "I have a mum and she died last year."

"She wasn't your mum. Sheila and Dave adopted you when you were a baby."

"Hey, this is too much, lady; I'm going to have to ask you to go."

"Yes, I expected this as it is a big shock for you to absorb, but I want you to know that I never wanted to give you up. I have loved you and thought about you every day since and I would be honoured if you would think about getting to know me and maybe coming to visit your two brothers and two sisters."

"I have brothers and sisters?"

"You sure do, son . . . Here, please take this. All of my details are on there. I know that you will need some more time to let this all sink in."

He takes the note and she slowly moves towards him to give him a much yearned for hug. She has obviously waited for this moment for many years and doesn't want to mess it up by pressuring him. To her surprise he responds by hugging her back. Some tears form in her eyes and he too has welled up. This is going to be a new beginning for them both I reckon. My heart warms to witness this reunion and I now have a better understanding about Lucy's character.

Jade

The next twinkle to shine is Jade's. To my surprise we seem to be somewhere very dark and quite stuffy. There are loud noises and men shouting at each other. The heat is intense, and dust fills the air. I am drawn towards an area where a man is standing shovelling a coal-like substance into a mine cart that is connected to other identical mine carts and they all roll along a track in a convoy straight towards the light.

I follow a man named Sam. He is strong and has brown hair peeking out under his helmet that has a bright light attached to it. He is wearing a dirty white vest, shorts and big sturdy work boots. His eyes look worn out, and the whites of them shine bright because of the blackness of his face. As we reach the light he squints and makes a noise as if in pain.

"Hey, Sam, what's the problem down there?" a short bossy guy calls at him.

Sam just walks on. He looks as if he is in shock. He is certainly dazed.

"Answer me, Sam, what the hell is going on down there?"

"Get everyone out of there. It's not safe."

"What are you talking about? There is too much work to be done for you to be starting these types of rumours. Jack, please escort this man off this mine site. He is a union man and we don't want his sort causing a ruckus with the men."

Jack, who is a bigger man, grabs Sam by the arm and starts to escort him away.

"On your head, be it if men die down there. The smell of gas is brutal. Sound the siren and get them out, I tell you," Sam shouts along the way.

"What am I supposed to take your word for? You are a mere miner. Surely you could just be avoiding work."

"Well, you go down and check for yourself. Then if there is nothing to worry about, go on. Go and see if I am telling the truth or not.

The man suddenly realises that this is not a joke and that he will have blood on his hands if he doesn't act straight away.

"Hurry before it's too late," he yells at his boss.

The boss says to another beside him, "Sound the siren, Jack; get the men out."

The man runs as fast as he can. Within moments the siren is sounding. A piercing sound it is too. I suppose it has to be to penetrate the ground and echo down the tunnels.

After a few tense moments the first miner comes running out to a cheer from the awaiting crowd of miners outside. One after another they come running out squinting and dazed. Then one man comes out crawling and two guys run to help him. Sam is one of them.

While dragging the weak man to safety, Sam senses something is not right and shouts to the crowd, "Take cover, take cover, it's going to blow!"

Everyone starts running as fast as they can to safety and then there is the biggest explosion I have ever heard. The ground shakes, dust shoots out of each of the open mine shafts. Grown men jump all around the place in a desperate bid to save their lives. When the dust settles heads start to rise and look around.

We are being drawn somewhere else. Sam is there with a woman and five young children. I am warmed to see that it is his family. The woman has long ginger hair that twirls down her back. Two of their children look like Sam and two like his wife while the fifth one looks like both his mother and father. They live in a small yet private homestead and there are animals in the paddock. Sam obviously works very hard to maintain all this for his family. I wonder whether they realise how much risk he puts himself into every day. He is a true trouper.

I believe that many lives have been saved because of this man's active intuition and his readiness to listen to it. How does this relate to Jade? I reckon that Jade's past lives have been hard. She knows nothing else other than toughing it out. Sometimes we need to step back and create a simpler life for ourselves as things are not worth sacrificing our lives or happiness for. In her past life he was sacrificing so much to provide for his family. But if he had died in that explosion, his family would have been worse off. They also need love, not absent parents who feel that they must provide as much money as possible for their family, as money can't buy you happiness. In fact, the happiest people in the world are those who have less as many of these people lower their expectations and are more easily fulfilled than others.

I feel that in Jade's case the struggle has always been part of the dynamic of life. Being so used to the struggle and making do with the struggle just brings more struggles. However, should she decide to move on from the struggle she will discover the serenity of the breakthrough. This is the next step on the journey of our souls. When this happens, things come together, and life seems brighter and more fulfilling. Intense joy is easier to maintain, and our heart chakra opens allowing us to attract similar loving experiences and people towards us. This is what I believe Jade needs; this is the essence of her true wish. This will allow true love to find her. This will be interesting. It is now time to move on.

Irene

Irene's is our last past life to visit. Her twinkler has not yet shone, and I don't understand why. I don't like to push the twinklers along as then there is a chance of incomplete visions. We decide to take a stroll along the countryside. Lush green grass blankets the whole landscape and when you are looking down on it you would be forgiven for thinking you could dive in and swim across.

"Claire, do you miss your physical form here on Earth?" I ask.

"No, not really. Why, do you?"

"Not now, because I know more and have fallen in love, but I have to admit that initially I did really miss my physical form."

Oh finally, Irene's twinkler starts to shine. I relax and allow myself to be drawn to where I am brought as I trust the process unconditionally. The setting is a vast countryside; there is a castle type property ahead that looks in disrepair as if it has been under attack. The weather is dull and chilly. This is something I don't usually observe, but it is a part of the essence of this environment, so I must take it into account.

Some men are shuffling along the ground – about two hundred in all – and they seem to have weapons with them, spears and daggers to be precise. I do not like the feel of the energy surrounding these men. Their intentions are not positive, and I can see that Claire is trying to shield her beautiful energy so that it does not absorb any of this intensely destructive force that is trying its best to penetrate her energy field. I too will shield myself although

I believe I have already been attacked by this intrusive evil. It is energy like this that mutates and sends shockwaves of negative energy around the globe that affect everyone who is not fully aware of energies and how damaging negative ones are.

There is some movement at the top of the castle, I hear a whooshing noise and one of the men who was shuffling along the ground a moment ago yells in pain. He has just been struck by an arrow and is now grasping on to life. He makes a noise of pure pain and within a moment arrows start shooting through the air at a mesmerising speed. Even in the darkness I can still see men dropping like flies and feel the essence of death. Unfortunately, I don't think that it will be the angels of the light that will be coming to guide these men to their eternal resting place, yet I do hold out the hope that they may find redemption during their next coming.

The arrows cease, and the remaining men stand and charge towards the castle with an intense vengeance. Suddenly a big drawbridge starts to drop, and a beam of glowing light shines behind a battalion of men. I am drawn closer to this group and see a man who I deem to be the leader standing strong at the front. He has long brown hair and deep green eyes which are quite mesmerising. He is wearing a sash-like band that crosses from his left shoulder to his right-hand side. And the most prominent thing to catch my attention is his skirt. It is made of a pleated checked fabric of green and navy blue. He is a warrior; he must fight to protect what is his as someone else wants to take it from him.

"Charge!" he shouts and all of the men behind him join him as he speeds towards the enemy. It doesn't take long for contact to be made and I can barely look as it is a total massacre. No mercy is shown by either side as they battle it out. I expect all of this horror is to do with principles and fear.

This type of energy is pure evil; it is fuelled by fear. Fear in any form, whether it be of a spider or of something catastrophic happening, can make people act in desperate ways in the pursuit of protecting themselves and those closest to them. The world has been speeding up over many years and it will soon stop as it has turned far too many times and the cog of the universe will be unable to keep turning if it keeps up this pace.

After some time, the battle ceases and I look around to see who – if anyone – is still standing. Anyone who survives such a torturous rampage must have someone shielding them from above. A few are able to stand up but not many. I look around to see if the one I was attracted to survived. I am drawn towards a mountain of bodies and I hear a groan. There he is, and he is still here with us, but barely. A man comes running over and shouts, "Earl, are you alive, man?"

Then a light, very tender response comes.

"I'm here," he says while trying to get their attention.

The guy is soon by his side.

"Get Connie, tell her I love her," he whispers.

"You hang in there, Earl. I will bring you to her," the loyal friend responds.

"Hurry," his weak voice demands.

His friend makes a makeshift trolley to bring Earl back home to the castle. The battle is over, but he still bears the scars.

As they make their way into the castle a beautiful lady with red hair, blue eyes and a dress made from the same fabric as Earl's skirt comes running out in distress and with one look at her dearly beloved she drops to her knees and gives him a big hug as she is so glad to see him alive. She pulls herself together by giving herself a shake and begins organising everyone to help set up a makeshift hospital in the big room.

"Don't leave me, Earl, I need you," she says as he lies in a sorry state on the canvas stretcher.

He tries to speak and open his eyes, but he can't manage either. He grabs her hand and she is delighted that he is able to communicate. She is now determined to nurse him back to full health.

The loving, healing energy that is projecting off this lady is touching us all. Miracles can happen with this type of love and one is certainly needed here if she is to save this man's life.

"Earl don't leave us. We all need you, and you are our warrior."

He slowly moves his hand towards hers and opens his eyes. He struggles for breath but finds the strength to say, "Eloise, I am not defeated yet. I love you. Will you marry me?"

Tears trickle down her face as her emotions transform from pain and sadness to love and joy. She knows he is a true warrior and that he will heal well because he is strong of mind. Challenges will always come to face him as that is the nature of his presence during this time, but he will weather any storm and defy all odds. Irene is very fortunate to have such a strong past influence; this will help her with her personal battle right now.

CHAPTER FOURTEEN
Claire

So much has been uncovered since our departure. I feel closer to Claire in this short time than I have with anyone else throughout any realm, apart from Rupert of course. The way she can pick up my thoughts and yet not be intrusive is simply amazing. I feel that she is a true friend, a girlie soul mate; I couldn't imagine my life without her in it now. One thing baffles me though. Claire can escape to different realms through her energy, so I don't understand how she has been directed to the Waiting Zone.

We have been working so hard over the past few days, so today I have organised a special picnic lunch for us to enjoy. We are sitting relaxing and allowing the energies of nature to replenish our essence so that we will be fully charged for the remainder of the task ahead.

"Claire, if you don't mind, I would like to ask why you have arrived in the Waiting Zone."

"I have to admit that I probably did not arrive in the usual way."

"Hey Claire, I don't know two people who arrived the same way, so don't allow yourself to feel that you are different from anyone else."

"Thanks for the reassurance, Syd, but wait until I tell you what happened. I promise you it is quite unprecedented."

"Go on, you have my full attention," I eagerly reply.

"As a child growing up, I always had increased awareness, so much so that I could pick on manifesting energies before they surfaced emotionally," she began. "Things happened when I was around. People don't like to allow themselves to understand this type of awareness and I was branded a freak in my family and community. There was one friend who didn't treat me differently. We got on so well, but he left me too, never to be seen again. I obviously scared him away just being myself.

"I never knew what I had done so wrong to be made to feel so isolated and different by everyone. I understand now that they were all reacting this way because of fear; they didn't understand what it was that I was doing and so to eliminate their fear of the unknown and in a bid to control it, they avoided me and suppressed me. I wasn't allowed to talk to many people and I was sent to a special school with children who had learning difficulties because everyone thought there was something wrong with me. The school wasn't so bad, as I could help some of the children. But when the teachers saw that I was assisting the other children in this way they also isolated me. I spent many days sitting on my own in the corner of the day room just because I would give someone who was emitting sad energies a hug and refused to let go before I had healed their energy.

"I was only doing what came to me naturally. Helping others with their energies was what I knew I had to do. I would have gone crazy if I had not been able to express myself in the way I was born to do. The only way I could keep myself from going crazy was to go within. When I first started doing it I could hear them all crowding around me. They would say things like, 'Look at the poor thing, she is unresponsive.' On more than one occasion I was taken for testing to check my brain function. They likened me to a vegetable. I started using my energy to leave my physical form more often as time progressed."

"Sorry, Claire, but where did you go when you left your body?"

"I went to different locations where there were energies in need of help. When our energies are distressed or lonesome or depressed it is very draining and it takes a lot of strength to break through the shadow that clouds our energy field at this time. I did spend a great deal of time with my mother. After I was institutionalised she found it hard to deal with things. She spent many days in bed and I would lie with her, hugging her energy. I don't know for sure if I helped or made things worse as I was feeling pain too. But on the good days she would get up, get dressed and even put on some make up. Then I would watch her as she left the house, caught the bus and visited me. She would just sit looking at me. Then she would catch the bus home and go back to bed. She used to drive you know."

"Really?" I reply.

"Yes. I remember when I was little she would drive me to big play parks and I would play on everything. She laughed a lot then, my mum did. But since being put on so many anti-depressants she was not allowed to drive. She always loved driving. It is terrible how the thoughts we have can consume our emotions and debilitate our bodies. Through these times, functioning rationally in the earthly environment can be quite challenging. I couldn't bear just sitting there with little stimulation to keep me going. I missed my family so much and I was being kept away from them so that the urge to be with my mum was uncontrollable.

"Eventually, because of my mum's depression my dad left her. He couldn't bear to see her like this any longer. It was going on for years and he figured that life was too short to keep trying to help someone who didn't want to help themselves. He had been going to work to pay the bills, hoping she would be okay when he returned. By caring for her every need he was feeding the problem, I mean literally feeding her at times.

"I sat with Mum during this time and I do believe she didn't realise that he was gone. My auntie Vera would visit a few times a day to make sure she was all right; my dad must have asked her to do that. One day I overheard Auntie Vera in the hall telling someone that she was going to have to get Mum sent to a caring facility. I couldn't bear the thought that my mum would be in the same kind of facility as I was in. The thought alone made me frustrated and so I decided to stop feeling guilty about what I had done to my mum and I shouted as loud as I could, 'Mum!'. As if by magic she sat alert and upright in her bed. She ran her fingers through her hair and got out of bed. Even Vera felt the vibrations as she came jolting into the room just in time to witness it all."

"Claire, it must have been wonderful to see the reaction."

"It was for sure, but it made me realise that sometimes, in order to help someone, we need to lovingly give them the wake-up call they need to catch a grip of themselves. 'Cruel to be kind' was a motto that I started to incorporate into my thinking. I know my dad was doing the same; he knew he was not helping her by doing what he was doing for so long. He was hoping to get her to wake up too."

"So, what happened after that?"

"Things changed then; Mum changed. She went to counselling and it worked and then she and Dad got back together. They worked together, and it brought them back together. They were strong again and their combined energies could fight against any challenge that came their way. Luckily enough I had departed from my body for too long this time and it had given up. I went into shock and my parents were called to the hospital to see me lying hooked up to monitors and lying unresponsive. They made the toughest decision ever, which was to turn off the life support machine. At that moment I decided not to return to my physical form. I was going to leave them be to get on with their lives together. Let them grieve for me and then they would be able to rebuild and eventually move on to doing things for themselves again. They were grieving every day for me anyway and this way I could set them free and myself also."

"I get the picture. Because you had neglected your physical form and chose not to return to it, you left humanity before your time and that is why you are here in the Waiting Zone."

"Yes, that is what I was told, Syd, and I couldn't be happier. I still check in on my mum's and dad's energies from time to time. I was visiting them the other day when you and Mr Boss found me. They are in good spirits and I feel a surprise presence with them. I think they have been sent a gift. Mum was told she could under no circumstances have any more kids after they had me because of some complications during my delivery. Anyway, their pain will soon be filled with joy and I no longer feel the urge to keep visiting them and sending love to their energies. I have now freed my spirit to pursue a different venture. I believe that wish giving is the perfect channel for my energies to be utilised to their full potential and with you having a little one yourself, you may need some help. Please, I am not being presumptuous or expectant; I would just like to help if you think I could be of use to you."

"Claire, I would love nothing more than for you to assist me and I am privileged that you would channel your beautiful energies in this way. What lucky wish receivers we now will encounter that will have your presence penetrating their energies."

"Thank you, Syd, you don't know how much it means to me that I have this focus. I will do my very best."

"So, have you felt more belonging since coming to the Waiting Zone?"

"To be honest, I have been distracted by the energy pull back to my parents. They needed me and so I was there. Maybe that is why I have not engaged fully with the community spirit here and I am sorry for that."

"No need to be sorry, Claire. We thought there was something not working for you and that your stay at the zone may be challenging because of it. But after what you have just shared with me I have a feeling you will start enjoying it from now on."

"Yes, my energy field has a dramatically different feel to it since my decision to move forward. I have learned that sometimes we need to let go and move on."

"It is a tough lesson for us all, Claire. It is good to remember that our hearts are just a part of our being. We love our families, especially those who have created us, but I truly believe that throughout eternity we will encounter their energy again and we must hold faith in this so that our spirit can be at peace within. The opportunity to re-engage will present itself if we so desire it."

"Sydney, you are so wise in your thoughts."

"And you are so gifted in your energy. We make a good team," I say as I place my arm around her tiny frame and give her a one-armed hug. She responds by hugging me back and I know we have fully connected. I now deem Claire to be my Waiting Zone sister. It is as if we have adopted each other. I won't tell her that yet as I don't want to overwhelm her if she does not feel the same way.

"Can I ask you one more thing, Claire?"

"Yes, of course."

"Have you ever been in love?" I don't know why I ask, but I see some pain in her eyes that I always see when there is an ache in a heart. I know because I used to see it in my own eyes for some time.

Looking down, she tentatively replies, "Yes, but it was not reciprocated."

The pain of this memory must be too much for her to bear because she slowly rises and leaves the room, leaving behind a gloomy atmosphere. That was a very moving interaction which was quite uncomfortable, but I stand strong in the conviction that I did it with a loving intention and maybe it will assist Claire with any healing she may need to address.

CHAPTER FIFTEEN
Sydney and Rupert

Later that day, Claire joins me for dinner. I was so happy that she chose to. I attempt to say sorry, but she soon stops me in my tracks.

"Syd, I hope you don't mind me asking but you and Mr Boss are so perfect for each other. How did you end up together in the Waiting Zone?"

"Thank you for saying that, Claire. I too think that we are perfect for each other. I am so very blessed. It took us a while to get together though."

"Oh really?" she replies, with interest.

"Yes, thirty-five years to be precise. We were really close friends all that time though."

"How come so long?"

"Well, it is a long story. So, let's take a seat over here, shall we?"

We go and sit in one of my favourite picnicking spots on the planet. Rupert and I have often picnicked here. I close my eyes and I can feel his presence with me. I smile as my heart rejoices at the feeling and the thoughts of our impending delivery.

"This is nice, isn't it?"

"Lovely," Claire responds, looking around.

"Rupert and I used to come here quite often. I always joined him for a while when he was completing his missions."

"So, is this where you fell in love?"

"No, Claire. That was the very first time I laid eyes on him actually. I was in the zone before him and when he arrived he was quite distressed as he expected to be reunited with his wife and child but was brought here instead. I hooked up with him then and tried my best to support him. I fell for his warmth and instant charm straight away but I knew my boundaries as his heart only sang for his wife and child and he waited for thirty-five years to be re-united with them.

"I had always accepted that he only thought of me as a friend throughout the years. We used to have quarters right opposite each other, which was good as we were always there for each other. When his time came to enter Heaven, I was so sad. I went into myself and stopped chatting with others and organising his leaving party was a real challenge, but I did it. My heart broke down when he left, and I realised that my love for him was eternal. I didn't know how I was going to survive without him. I thought he was gone forever and then as if by magic he came back. It was like all of my wishes came true at once. He told me how no one was there to meet him at the gates of Heaven and that when our previous Boss explained why that was, it freed him. Once freed in his mind he came to the realisation that I was the one he wanted to spend the rest of eternity with, so when the Boss offered him the opportunity to return to the Waiting Zone and take over the role, he took it with open arms. He then declared his undying love for me and asked me to stay here with him as his wife. Of course, I was happy to be anywhere he was and so I signed away my chance of entering Heaven. But I am happier here. Heaven for me is in the Waiting Zone and hey, it is not a bad existence at all. Have you seen our penthouse?"

"Yes, I sure have, and it is gorgeous. Can I ask you something more personal?"

"Yes, go ahead."

"Is it normal for people to have babies in the Waiting Zone?"

"This is the first little Waiting Zone cherub, right here," I say, rubbing my ever-expanding bump.

"Wow, you must feel wonderful to be the first to ever have experienced conceiving here."

"It is pretty special, isn't it? I just feel so lucky to be the one to create another life in this way. I can only say that I am living my perfect dream.

"This has been the thing that I never thought I could have or even that I deserved. When I changed my thinking pattern and awakened to the possibility that anything is possible, well, it was then that unprecedented things happened for me and I believe it is that way for every being in the universe. When Rupert left to go to Heaven I was imagining what we could have had together. I felt it and I craved it; then it came to me. Quite simply, that is the law of the universe. If you want to attract something to you, close your eyes and feel that you have that something; it will soon find you."

"Really, Syd? And what about wishes?"

"Wishes are special; they are the magic that finds us in life. When they find their place in our timeframe it is an extra gift that is bestowed to those who choose to believe."

"Just like the extra gift my mum and dad were sent?"

"Yes, that is a prime example, Claire." What she has said has sparked a light bulb in my mind that I must question Rupert about. It all seems a little coincidental and as I don't believe in coincidences I must investigate further. I think it is time to call my darling husband to see if he has been tampering with my wishes.

"Claire, if you would excuse me for a moment, I must send my darling a message."

"I am fine here, Syd," she replies and tucks into some of our heavenly food.

I message him, '*Roo did you use a wish for Claire's parents?*'

In an instant a message is returned. '*Stay where you are, will be there soon.*'

Oh goody, I get to see my dearest in the middle of this assignment. How wonderful!

"Rupert is coming to visit us," I tell Claire. "I am not sure why, but I am sure it will all be revealed to us in due course."

"Oh, are you excited? You must be a little excited surely," she keeps quizzing me.

Just as I am about to reply Rupert appears and my heart sings. He comes straight over, feels my bump and gives me a kiss. I can see Claire looking at us, thinking it is so romantic and that it is the stuff of fairy tales.

"Would you like to join us for our picnic?" I ask Roo invitingly.

"Sure, I would love to." He looks around and in a moment of realisation that is written all over his face he says, "This is our special spot, isn't it?"

I confirm his suspicion.

"So, why do we have the pleasure of your company on this assignment, my dearest? Not that I am complaining or anything of course." I beam a smile.

"Can I not visit my wife and unborn child without suspicion?"

"Sure, you can but it is a bit timely."

"I don't know what you mean. My intentions are purely innocent, I assure you, my lovely. So how have my gorgeous girls been?"

"We have been fine. I have had a few interesting encounters of late, but other than that, my dearest, we have been wonderful. How are things back home?"

"The Waiting Zone is functioning well. But of course, I am not functioning as well without my left-hand lady," he says, putting his arms around my waist, hugging me.

Oh, he is such a charmer and I cannot resist his charm lately as I know it comes from a deep loving source.

"Claire, what do you think about your training mission with Syd?" he asks.

"I am really learning a lot. There are some very interesting cases and I am embracing the way in which Syd conducts her assignment."

"I am happy to hear that, Claire, I really am. So, are you thinking you would like the task of wish giving as you're . . . ouch!" I nip him to get his attention. What is he doing? He said he wouldn't butt in.

"Claire, would you mind excusing us for a moment?" I ask politely.

I start to walk down the path and Rupert follows, still with his arm around my waist.

"Why did you say that, Roo? I haven't talked to her about becoming the Wish Giver yet and I don't want to pressure her."

"Oh, I have done it again, haven't I?"

"Yep, and another thing just dawned on me while I was in momentary thought..."

"Uh oh."

"It was something that Claire said when she was telling me about herself. She said, 'It is like a mini miracle because Mum was told that under no circumstances could she have any more kids after me.' Now call me paranoid, but it seems a little coincidental that I need of a replacement so that I can focus on our baby and you being the Boss of the Waiting Zone . . ."

"Syd, I can explain..."

"No, please wait until I finish."

"Okay, fair enough."

"Well, with you being the Boss of the Waiting Zone you know everything that goes on. You surely knew all about Claire's travelling energy and her dilemma. You are also in control of the Waiting Zone gifts and as a miracle occurred for her parents to conceive again, I reckon you have made way for that to happen. Well, am I right?"

He lowers his head. "I only did it for the best possible outcome for everyone. It just seemed so simple a resolution and you know me, Syd. If something flows smoothly then it is meant to be. It is when events start occurring that shield you from achieving your goal that it is time to pull the plug, but this did not happen in this case, it was meant to be."

"Oh Rupert, you are wonderful. You know that, don't you?" I say as I embrace him.

He looks relieved. "I thought you were cross with me."

"How could I be cross with you when you do everything with the right intentions?"

"Well, that's a relief to say the least."

"Had you going there for a while though, didn't I?" I tease.

Laughing, he says, "Come on, you, we had better get back to Claire before she disappears on us."

It is not long before we are back at the spot and, to our dismay, Claire has left her entity. We look at each other in desperate search for a solution.

"I think we should follow her energy to observe what she is experiencing," Roo says. "I know it may be a little intrusive but at least then we will know where she is."

"You can do that?" I ask, amazed.

"Yes, sure. A man of many talents, that's me," he says playfully.

I giggle and await direction. We hold hands, then Rupert leads me to Claire's location, and he takes her hand.

"Close your eyes," he says quietly and then he guides me deep into the karma I need to visit the energies. "Now allow yourself to connect with Claire's energy. Don't force; just let it flow breezily. My energy will be there waiting for you so that we can travel along the Quantum spectrum together."

I follow his lead and in no time at all we are there with Claire. She acknowledges our presence by putting her finger to her mouth requesting that we remain quiet. I suspect she doesn't want our energies to impose on those that she is witnessing.

We are in a dainty little hospital room. There are beautiful flowers spreading a scent of floral aroma to every inch of the room. A woman lies in the bed; she is heavily pregnant and glowing. Her husband is sitting beside her, holding her hand.

"Imagine, soon we will have a new life to take care of, love," says the man happily.

"Yes, I know, darling, and I believe that our Claire is with us sharing this with us right now," the woman answers. Then suddenly she sits up and looks to the roof saying, "Claire, if you are with us, please know that we love you and you will always be in our hearts."

I look to Claire and a tear trickles down her face. "I love you too, Mum and Dad," she whispers.

As if she heard Claire, the woman pulls her hands to her heart and smiles.

"It is time for this baby to join us, darling," she says calmly.

Just as she says that a nurse pops into the room. "Okay, it is time to meet your new addition now that we have a theatre available."

They leave the room and so we wait for their return.

"Thanks for joining me, guys," Claire says.

"Our pleasure. We were a little concerned to discover that you had departed."

"Sorry about that. I got drawn here; I am sure you can see why."

"Sure, Claire. How are you feeling about it all?" I enquire.

"This is the last time that I need visit for a while as they will now be happy and fulfilled again."

"That is a big step forward, Claire. I for one am very proud of your decision and I respect that it was not made light-heartedly," Rupert returns.

"Yes, and now that I have said my final goodbyes I will be able to focus on my new position of Wish Giver. Well, that is if you still want me, Syd," she enquires cautiously.

"Want you? Of course, I want you. You are the perfect one for the job," I say excitedly.

Just then the door opens and four return instead of two. Claire is jumping for joy; even she hadn't predicted that they were having twins. It looks to be a happy ending indeed as we leave them cooing over a little boy and a little girl.

We all return to our picnic spot that has been picked over by some birds.

"Syd, I must return to the zone. I trust that you guys are good to go now." He gives me a kiss and finishes by saying, "See you, Claire. Congrats on your becoming a big sister today."

He is gone in a flash. I turn to Claire and say, "You are officially welcomed on board, Claire. You will not regret your choice of position in the Waiting Zone. I have been doing it many, many years now and I still love the joy it brings."

"I feel that it is going to be a good thing for me that I am following my heart's desire. The opportunity to connect with others at this level delights me and gives me a glowing feeling within that is telling me I am on my right journey. I am fulfilled."

"How wonderful that is, Claire! I am so happy that this has all fallen into place for you because if it is going to work it has to work for everyone and I think if it does we are all winners. Now shall we try to salvage some of this picnic?"

We chase the birds away and salvage anything they haven't touched. Again, I must say that I never cease to be amazed by the flow of life. The synchronicity of events that combine in every given situation is amazing and goes to show the complexities of the universe.

I glance at Claire. She is in a daydream and I sense that there is something still hidden, that she has a missing piece of her puzzle to find. This girl certainly does have many hidden depths. I am sure that if I am to be the teacher that enables her to connect with this challenge then all will be revealed in time.

"Are you ready, Claire? It is time to move on."

She shakes herself out of her daydream and gently replies, "Yes, I am ready, Syd."

"Okay, let's go then."

CHAPTER SIXTEEN
The Power of Now

Now with a clearer perspective we decide to revisit our cases. On this visit we will be determining how, if each individual incorporated the power of the now instead of living as victims of the past or slaves to the future, their lives would immediately prosper.

When we are born to physicality we are pure, untampered with little innocent beings. Intentionally and unintentionally, influential figures manipulate our thoughts and it is all of these influences combined that determine our personalities and what makes us tick. Until we recognise that this is the case nothing will change. Only those who visit their inner sanctum discover their true essence. When this happens, they can live each day feeling fulfilled in the knowledge that they are the controllers of their own destiny. Others can influence the practicalities, but the essence is what only they themselves can embrace. It is within each person's power to control how they react to a given situation. If someone were to change their thought process to a more positive outlook, more positive things would come to that person because everything is perceived positively. Alternatively, if someone were to think of things in a more negative manner then negative things would ultimately follow. It is simply the laws of the universe and quite logical to any inner thinker.

Jade

Jade is a very intelligent lady; however, she is quite emotionally vulnerable. She doesn't like to make decisions that hold personal consequences for her as she doesn't want to be responsible for hurting her own feelings or those of someone else. Jade lives her life with a deep root growing in the past and an unrealistic expectation for her future. She does not live in the now, ever. Everything she consciously does is with the future in mind and with the shackles of the past pulling her back. The strange thing about Jade is that she has a job that requires her to be very responsible. Making decisions is a daily task, the difference being that these decisions are in the best interests of other people. These character traits most definitely do stem from childhood experiences. Jade would benefit from living in the now more often than she currently does.

We enter her home. I am so delighted when I discover that she is sitting cosily on her sofa snuggled up in a duvet, her daughters snuggled at either side. They are eating popcorn and they have just started watching a family movie. The fire is blazing. This is a heart-warming sight to behold. Clearly, I was not one hundred percent correct; this certainly is living in a moment. The love is evident in the room and laughter and hugs are abundant. This is a healing room. Love is a great emotional healer and there is a lot of love here. I even feel it embracing me. It is like receiving a lovely hug. I look over at Claire and she is smiling.

"Shall we order a pizza or Chinese?" Jade asks.

Both kids shout together, "Chinese."

"All right. Then pass me over my mobile and I will order it now. Will we be lazy and get it delivered?"

"Yeah," say the two happy siblings.

For the next few hours the wonderful energy keeps flowing through the home, eradicating all of the less positive energies that so consumed this home when we first arrived.

The telephone rings. I don't have a positive feeling about this call, so I would have to recommend that Jade does not answer it.

"Mum don't answer it," says her little girl, who I believe has a sixth sense.

"It's okay, love. Mummy will just be a minute," Jade lovingly replies as she hurries to get the call.

But in doing so she trips on the duvet and bumps her head. She is quite dazed and her daughters rush to her side. The answering machine picks up the message which is from a man who says in a slurring voice, "Jade are you there? Can I come over? I didn't mean what I said . . . I have decided to forgive you."

This is not a positive for Jade as she is focusing on the love that surrounds her family tonight and they so deserve it. I try with all of my might to disconnect the call and I do. When Jade reaches the phone, she discovers that he is no longer there. She is disappointed, but her children run to be at her side and they hug her. She looks at them and then the telephone. I feel that this is a poignant moment for her as she chooses whether to call him back or not.

She smiles. "Come on, guys. It's time for the ice cream."

"Yay yummy, in my tummy," calls out her youngest girl.

Jade's older daughter gives her a knowing hug as she is old enough to recognise exactly what it is that her mum has done tonight.

The healing love continues. This is a simple yet powerful example of living in the power of the now. We shall move on to witness another example of this powerful moment in existence for another.

MELODY

I am drawn towards Melody. This lady does live in the power of her now; it is repetitive for her and keeps her safely in her peaceful place. Life, however, is not just about us; it is about others also and when we limit ourselves to interaction we are limiting ourselves to the number of lessons we are going to make in this lifetime. She will in time draw herself out of her sanctuary as her wish will guide her to.

At this moment she is sitting in her living room, in deep thought. Claire indicates that she would like to penetrate Melody's energies to visit her thoughts. I nod in agreement. This is a complex process because when we do this we need to ensure that our own thoughts are void; otherwise remnants of these invasive thoughts will remain in Melody's mind and create confusion.

I watch as Claire's energy infuses with Melody's. The energy this creates is beautiful to witness. It is generating a unique combination that releases gorgeousness out into the universe. This is a healing energy.

I wait in this peaceful stance for a time, embracing the beauty of the moment which is enhanced by the tranquillity of the setting. Through the quaint little window pane, I observe the lush meadows that swoop over the hills, a picture-perfect scene gifted to us all by Mother Nature. If only more people were open to accepting remedial treasures that we have free and in abundance! A walk amongst nature will have a more positive influence on our healing than visiting a chemist.

I am drawn back to the moment and witness Claire returning to her form. I will never cease to be amazed at the ease of this process for her as she glides from one form to another.

Melody senses our presence. She calls out, "Who is there? Why do you feel the need to visit me? Are you here to guide me?"

I go over to her and stand right in front of her face. I absorb the sweet fragrance of her perfume that dances all over her body. She stares into my eyes as if she can see right into my soul, searching to discover what it is that she needs to know. She feels no fear, only curiosity about why she is being visited. Her awareness is astounding; she is open and receptive to the moment. I lift up my arms wide; she does too. I wrap my arms around her in a peaceful embrace and she responds accordingly. We stand there for a few moments indulged in the magnificence of our two energies combined. I loosen my hold and she follows suit and so I retreat and follow Claire outdoors.

Melody calls after us, "Please call again, ladies; it was lovely to experience your energy."

Even Claire is amazed; we dare not speak to each other until we are out of Melody's awareness. When we go to the top of the hill, the views are breathtaking, and we position ourselves under the huge tree that stands majestically alone here.

"Well, Claire, come on and share," I eagerly request.

"Syd, she was deep in thought thinking of the poor children in another land. She was sending them love and comfort with a sense of hope for them. She would not let sadness intrude on her thoughts. Only positive thoughts were allowed to penetrate her vision as she focused on sending the loving donation of positive energy their way."

"So, she was living in the now by sending her beautiful energies to others. Even though she cannot physically be with these children, her heart is still open to sending them all that she has in a bid to brighten up their lives by unselfishly sacrificing some of her moments from her day in a positive prayer-like way. Claire, can you imagine what would happen if there were more people in the world focusing on the positives and sending this type of energy to each other?"

"You are right, Syd. It would be ideal. This type of knowledgeable awareness comes from an advanced spirituality; it is all part of the gift of wisdom that we receive when we go inward, and well, that's what I feel anyway."

"You are so right Claire . . . Okay, I think we are ready to move on. Is that good for you?" I ask.

"Yes, wonderful," she replies.

IRENE

When some people fall ill they use a lot of their power in the now on trying to get better or feeling sad contemplating the outcome about what might happen if they were to depart. Irene is using a lot of her power to find a cure and keep things as normal as possible for her boys. I want her to embrace the moment that she has when she focuses on the healing energy that surrounds her every day. She can access this energy by not feeling sadness about leaving her boys but instead living in the joy of each and every moment that she spends with them. She needs to stop continually affirming to herself that she is ill and desperate to get better. It is of course human nature to automatically think this way but by doing this, she is ensuring that her healing will be a steeper hill to climb than is necessary. Instead, if she takes each day at a time, lives in each beautiful moment, and seeks a positive to eradicate any negative, she will recover so much more easily.

When we are physically or mentally unwell we are being called inward. We need to focus solely on ourselves and listen to the signs sent to us by our inner spirit because it is there to guide us through our lesson and heal and recover. While spiritually we will have evolved during the process it can be really overwhelming as it consumes the person's life and they feel battered and bruised physically and emotionally. The truth is that we all choose what lessons we want our spirit to experience during each lifetime. This is why so many people have a rough ride through life and others have all of the luck in the world. Those who experience the bumpier journey through life will have had many lessons to learn as their spirit was ambitious this lifetime, but generally an easier ride through the next existence will follow when the spirit chooses to return again.

I want Irene to experience the healing of now. So, I am going to do something that I don't usually do. I am going to take away her pain for a time and store it within my body so that she can be relieved of her suffering for a while and have some quality time with her boys.

I am about to conduct the exchange when I feel someone placing a hand on my arm. I turn around to see Rupert standing there.

"Syd, honey, you cannot do this. No matter how much you want to, this darkness may affect our child. I am sorry to intervene, but I know you would not be happy with the consequences of your actions should anything go wrong."

"You're right. I am sorry. I got carried away by the desire to help this lady feel well for a time."

"I will do it." Claire steps forward.

She is such a slight little thing and from past experience I know this is not an easy thing to do even for a sturdier person. But she is adamant about it and insists that she would like to assist in this process.

Rupert shrugs his shoulders. If she so chooses, then who are we to stand in her way?

"Right then, Claire, if you are sure you want to do this, I must let you know that when I indicate it is time to return the toxic energy back to Irene, you must do it immediately. Do you understand?"

"Yes, Syd, most definitely," she agrees.

"I shall leave you two ladies to it," Rupert says.

He comes over and kisses me and our little bump and in response it jumps for joy. The surprised delight in his eyes lets me know that he felt it too. This is a very intimate moment, one that I am so grateful to experience. I have been so distracted by the mission, I have not given much thought to the beautiful being inside of me. I shall be more mindful from now on. Rupert looks at me with a loving glance and I know that he knows my thoughts. I blow him a kiss and he returns to the realm.

"Let's get started then, Claire. Are you ready?" I ask.

She indicates that she is and so she takes a comfortable position and the process begins.

Irene is lying on the sofa in her living room. Her boys are sitting on the floor in front of her building a train track and having a little quarrel about who is going to do what bit. Irene struggles to intervene, and I can see by the expression on her face that she is heartbroken that she cannot parent successfully.

Claire summons the toxic energy to her body and it comes without any extra persuasion. It leaves Irene's body like a black toxic plume and travels into Claire's, which will be its incubator for a short time.

Immediately Irene has perked up, colour starts to come back into her cheeks and she sits upright and firmly tells her boys to stop quarrelling. They both stop what they are doing and look at their mother. She holds open her arms and they both jump up and run into her warm embrace. She holds them there, not wanting this moment to ever pass. Then she pulls back her duvet and says, "Right then, boys, let me show you how to make a track."

The boys cheer, "Yay!" and help their mum with every piece and in no time, there is a vast structure covering the whole floor space. The boys don't waste any time in getting to play with their new and fantastic track and when the door opens, and their uncle walks in they shout in unison, "Uncle Joe, look what Mum made for us." His face speaks a thousand words. He did not expect to witness so much joy when he entered.

It is to be short-lived though as I see Claire struggling and tell her to release the toxin, but it refuses to leave her body because it has new vibrant energy to feed on. She begins to shake intensely, and I know that I must intervene. I reach in and pull it out. It battles with me and tries to penetrate my energy field, but I block it out. It races back towards Claire's exhausted energy force and I quickly move to shield her. It is losing energy, so it rushes back to Irene who in an instant collapses on the floor.

Her boys cry at witnessing the occurrence. Joe picks up his sister and places her gently on the sofa again, snuggles her up and calls the doctor.

I am saddened to observe this misery. Irene is strong though and she will fight for her life, if not for herself, most definitely for her boys. I am happy that we intervened and gifted Irene with some pain-free time with her boys. She truly did live in the power of the now, ensuring that each given moment reached its positive potential.

Suddenly Joe starts looking around the room and starts to say, "Claire, are you there? Claire, Claire, I can feel you close. Are you there?"

This catches me unexpectedly and I look straight at Claire whose small frame is in a weakened state after what she has endured. Her expression indicates that she needs to leave the room now, so I lend her a hand to flee the scene.

I decide to give her the space she needs to revive her beautiful energies. I will not probe about what just happened. I can only hope that she finds the strength within to share what troubles her. I shall move on now.

JOY

Living joyful in each moment is what Joy does best. She gives every moment to others and her quest to be joyful. But what about herself? She is sacrificing so much of her happiness for the joy of others; if she doesn't begin navigating some of that positivity towards her own joy then she may lose passion for her vision. That would be a travesty for mankind. The positive energy that she creates is extremely powerful. As it pulsates from every molecule of her tiny frame and spreads from her to another and then to another like a wave of optimism sweeping the world, it will become widespread. The world needs more joyful people eradicating the dark plume of negativity that lingers, constantly waiting to strike at any weak moment.

So, I focus on sending some selfish energy for Joy. She is in her garden. Flowers of all shapes and sizes in an array of vibrant colours surround her. This is a vast area of beauty. When we surround ourselves with beauty and take moments to absorb the energy that throbs from each natural blossom, then we have tapped into one of life's little treasures, the gift of natural beauty. It is ever energising and explains a lot about where Joy's vibrant energy originates. I am aware that she understands the importance of nurturing her spirit even more so now for witnessing her sanctuary. I understand that she resides in the power of the now every day, re-energising herself and spending time with Mother Nature, the beloved provider of beauty.

Is this what I am to witness? Claire too is in awe of the splendour that surrounds her vision. I indicate that we could now leave as I was sure we had observed enough but then a mobile telephone rings.

Joy lifts up her phone and looks at it for a moment, obviously knowing the number. A bright spark shoots from her heart and she holds the phone close to her chest. She heads over to a pergola area that has a romantic table and seating situated inside. She checks her phone again and smiles but just as she is about to answer the call she loses faith and places the phone on the table in front of her. Pulling her knees up to her chest and sinking her head into them she lets out a little moan as if her heart is aching. My heart aches for her. Why is she not allowing this love into her life? She has gone against her heart's desire and is now bearing the consequence of it because her mind and body are telling her otherwise. Her phone beeps a message alert. She leaps in an instant to grab it, presses a few buttons, holds the mobile out in front of her and eagerly listens.

"Hello, Joy, it's Ben . . . remember, the guy you were chatting to at the benefit lunch on Saturday? . . . Well anyway, I was hoping that you might like to go out for dinner with me this weekend. I felt that we had something special happening when we were talking . . . Please will you call me back if you would like to go out with me . . . Okay . . . Hope to hear from you soon, Joy." Then a beep as he hangs up.

At that moment a small white shaggy-haired dog hops up beside Joy and starts licking her arm. She instantly picks it up and playfully hugs it and ruffles its hair.

"Oh Ruffles, what should I do?"

She is obviously letting doubt overshadow her impulses and I look to Claire, who nods. She knows exactly what to do and stands straight, focusing with all of her might on Joy. A courageous energy ball emerges from her energy field and makes its way towards Joy. As it slowly enters her she sits upright, lifts her phone and presses the redial button. She sits confidently awaiting an answer then for a moment I see doubt trying to creep back into her; but it is too late, and the phone has been answered.

"Hello, Ben, it's Joy. Sorry to have missed your call a moment ago."

She listens carefully, engulfed in this moment of bliss, sparks of love and lust floating all around her and from the device she holds to her ear.

"Yes, I would love to go out with you tonight." She smiles from ear to ear as she receives his reply.

"Okay, so I will meet you there at seven?" she enquires.

Then, a little startled, she says, "Oh, pick me up? . . . Mm . . . yes, that would be lovely. I will send you my address in a text later. Is that good for you?"

A brief pause, then, "I look forward to it, Ben. Thank you for calling." Joy switches off the phone, sits back and embraces the moment as if she has overcome a personal barrier. Suddenly she seems startled.

"Oh, Ruffles," she says to her bemused pet. "What am I going to wear?" This with a glance at her relaxed attire.

"What about my hair?" she says more anxiously and brushes her fingers through it.

"I must get myself sorted," she says and rushes off to her house of beauty, taking a moment to stop and smell the roses along the way. As she does this she twirls around, puts her hands up in the air and cries, "Wheeeeeee!" She has allowed herself the pleasure of living in the power of the now to guide her through a nervous experience. She will now allow herself to also enjoy the night ahead.

I try to move ahead and am pulled to another phase of Joy's day. A limousine pulls up outside her home and a handsome man with blond hair and a clean, crisp, smart appearance gets out of the back of the car. The door is being held open by the driver.

"Your chariot awaits, my lady," the handsome guy says as he bows and gestures for Joy to get into the car.

Joy smiles from her heart as she approaches. When she comes closer to the car she is handed a flute of champagne and her handsome prince swoops her into his arms and gives her a very affectionate kiss. They are in sync, both hearts beating as one. This is a match that has been encountered in a past life and they have now been reunited. The connection has already been established and the sparks are flying high. I don't think either of them will be able to resist this union even if their circumstances do not allow it. This is a relationship that is concrete from the beginning. The phrase 'They were made for each other' pops into my thoughts and they probably were. Even as the car moves along the highway they glance into each other's eyes. They are both love-struck. He gently strokes her jaw line and leans into yet another tender embrace. It is a beautiful sight to behold. The love radiates, and Claire and I absorb this priceless power, especially at this stage of our journey. Before long we are given access to depart and so we will move forward and leave this adoring couple to familiarise themselves again. I look forward to seeing more of this connection. It is now time for us to move on to Lucy.

LUCY

Oh, I am happy to revisit Lucy; I feel a connection with her. I sense she has a true spirit that will shine in time. She will have lessons to learn which will strengthen her character and make her life more fulfilling when she gets the opportunity to reach her potential. Her spirit will be wise at a young physical age. Pondering on her situation, I suppose she has had to endure what it feels like to be restricted so that when she does experience freedom she will value it and utilise it to its full potential. There are so many people who take too much for granted; Lucy will be grateful for all of her treasures.

We join her in the presence of her mum and dad. There is a heated discussion going on.

"I just don't feel that I belong with you. You never make me feel loved; you just want me to be your puppet. Well, I won't, I tell you I won't!" she shouts and storms out slamming the door as hard as she can.

They stand there bemused.

"She is getting to be more trouble than she is worth," her father comments sadly.

"Love, she is just feeling unsettled. Maybe deep down she knows that she is not of my blood."

Just as her mother had her words out, Lucy charges in through the door.

"What do you mean not of your blood?"

"Well love . . ." her mother stammers, shocked at the confrontation.

"Let me get this right . . . You mean to say that I have been here suffering for all these years and you are not even my real parents . . . you have got to be kidding me," she says in disgust and runs out of the room without waiting for a reply.

"Lucy, get back here this instant," her father calls but she keeps running.

She runs as fast as her legs will carry her right across the vast green garden that slopes towards the prominent stone pillars that surround the closed entrance gate that acts as a barrier against her desire to be released. But this feisty young lady does not take too long in charming the gateman to open the gate.

"Have a nice day with your friends, young Lucy," he says, waving as she calmly walks in the direction of freedom.

Then the gateman unexpectedly hears a message bellowing from his walkie talkie.

"Don't let Lucy out of those gates, Norm; she is trying to run away."

He starts to panic and his and Lucy's eyes meet. Her returning gaze is one of desperation and she also begins to panic. Norm goes to catch her but after seeing her reaction he calls, "Go on, Lucy love; it won't be long before they are following you."

He then lifts his walkie talkie and says, "Sorry Gov, she has already left the premises. I did try to catch her but to no avail, sorry Gov."

Lucy sends a glance of true gratitude his way and then takes off as fast as she can to find her sanctuary.

We choose to stay with her until we see that she is safe. She continues to walk along the tree-lined rural road as fast as she can. She hears a car coming and swiftly hides amongst the trees. She is in a position to observe the passing vehicle. It is her parents' station wagon. She is relieved they did not discover her hiding place. She goes back onto the road and resumes her journey.

Soon another car comes zooming past and catches her off guard. It is a red sports car with the registration plate displaying the word RACEY. It passes her by but then quickly comes to a halt so fast that its tyres screech, leaving a trail of black marks on the road. The reversing lights turn on and the driver pulls up beside her. He puts down his window and we see he is a young lad of about nineteen. He is quite handsomely confident in his appearance and energy. When he sees how nervous and shocked Lucy is after what he had just executed before her he says, "Ah sorry, I didn't mean to startle you. Are you okay?"

"Mm, I have always been told not to talk to strangers," she responds and starts walking speedily away.

He slowly follows her in the car. "Hey Lucy, I am not a stranger. I live up the road from you. I need to know that you are all right before I leave you because it is going to be dark soon and it won't be safe on this road as even your clothes are dark."

She stops and thinks about that for a moment. "I have just run away from home," she declares.

"Listen, hop in. I will drop you off in town," he offers.

"Oh, I don't know," she says hesitantly and then, after a few moments of contemplation she agrees. "Okay, thanks very much." She jumps into the car.

Lucy certainly is living in the power of her now. She is making some big life-altering decisions.

Along the way Lucy fills the guy in on everything that has been happening to her. His name is Jay, he is eighteen and he tells Lucy his parents bought him the car for getting high honours in his exams.

When they reach town, he does as he had promised and pulls up to let her out.

"So, what's your plan now, Lucy?"

"I don't know. I might ring my aunty Gina. She is always nice to me. But she isn't really my true aunty. So how can I call her?" This realisation brings tears into her eyes.

Jay puts his hand on her shoulder and says, "Well, I can't leave you like this, can I? I may be a bit crazy in saying this, but I will call my parents and tell them I am away with friends for a few days and we can go visit a few places that might help you find your real family, like libraries and stuff. I know it is a crazy idea, but you do have strange circumstances, don't you?"

"Would you do that for me?" she asks.

"Yeah, sure. I have nothing else on and it sounds like fun."

"Thank you so much. I won't ever forget this," she says gratefully.

"No probs. We will go stay at my college mate's flat tonight. She lives in the next town and won't mind us staying with her. She may even be able to help us find out a few things."

We shall leave now and revisit in the morning when things have settled. Jay seems to be a genuine enough character and I detect no malice in his intentions, which is quite refreshing, taking his age and class into consideration.

"Well, Claire, all of our assignments are experiencing new levels of awareness which will help them to realise what will make them truly happy. The power of living for each moment can be intense but also rewarding; moving forward in the trueness of being, moving forward along the true path that is awaiting our presence."

"I am hopeful for each of these ladies, Syd. Their potential to successfully receive the gift of a wish is getting stronger," Claire replies.

"Ouch . . ." I double over in pain.

Claire comes to my aid quite concerned.

"Syd, what's wrong? Is it the baby?"

"I am fine. It was just a . . . ouch," I say again as I hunch down on the ground.

"You cannot be having your baby yet, Syd. It is too early." Claire panics, which is strange because I have never seen her panic before.

Sensing the danger, Roo is swiftly on the scene.

"You need to come back to the Waiting Zone now, Syd."

"I . . . oh . . . can't leave . . . now . . ."

"You must go," Claire exclaims. "I will be fine; we can connect through our energies."

I look at Rupert and Claire and I feel the pain and it is my baby who needs me now. My choice is easy. I know that Rupert has insight into everything and he knows that if at times we don't retreat then the outcome of our actions can have dire consequences. I trust him.

"Okay, I will come," I say. "Claire, the twinkles need to be released and it is important to stay close to Lucy. She is our priority at the moment. The voice is yours."

CHAPTER SEVENTEEN
Inner Meeting
Claire

The shock of what occurred with Syd has mellowed. I can now think more clearly. When a bolt from the blue occurs like that without warning it can be somewhat unsettling. I am fortunate enough to have the inner wisdom to know that a reaction should not commence straight after such a moment because our thoughts are not crystal clear. When the cloud passes, and the sun starts shining again then clarity will follow, and our inner spirit will ignite to guide again instead of comforting us.

I am a little nervous about what awaits me. I shall move inwards to receive some guidance; here I shall summon the energies of those I wish to talk with in the safe environment of my sub-conscious and have faith that they will respond.

I unearth for myself the most perfect place for me to transcend. I relax, close my eyes and leave my present consciousness. I open the door to a new inner room. Within this room are two floor pillows and a table with short legs. I sit down on one of the cushions with my legs crossed at the ankles. I am wearing white linen trousers and a linen top with a V-neck. I empty my head of all restrictions, expectations and distracting thoughts. I focus all of my energies on connecting with the energy of the entity I wish to call in the hope that it will subconsciously respond. After a moment I feel something related come closer and in walks Syd. She too is dressed in white linen. She takes a seat on the pillow at the other side of the table.

"So lovely to see you well, Syd. Thank you for coming."

"Thanks for connecting, Claire; I have been worried about deserting you."

"I will be fine, Syd, once I know that you and your baby are well."

"I have to rest; she needs to grow and needs my energies right now, so that is where I must be."

"Oh, a girl? How precious! Please know that I will do my best, Syd. You have taught me so much that I trust I will be guided."

"That is all any of us can do, my beautiful friend. I look forward to seeing how you progress. Be true to yourself, Claire. I will connect with you as soon as I can. Oh, Rupert said to contact Jayden if you need anything. He will never be too far away at any time."

"Bye, Syd."

She leaves, and I quickly connect with another before I change my mind. In walks Joe. He too is wearing white linen which further enhances his handsome looks and I cannot help but notice that he still has the beautiful eyes I fell for all those many years ago. I feel that he has been humbled by what happened between us and that is why I want to give him the chance to express what it is that he is trying to say, if for no other reason than to help him to stop embarrassing himself in public places when he comes into contact with my energy.

He rushes towards me and I gesture to the opposite cushion.

"Claire, you don't know how long I have waited for this moment. Please do not let us be apart anymore. Take me with you now; I do not want to return to my body."

"Joe, I don't understand the way you have reacted when you sense my energy. You are obviously very aware of surrounding entities. Why do you hold a candle for me? We had parted a long time before I departed."

"You don't know, do you, Claire? I know that we were only young when we were in love, but it was real."

"What? You left without even saying goodbye or offering me an explanation. I don't understand what you are trying to say, Joe."

He rises from the cushion and comes and kneels beside me, holds my hands and those big blue eyes gaze lovingly into mine while he explains. "Claire, our parents kept us apart. They told me you didn't want to see me anymore and that you had a new love and

I suspect they did the same to you. For many months I was so heartbroken that I could hardly eat. I was moved away to my granny's house and when I was finally allowed to return they told me how you had deteriorated. They let me visit you, but I knew you were not in that body that I visited. Your spirit was not within. I have waited for this day ever since. I am not prepared to lose you again, Claire." And then he hugs me passionately. It feels so good to have him hold me again, as if all those years had never happened. All the pain, all the emptiness, all the sadness, has just disappeared.

"Thank you, Joe, thank you for loving me," I say with a full heart.

"I will always love you, Claire," he says, holding my face in his strong hands.

I smile a knowing smile. "I must move on now, Joe."

"I can't leave, Claire, not when I have you here so close."

"I will come again, Joe, but for now we must part," I try to comfort him.

"Bye, Claire," he says as he leaves, and I wave.

I prepare to leave but choose to call one more person before I depart from my sanctuary.

I call and there is no response; they have chosen not to come.

I choose to clear my thoughts again and understand that I will be guided. Lucy enters straight away; she is the fundamental link in the chain. Next, I am guided towards the twinkles; they are shining bright and awaiting release. I will lock the door of my subconscious and return to my entity.

I listen to my inner guide to lead me along the path to directing those whose twinkles I now guard. I trust that decisions will come naturally and in a perfect sequence. After taking a short time in solitude to organise my thoughts and feelings about the immediate task ahead, I have come to the comfortable knowledge that I will follow my inner heart when I come to moments of uncertainty. I feel as though Syd has passed all of her strength and wisdom to me and I find comfort in that.

Karen Weaver

CHAPTER EIGHTEEN
Twinkles Released

When I hold this box of twinkles close to me I feel their strength. I know that each and every one of them comes with the gifts that each candidate has chosen for themselves. My understanding is that once the gifts are released they cannot be stopped as a chain of events has been instigated. Each twinkle will begin to shift things in order to make way for their coming. Their energy is very powerful and that is why we should be careful what we wish for because we cannot be in full control of how that wish finds us.

I stand at the top of the hill where many of us from the realm find ourselves located during our stay here. It is dark, the sky is clear, and it is time for these rocks of splendour to facilitate their arrival by initiating changes that will create an opening in the lives of those who have requested their presence. I unlock the latch; the enthusiastic energy within is too powerful for my timid little hands and the lids burst open releasing the twinkles. They shoot straight up into the sky above and momentarily hover there and in an instant, they dart in all different directions. I have never witnessed anything so naturally spectacular before.

I imagine that many people will wish upon these twinkles as they zoom across the sky tonight without knowing that they are wishes on route to those who summoned them. Nevertheless, each wish wished is another twinkle created, so as long as there are people who wish upon these shooting twinkles, there will always be the likelihood that they may receive a twinkle of their own.

Mesmerised, I stand gazing at the sky absorbing the energy being generated.

Out of the blue a familiar voice says, "So, releasing the twinkles, are you?"

I practically jump out of my skin as in my constant awareness I am rarely caught off guard.

"Oh whoops, I didn't mean to scare you there, keep your skin on, Claire."

"Jayden, sorry. I thought I was alone and . . ."

"Yeah, yeah, I know. Maybe next time I will knock. Get it, knock?"

"Yes, very funny," I reply in a solemn tone.

"So, you are on your own now, are you?"

"In a way I suppose, but Syd's energy is always close by. I am sure I will be fine."

"We may be crossing paths a few times on our missions and I don't want to be stepping on your toes, so small they are and all."

I choose not to respond as I feel that he is mocking me.

"Okay, little lady, I will see you around. Should you need me just call. I know the ins and outs of all of the missions."

"I am grateful for your offer. I will be sure to take you up on it should I encounter any complications."

He looks at me confused, as if I am talking another language. He tips his hat, and, in an instant, he has departed.

I am astonished by what just happened and a little uncomfortable about this person. I also can't help but wonder why he didn't respond to my request to connect in my subconscious room. Perhaps I will never know, but I am relieved that he didn't.

I must compose myself in preparation for what is before me.

CHAPTER NINETEEN
Unearthed

I return to where we left Lucy sleeping to discover that she is still there. This is a relief for me as I have been unfocused slightly since Syd and I were with her last. My heart is with her; she feels so unloved. It is as if she doesn't fit into where she has been placed in this world and I can connect with her. However, she has a strong spirit and a passion for life that refuses to accept the unreasonable demands made by others, and that don't fit with what she believes to be her purpose even if that is not crystal clear. She is inspiring to me.

Lying wrapped in a sleeping bag on a make-shift bed, Lucy is being awakened by Jay.

"Luce, wake up, Luce . . . we need to get going," he gently urges.

She groans in response and rolls over into another dream as if it hasn't fully registered with her.

"Luce, Luce, wake up. Are you coming to find out who your parents are or not?"

She jumps up out of her sleeping bag in an instant. Her hair is all messy and she is slightly unsteady but her desire to continue with her journey is there for sure.

A young lady walks in. She is confident and casual. Her blonde tresses are formed in tightly sprung coils. This, coupled with her green eyes and distinctive style in clothes, provides her a unique appearance.

"Morning, you two," she says in a friendly way. "Breakfast anyone?"

"That would be cool, Sara, thanks," Jay responds.

They all make their way to the breakfast bench.

"So, what's the plan of action for today, guys?"

Lucy seems to have lost her tongue and so Jay explains their mission.

"Lucy has just found out that her parents are not her real parents, so she has run away from home. I am going to help her find her real parents and I was thinking that as you have done some work in the records office you might know how we could make a start."

Sara looks at Lucy, who shyly drinks her hot chocolate. She smiles at her. "Lucy, are you sure you want to do this? It is going to change your life as you know it."

Finally, Lucy finds her voice. "Yes. I have never been surer about something in my entire life. I have never fitted into my surroundings while I was growing up. My parents . . . well, those people who brought me up, they have just used me as a puppet. They have never loved me. I don't know what we are going to discover but it is better than not knowing anything. I have to find out."

Sara gives Lucy a warm hug. "You poor thing, it must be terrible for you to grow up feeling so unloved. You had everything you financially needed but nothing you emotionally required. Of course, I will help get you on the right track." She beams free love from her inner self right onto Lucy. Lucy absorbs every molecule of it as she rests her head in the bosom of this free spirit.

"Okay, where do we start?" Jay asks.

Reluctantly they separate.

"In this instance I would say your birth certificate is your best bet," Sara says. "It has to state who the birth mother and father are. Have you ever seen your birth certificate?"

"We had to have it when I was starting school, but I have never read it; come to think of it, I was never allowed to."

"Well, there is your key," Sara exclaims.

"But I can't go back to my home. They might see me. Nor can I go to the school. It is closed."

"Do you know anything about where you were born? Your birth name? Date of birth? They should be able to find something out down at the records office."

"Oh, I do remember one time when we were registering for something and someone asked when it was that we moved here from Madison Valley. I knew something was up because my mum got all anxious and quite snappy at the lady. I thought it strange because I believed we had always lived on our estate."

I am taken aback at first because my childhood home was in Madison Valley. But I refocus and listen closely.

"That is where I would try first then," Sara suggests. "Give me your details and I will ring and make an initial enquiry. I will pretend to be a government institution and that should do the trick."

"Thanks, Sara, I really appreciate it."

"No worries, Lucy. It is all very exciting. It's like being a part of a movie investigation squad and besides, I like to help others."

"Okay ladies. Can we start getting things moving along here? If I am supposed to be driving to Madison Valley today, we had better get started."

"You would do that for me?" Lucy asks in a haze of disbelief.

"Sure, I have nothing else planned for the holidays."

"Oh, thank you, Jay." Lucy gives him a grateful hug. He gets a little flustered.

"Hey, maybe you should get yourself ready to go," Sara says.

"Yes, you are right. Can I use your bathroom?"

"Yes, go for it and if you need any toiletries or clothes you can borrow some from my room."

"You guys are so fab. I won't ever forget this," Lucy says and leaves the room.

As soon as she is out of sight Sara says, "Okay, Jay. You really like this girl, don't you?"

"Don't know what you are talking about, Sara. Can I not help out someone who needs it?"

"There's more to it than that, Jay. You are giving too much of yourself just to be helping someone out. You really like her, don't you?"

"Sure, I like her, Sara, but I haven't any intentions of doing anything about it. I just want to help her. I know what she has been through as we are neighbours."

"Okay, Jay. I will believe you but remember she is still young and fragile; that's all I am saying."

"I hear you, Sara."

Lucy walks back into the room all freshened up and ready to go.

"Ready, Lucy? Great, we will get going then." Jay hops up from the bar stool and grabs his keys. "It's going to take us a while to get there. Are you certain you want to go?"

"Yes," Lucy says confidently.

"Before we leave, do you want to ring your parents to let them know that you are all right?" Sara suggests. "I am sure they are worried about you."

"No, they are not my parents and they probably won't even care that I am gone anyway."

"Okay, well, I will give you a call to let you know if I get any leads. Good luck, Lucy, nice to meet you. I hope you find what it is you are after."

They take off in the sports car, Lucy looking adoringly at Jay. It will only be natural for her to engage in some romanticised feelings for him. At this moment he is her prince charming who came to free her from her captors. This is what fairy tales are made of.

I continue on the journey with them as Syd has requested that I stay close should my intervention be needed.

After a few hours the phone rings and Jay glances at it and throws it to Lucy to answer. "It's Sara," he explains.

"Hi, Sara, Jay is driving so he can't answer the phone right now . . . Oh okay . . . Yes, I got that . . . Sorry, hold on, I am just going to grab a pen . . . Yes, I got the name and number . . . What? That's not good . . . okay, I will think about that. Thanks, Sara," and she hangs up.

"Are you going to tell me what's happening or am I going to have to squeeze it out of you?" Jay asks.

Lucy laughs slightly and gives him the full message. "Well, Sara contacted the records office and there is a birth certificate for my date of birth and surname in their records but not with my first name and they explained that may have been changed. They obviously couldn't give out too many details, but Sara did manage to squeeze out of them my mother's surname, which is Harvey. So, she has looked up that surname in the area and there is one. She reckons we should call them and see if there are any leads from it. What do you think?"

"Yes, that sounds good enough to me. Are you happy with that?"

"Yeah, I'm happy but a little nervous too . . . Oh, I almost forgot. She said there are people out looking for me and that I should think about calling home. It was on the news apparently and they are concerned for my safety because of the skid marks they found on the road."

"Ah man, I didn't see this coming. Best you call, or they will be on our tail."

Reluctantly Lucy dials a number into the mobile. She listens for a minute and just as she is about to hang up there is an answer. "Hello, it's me," she says. "I am just ringing to let you know I am fine. You need not worry. Anyway, you are not my parents. Bye." Then she ends the call.

"You didn't hold back there, did you? Where is shy little Lucy now?"

"I am not shy and if you knew what they have put me through you would understand my hostility. If I was happy would I have run away?"

"Sure, you are sixteen . . ."

"Nearly seventeen actually."

"Well, there you are. No worries then. We will pull over soon and get some lunch if you like."

"That would be nice," she says.

"Ooh feisty and all cashed up, you surprise me now."

"One of the very few benefits of being brought up rich, but you know all about that too."

"I have been lucky enough to have loving parents and money, so I hit the jackpot when I was born."

Lucy drops her head and Jay puts his hand on her leg to comfort her.

"Don't worry, you will strike it rich too. We will find your real family."

Lucy is smiling.

I am being called to Melody and so I must trust my intuition as it is my faithful guide.

CHAPTER TWENTY
Spiritual Entanglement

I reach Melody. She is basking in tranquillity. The natural glow of her fireplace warms up not only the room but also my heart. She is sitting with a cup of hot cocoa in front of the fire in deep contemplation. I love how she chooses to live in such peace and embraces it wholeheartedly. Her time alone is spent wisely, recharging her energies so that when those in need call she is ready to help.

It seems late in the evening and so when the telephone rings it takes her off guard. "Oh, who could that be at this time?" she says aloud as she goes to answer it. The telephone is a traditional dial phone made from white ceramic with a white and brass handle. There is a pink floral pattern on the handle and at each side of the round brass dial. It is a romantic out of date telephone, but it is beautiful.

"Hello," she says cautiously, lifting the receiver.

"Yes, that is me . . . how can I be of assistance?" After listening for a moment, she goes a little pale and reaches for the magnificently crafted mahogany chair with a cream satin padded seat, so she can sit down.

She continues to listen without uttering a word, then says, "Yes, yes, I am still here, love . . . that will be fine . . . can we say tomorrow morning around ten . . . see you then . . . bye."

She sits back and absorbs her thoughts, the receiver still in her hand. Then she slowly dials a number, carefully slotting her finger into each circular hole and turning the dial clockwise.

"Hello, Joan . . . yes, it has been some time, hasn't it? How are you all? . . . Oh, I am sorry to hear that . . . I will be needing you to call . . . oh you can't? . . . okay, yes, if he could come that will be fine . . . tell him I will make up a bed for him and I will see him in a few hours . . . Joanie, I will call you tomorrow if that is okay . . . speak with you then."

After Melody replaces the receiver, she sits for a brief while and then jumps up. "Oh, I must get some things ready for my visitor. I didn't expect company," and she whizzes around making beds and preparing some supper. She then stops and takes a moment to look around. "Yes, that will do," she says and takes her place beside the fire again.

"I know you are there with me, you know," she exclaims quickly. "Why don't you communicate with me? Do you know why this is happening and why she has been guided to me?"

"You can sense my presence?" I reply softly just in case she is not talking to me.

"Yes, you have visited before with the pregnant lady. Come take a seat beside me. I can't chat for long as I have company coming and they think I am crazy enough without adding speaking to spirits to the mix." She chuckles.

I move over beside her and sit close by.

"Now that's better than standing in a drafty corner, isn't it?"

She is right. "Yes, thank you."

"Why do you visit? Am I going to die?"

"No, Melody. That is not why I visit you."

"Well, that is a relief. I am not ready to die. I have so much that I need to do first."

"My visit is for good. I am here to guide you towards positive change."

"So that's why things are happening, and changes are occurring. They are making way for something I have wished for to come into my life. It is time, isn't it?"

"Your awareness astounds me, Melody. Please continue with your awareness and trust in the process of your intuition."

"Oh, I will," she says happily.

We sit for a time in silence.

Then there is a loud knock on the door that can only be made by a big steel door knocker. It catches us both off guard and we jump slightly.

"Oh, that will be my guest. Do you mind? I am sorry to be rude."

I move back to my position in the corner.

Rushing to the door she stops to fix herself. She opens the big heavy door and I am astonished to see who is standing there. It is Joe. Melody holds out her arms for an embrace and the two of them hug for a time. My heart is crushed. Thoughts start rushing through my mind at an accelerated pace. Surely, they can't be together . . . Melody is a beautiful radiant woman, but she is old enough to be his mother . . . please, please, no . . . I can't watch.

"Claire are you here?" Joe asks, obviously picking up on my energy.

"You can see her too?" Melody enquires in delight.

"Yes, I can. You can too, Mel?" he asks excitedly.

"Claire, love, it is okay. You can come join us," Melody invites me.

I don't know whether to accept the invitation or return to Lucy. My heart is fluttering, and I don't want to leave Joe like this, so I accept and join them. We all sit together and Melody delights in it all. "Now you two, how did this happen?"

We explain our history and Melody begins to shed some tears for us. "That is so sad, forbidden love. I have to say that your mum has made some very harsh parenting decisions, Joe. Poor Irene all those years ago and you also and now, well, she may be given the opportunity to help make up for some of her wrong doings and she chooses to not deal with that either. This is very disappointing."

Joe doesn't let go of my hand. How can he feel it? He must sense it. "Oh yes, Mel, why did Mum send me here? She didn't say anything. Was it so that Claire and I could see each other again?"

"Joe, love, I would love nothing more than to say that I masterminded the plot to get you two beautiful souls together but alas that was not my doing. I got a call from a young girl who wants to come visit me. She says she is looking for her biological parents and that she was given my name as a point of contact. I just know it is that young child your mother forced from the embrace of your sister, Joe, so I told her she could call in the morning."

"Does Irene know about this?" Joe asks.

"I don't know. Surely, we all know that your mum doesn't think of me as family because we are not blood sisters even though we were brought up with the same parents and spent every moment of our young lives together. Surely I have been part of your life."

"No, not really except in those few months when I was sent here to stay with granny, and you were here too, and Mum didn't know."

"I would have been a great aunty you know."

"I am sure that you would have been, Mel."

"So how is Irene?"

"Don't you know?"

"Know what?"

"Irene has cancer."

"What? The poor girl? This is because of your mum's poison, you know."

"Ah you can't say that, Mel. She is really sick, it's hard to know what to do."

"Well, I know what to do and I will be doing it whether your mum lets me or not. The poor girl must be going through hell."

"Yes, pretty much."

"I feel that I must go prepare for this healing. I hope you will not mind excusing me. I will be deeply inward for some time, so I would like to offer Claire the use of my body should she so wish to utilise a physical presence."

"That is very kind of you, Melody, thank you," I say in utter gratitude.

"That can be done?" Joe asks in amazement.

Melody has already abandoned her physicality to pursue her spiritual guidance. So, as Joe seems slightly uneasy about it, I choose to begin the transition from entity to physicality. It will be strange to experience being in a bodily form. For some time, the strangeness is further enhanced as this form is not one I have known. Melody's frame is of entirely different proportions from that I occupied in my previous presence, the one Joe was familiar with.

Slowly lowering myself into Melody's body, I feel strangely comfortable. I adjust myself to examine if I am able to manoeuvre correctly and when I raise my head to look into Joe's eyes, I feel the rush of love shine through.

"Claire is that you in there?" he asks in astonishment.

"Yes, it is me, Joe, please hug me."

In his warm embrace I feel safer than I have ever felt before. I am immediately brought emotionally back to the years when our forbidden love was at its peak. We should never have been separated; our love was too strong, strong enough that separation through the intervention of others forced me to become completely introvert and my body to suffer unimaginably. I feel sparks whizz all around the body I now inhabit.

Joe has his eyes closed; he is absorbing every morsel of this moment. He holds me firmly as if he never wants to release me from his embrace. Lifting his head and placing his hands to cup my face while still keeping his eyes closed, he kisses me. I melt in the deep true love that is projected through to my heart from this kiss. This magical gift of love is solely just for me, right in this moment and with all of the love in the world I shall keep it close for eternity.

"I love you, Joe," I say softly in his ear when the kiss ends.

"I love you too, Claire, forever," he says as a tear drops from his eye.

We lie in front of the fire for a long time and when I know that he has drifted soundly off to sleep I release myself from his arms and place Melody's body back in the position it was in when she so generously lent it to me. I do hope I have not wasted too much of her beautiful physical energy. It takes a lot of physical and emotional energy to transcend between the domains.

I have been selfish in tending to my own emotional needs and been neglecting my duty to this mission. I have disappointed myself and I must keep myself focused for the rest of this mission or risk jeopardising the process of wish giving.

CHAPTER TWENTY-ONE
Alterations

LUCY

Returning to Lucy I am astonished when I witness the scene that greets me. The setting seems to be an inn. They have obviously stopped driving for the night and taken refuge in a roadside motel. They are both asleep in a spooning position and I get the impression that intimacy has occurred here. The thing that concerned me the most was that when I was transcending here I encountered the gift carrier. As the Wish Giver I must trust in the process of adjustment that occurs when the twinkles are released. I do hope that this is part of that process and not just a result of me being neglectful of my duties.

Looking at these two young individuals I can't help smile. They are both young, but they are listening to their desires and although it may not be ideal for things to happen so fast for them it is all part of the process of learning, loving and receiving that comes hand and hand with the true existence of being. The feeling of knowing and living for the moment is one of the most alive sensations possible.

As I contemplate the mission so far, I am drawn towards the thought that many of the wishes have a link with intimacy and creation of life. I deduce that this is because one of the most natural processes of life is creating life. Each life is a miracle that is gifted to a parent for the purpose of nurturing, learning and wish receiving. Many avenues of desire all navigate their origin back to the creation of life. Lovemaking is one of the most sensual and exhilarating experiences anyone can have. It connects people on another level of being that can link them for life; it is that powerful. I find it concerning when this beautiful gift is ill-treated by those who choose not to consider its true purposeful intention. Then there are others who attempt to mimic the exhilarating sensation of satisfaction through extreme sports and other such pleasures which is all very well so long as it doesn't hurt anyone else in the process. However, it may all also be in the learning process for someone to experience. There is so much to consider.

I am being called away and because Lucy seems to be safe for now I choose to move on and return again soon. I listen to my intuition and I am drawn to Joy. It must be time for some adjusting to occur for her, even though there have been a lot of changes already in her life.

JOY

Navigating to Joy was not as I expected. She is located in an entirely different setting from that of previous visits. The energy where we are is filled with romance; it is as if every breath not only fills your lungs but also fills your heart. I am not surprised to find Joy in such a place. I am delighted to see that Ben is accompanying her. They are both very much in love as they hold hands and gaze lovingly at each other as they walk around this beautiful city of Paris. Ben is enchanted by Joy. It is obvious she has captured his heart. They visit monuments that are filled with the energies of past and present which exhilarate in their sheer magnificence.

Finding a nice spot for lunch, Ben spreads his jacket on the grass for Joy to sit on so that she doesn't get grass stains on her light-coloured trousers with matching lemon top.

"I will just pop over to that cafe and grab us a sandwich or something. Would that be good for you?" he asks as she seats herself in a position to get the best view of the surrounding landscape.

"That would be divine, Ben, thank you."

While he is away Joy is approached many times by French men exclaiming that their hearts have been captured by her beautiful glow. One certain man with his charming French accent and unique appearance says, "Oh beautiful lady, you have stolen my heart. Please say you will be mine forevermore."

Joy laughs at him and he is slightly insulted. "You think that what I say is funny?"

"Sorry, it is just that you have only known me for less than five seconds. How can you declare undying love for me?"

"You shine like an angel and your beauty is pure. There are not many like you."

"I am flattered, honestly, but I am here with someone. In fact, here he comes now," she says as she waves her arm at Ben who is walking back from the cafe with two baguettes and two bottles of water."

He passes the refreshments to Joy and faces the French admirer.

"Bonjour, Monsieur. I am Jean Paul. You are a very lucky man, my friend," he exclaims.

"Yes, I know that," Ben says. "Thank you."

They shake hands and Jean Paul hops back on his bicycle.

"She is a beautiful angel shining her light on our world; help her shine," he says and races off.

Ben and Joy sit for a moment and then both begin to laugh at once.

"Oh Joy, you surely attract them, don't you?"

"Yes, he was an interesting character, wasn't he? He asked me to marry him."

"Well, if I had known that I wouldn't have been so polite."

"He is not a threat to you, my darling," she says and leans over to kiss him affectionately. "Thank you for bringing me here." She unwraps her baguette. "If only everyone could feel such joy as I am experiencing right now."

"Joy, I love you and support you in all that you do. I love your stand-up comedy shows, I love that you want to share joy with the whole world and I want to help you. Your energy is amazing, and it would be selfish of me to want to keep you to myself, but I am not giving up on the joy that you are able to devote to me. So, will you marry me?"

Coughing momentarily on a morsel of bread, Joy cannot believe her ears. "Really? Really? You want to share the rest of your life with me?"

"Yes, I do," he exclaims while getting down on bended knee and drawing a little red velvet box from his pocket. He opens it and she is stunned to see a big diamond on a tiny gold band. "Well, what is your answer, Joy?" he asks in anticipation.

"Oh yes, yes, yes!" she says and leaps towards him in excitement, lunch forgotten.

Ben takes the ring out of the box and places it on her finger. It fits perfectly, and they melt into each other's arms and kiss lingeringly. A small crowd has gathered, and they begin to cheer and clap in celebration.

Ben and Joy break from their embrace and share a warm hug and a giggle with those who are watching. Then Joy holds out her hand to show off her dazzler and the ladies come to admire it, exclaiming in French accents at its beauty.

The birds have since helped themselves to their baguettes and Ben puts his arms around his wife-to-be's waist and asks, "Shall we make our way back to our chateau, Mademoiselle?"

"Oui," Joy happily replies.

And off they go hand in hand across the park surrounded by the magical, combined loving energy they are projecting out into the world's atmosphere. They are invincible right now.

I am aware that the twinkle is at work here, moving things along at a rapid pace. Things happen faster when there is intervention from a miraculous source. I feel a pulling energy towards Jade, so I swiftly move forward trying to make up lost ground along the way.

JADE

Jade is not in such tranquil surroundings and this is also reflected in her mood. She has red eyes and has obviously been crying. I would love to take some of her pain away just as Syd did earlier, but I am being advised not to intervene as sometimes we must walk through the valley of tears to appreciate the glorious magnificence that is reaching the summit. Once she chooses to embark on the journey to the top, towards her true happiness, then her path will be revealed. One step at a time will get her there and the biggest challenge is discovering where the first step begins as it may not be where it is initially perceived to be. I know this because I am on my journey and each step is concealed until I am ready to take it. Then it is uncovered, and I take that one step and will always be prepared for the next, knowing that I am one step closer to the tranquillity of my destination. I trust in the process and it rewards me every time. I am grateful for this knowledge.

Jade has not discovered her path so far and feels stranded in the valley of tears. She has taken to her bed again in physical pain about what has happened in her life recently. If only she realised that everything happens for a reason, even the bad things! If only she realised that her wish is on its way! But she must begin to listen to the signs to allow her to receive it.

A little girl is standing at the doorway. She sees me and asks, "Hello, lady, are you here to help my mummy to be happy?"

"Oh yes. I will try princess. Why don't you go and give your mum a big hug?"

"She might not want me to."

Just as she says it, her mum throws back the covers and welcomes her into her loving embrace.

"I love you, Mum."

"I love you, Nicky."

They both snuggle, and Nicky falls asleep in an instant. Jade hugs her daughter just that little bit tighter, absorbing every bit of the unconditional love she is being given right now.

Then Jade's phone beeps to indicate a message has come through. She hesitates at first but then she slowly releases her arm from around her sleeping daughter, ensuring she is comfortable before viewing the communication.

"These two men of yours are fighting up the town."

"Oh Jesus, that's all I need right now." She buries her head back into the pillow without responding to the message.

After a short while there is a knock at the door. Jade is reluctant to answer but curiosity prevails, and she looks out of her window but can only see the shadow of a man. She cannot make out who is at her door. Then he starts shouting, "Jade I know you are there. I need to talk with you." He backs out into the street and she can clearly see that it is Sean.

"Jade, I need to talk to you," he hollers.

Jade hides behind the curtain.

"I'm not going anywhere until I talk with you, Jade," he continues determinedly.

Then he starts to sing. Out of sheer embarrassment Jade rushes down the stairs to open the door and lets a slightly intoxicated Sean into her home and storms into her living room in not the best of humour. Sean shuts the door and follows her.

"Hello, Jade," he says cautiously.

Jade replies reluctantly. "Hello, Sean, what are you doing here? And why are you and Jason fighting up in the town?"

"Oh, ye heard about that, did ye?"

"Yes of course I did. We live in a small town, Sean, and it doesn't take long for news to reach anyone. Why are you here?"

"Oh yes, I have come here because, well, because I heard that you are expecting, and you know we . . . well, that night . . . the baby could be mine and I want you to know that I am going to stand by my responsibilities . . ."

"Hold on, Sean. Who said anything about me being pregnant?"

"Well, as you so rightly said Jade, we live in a small town and well, you were at the doctor's the other day and you know how . . ."

"Don't say any more, Sean. I have heard enough. Yes, Sean I am pregnant and yes, it is yours, but I don't know if I can possibly keep it. I have two other children to think about and to be honest, I can't be a single mum again."

"Definitely mine, are you sure?" She gives him a look and he retracts by saying "Ah you know, I mean you are with Jason . . ."

She cuts him off. "Let's just say we never got that far."

"Oh, oh, right, well, that changes everything then." He manoeuvres his way over to where she is seated, takes her hand and says, "Jade, from my heart I love you ever since the day I met you in preschool. Will you please marry me?"

"Sean, you don't mean that and anyway I don't love you."

"That's only because you haven't considered it yet, Jade. I am a good man and you can't say that we didn't make sparks fly that night. We could be good together."

"I am with Jason and he has been through enough already . . ."

"Jade, the guy is gay. I don't see why you can't see that."

"No, he is not."

"Has he ever made any moves of a sexual nature towards you?"

"Well no, but that's because he respects me and to be honest, Sean, you don't."

Noticeably hurt by what she has just said, he stands up and before he leaves he says, "Well, if that is what you want to believe, then you go ahead." He walks over and gives her a long passionate kiss that makes her go weak at the knees. He makes sure she is standing safely and then says. "You can't say that you didn't feel anything, Jade. My offer still stands." And then he walks out.

Now things are clearer for me. Jade is searching in the wrong place for love. She is hoping the love will suddenly appear in the relationship that she already has whereas all of the changes she is experiencing are forcing her to realise she needs to look elsewhere. Jade strives to find love and she must just listen to the signs the universe is screaming at her by putting obstacles in her way. If she would only realise that what she seeks she already has but blocks it because of fear and lack of awareness. The vibrational frequencies that Jade radiates can only attract more sadness. When she simplifies her expectations of herself and others and allows herself to forgive past hurts then she will be equipped with the tools of life she needs to move forward into her power. Right now, she cannot see that but hopefully she will open her heart soon or her wish will not be able to reach her. There is so much potential for happiness here and if anyone can help Jade to find her path I believe that Sean can, if she doesn't push him away too far in fear.

I shall move forward and let the magic of the twinkle do its work.

CHAPTER TWENTY-TWO
New Connections

"Jay are you awake?"

"Yes, Luce . . . I am sorry. I shouldn't . . ."

"Oh, did you not want to?"

"No, no, it's not that. It's just that I shouldn't have taken advantage."

"But you didn't take advantage; I wanted to as well. You do like me, don't you?"

"Yes of course I like you. I have since the moment I saw you walking along that road."

"Well then please don't be sorry."

They look into each other's eyes and he kisses her nose. "Come on then. We have an important meeting this morning."

"Oh yes we do, don't we?" she says excitedly. "I want you to know that I really appreciate everything you are doing for me, Jay."

"My pleasure. I just hope that it all works out."

"It will. I can feel it."

They get dressed and leave the motel hand in hand.

I am drawn towards Melody's house. I am slightly nervous but excited at the prospect of seeing Joe again, but our love cannot go anywhere after my mission, so I am reluctant to get any deeper with him. It would be unfair and would just create more sadness for us both. Our love can never be in this lifetime for him as I have moved to another realm and although my heart still holds the same feelings as it did when I transitioned I know we will come together again in time. Until then I must respect the reality of our circumstances.

When I arrive Melody and Joe are sitting at the breakfast table talking about me. As always Melody's awareness is second to none and she acknowledges my presence immediately.

"Claire love, come and join us."

Joe smiles from ear to ear to know that I am here. My heart beams for him and I try my best to shade it with the shadow of sadness.

"Claire dear, why are you so solemn?" Melody enquires.

"Thank you for allowing me to utilise your body last night, Melody. I do hope I didn't drain your energies too much."

"Claire, my dear, my body has never felt better. You filled it to the brim with love and every muscle, organ and cell rejoiced in the healing it received. I focus so much on healing others that I forget about my own needs sometimes. You can utilise my body anytime as I depart to the inner pursuit of healing others on quite a regular basis."

"Yes, I feel that from you, Melody. I hope you don't mind me saying but you must also work in the power of your existence on earth. It is wonderful to be so connected to a higher source, but others would also benefit greatly from your physical presence if you navigate it towards those in need. You have so much to give that you are a gift to the world."

"Certainly, it is something to consider, Claire. I am enlightened by your words and inspired by your wisdom of such a young spirit. Thank you."

"She is special, isn't she?" Joe responds.

At that moment a car is heard pulling into the driveway. Melody gets up to look out her window and sees a red sports car pull up outside.

"Oh, it is her already; she is early." And she attempts to fix her hair by patting it.

"Don't worry, Mel, I will get the door if you want to go sort yourself out quickly."

"Okay, I won't be a moment," and she dashes away while Joe goes to open the door.

"Hello," a shy voice speaks, "I have come to see Melody Harvey. Have I come to the right address?"

Joe doesn't respond, instead he stands there staring.

Melody has picked up on the awkwardness from her room and comes running out while still fixing her clothes.

"Yes, yes love, I'm Melody. I wasn't prepared for your arrival and Joe here answered the door. Please excuse him. He is a little speechless right now." She gives her visitor a warm welcoming hug.

"Oh okay," Lucy replies. "We are early but thought that you wouldn't mind . . . oh, this is Jay by the way," she says, glowing in her feelings for him.

"Oh, young love, how beautiful!" Melody remarks. "Come in, come in, and take a seat."

They all sit in the cosy living room and Joe still has not said a word.

"I shall make some tea and we can have some cake, wouldn't that be nice?"

"Yes, thank you, Mrs . . ."

"Oh, please call me Melody . . . Joe, could you please accompany me?"

He rises and follows her.

When they get to the kitchen Melody slaps Joe right across the face, catching him off guard. I find it quite amusing and giggle.

"Hey, what did you do that for?" Joe asks, hurt.

"What is wrong with you? She is nervous enough as it is without you acting all strange."

"It's just," he hesitates, "it's just that she looks exactly like Irene. When I opened the door there was my sister standing there all healthy and vibrant; it caught me off guard."

"I do understand, love," Melody comforts him, "but we need to concentrate on making this work out properly and at least we know for sure that she is Hope and we can move forward in this knowing."

"Okay I shall carry the cake," he stalls again. "Oh goodness, what date is it?"

"The fifteenth of November. Why?"

"I have just realised that it is her seventeenth birthday today. Let's put a candle on the cake and see her reaction."

Melody scuffles in the drawer. "Here, perfect," she exclaims and places seventeen pink candles on top of the cake. "Are we ready now?"

"Yes of course," he says enthusiastically. Then they return to the room where Lucy and Jay are seated.

"We believe it to be your birthday, young lady. We hope you don't mind but we prepared a cake."

"I can't believe it. How did you know?" Lucy asks, tears filling her eyes.

"It's your birthday, though you never said." Jay wishes her "Happy birthday" and kisses her as if this is significant for him that she is now seventeen and he can give a little more of himself to her.

"Well love, Joe here is your uncle," Melody explains.

"My uncle?" Lucy asks emotionally.

"Yes Lucy, you look just like your mum. So, we know that you are our lost little Hope."

"Hope is what she called me?"

"Yes, and she never wanted to give you up but my mum, your granny, made her. She has regretted it ever since."

"But why did she make her? I didn't do anything wrong to deserve to be given to those people."

"No, of course you didn't, love," Melody says hugging her. "It is just the way it was then."

"What is she like?"

Melody and Joe look at each other.

"What? What is it, tell me. She's dead, isn't she?"

"No, no, love. She is not dead, but she is very ill right now." Melody explains.

"Then she needs me," Lucy says determinedly as she stands up.

"Do you know what, she probably does. The torture created in her by the thought of losing you all those years ago has been a heavy cross for her to bear. You will also want to meet your brothers."

"Brothers?"

"Yes, you have two younger brothers. They are twins and they will love you," Joe informs her.

"Please, can we go now?"

Joe and Melody look at each other again and smile. "Why not? It has been long enough," Melody says. "Then I can do some hands-on healing for your mum; she needs me regardless of what that mum of hers says."

They all prepare to go, and Jay pulls Lucy aside.

"You don't need me any longer, Lucy. This is private, and I will only be in the way."

"Oh, you don't want to come with me?"

"No, it's not that, Luce. Of course, I want to, but it is important for you to focus on your future with your family right now."

"Yeah you are probably right, Jay. I am going to miss you."

"I will miss you too, Luce."

He kisses her and gets into his car and drives off.

My heart aches to see them separate.

"Okay, so we are all going together in my car then." Melody goes into the side door of her garage and pulls up the shutter to reveal a Volkswagen camper van in pristine condition.

"Wow, that's so cool," Lucy says.

"Yes, it is, isn't it?"

Joe puts his arm around Lucy's shoulder. "Come on, young lady. Let's go meet your mum," and he guides her into the back seat and sits with her while indicating for me to occupy the passenger seat with Melody. I take a moment to check my intuition and it is guiding me to go, so I do.

Along the way Joe and Melody tell Lucy wonderful stories about her mum. Lucy listens carefully to everything they say. Revelling in the wonderment of the beautiful picture they are creating in her mind of this woman, she realises it is a far cry from the woman she believed to be her mother a few days ago. Relief consumes her, and she begins to cry.

"Oh Lucy, we didn't mean to make you sad," Joe says.

"These are tears of joy that I have a loving and kind mother. This is what I always dreamed of when I was growing up."

"You poor thing, every child deserves to feel the love of their mum," Joe replies.

"We're here," Melody declares as they park outside Irene's home. It is a two-storey residence surrounded by evergreen trees to create privacy from the busy road that runs alongside its perimeter.

A lady who looks slightly older than Melody burst out the front door and comes storming towards us.

"What are you doing here?" she shouts at Melody, "and as for you, Joe, why did you bring her here?"

"Hello, Joan, so lovely to be welcomed so graciously," Melody says.

"Mum, this is Lucy; she has come to see her mum."

Joan is quiet. She cannot believe her eyes. Here is a young lady that she deprived of motherly love seventeen years ago to the day. Everyone awaits her response as it has been one of defence for so long. She stands aside as if defeated and makes way for them to enter the house.

They run up the stairs to where Irene is lying, so poorly that she can barely open her eyes.

"Oh, dear girl." Melody's heart yearns. She swiftly makes her way to the bedside and takes Irene's hand.

"Irene love, I need you to focus and have only positive healing thoughts. I am going to give you some healing to help you now, and then again later."

Everyone is quiet, patiently waiting in anticipation for the next response.

"Hope is that you?" Irene weakly holds out her arms. "Is it really you?"

Lucy runs straight into her embrace and this healing love is getting to work.

"I can't believe that this moment is finally here, happy birthday my precious," she says cupping her long-lost daughter's face in her frail hands.

"Thank you, mum. I am so happy to meet you."

"I am complete again," Irene says as she hugs her as tight as she can.

I will leave them to bond and for Melody to work her magic healing on Irene. This is an exceptionally special moment.

CHAPTER TWENTY-THREE
Arrival

So much has happened since I have acquired the role of the Wish Giver. Each one of the assignments has progressed towards the possibility of receiving their true wish and some of them have even connected with each other. I am becoming more and more fascinated by the process of wish receiving. There are no constraints within the universal laws, only those that are self-imposed. When something is pursued with belief, then there is no reason for limitations other than those that are imposed by entities like us that are working for the higher good of all.

Deeply immersed in my thoughts, I am startled when my messaging watch sounds. I am being summoned by the Waiting Zone and so I must make my way to the porthole to discover my fate. Maybe they know about me connecting with Joe. Oh, I do hope I haven't mucked it up. I really love this role and don't want to return to being insignificant in the Waiting Zone. I am enjoying having a purpose.

As I reach the porthole it is open and ready for advancement.

At the dispatch area I encounter a message. I open a small quickly scribbled note.

"Please come quick." I know it is written by Syd and so I hone in on her energy frequency to discover that she is in labour.

I quickly make my way to her side. She is lying in her room with one of the messenger nurses assisting her. Holding her hand, I enquire where the Boss is.

"Oh Claire, thank you for coming. Rupert is in a bit of a tizzy because the baby is coming early, and he has not been gifted the insight of knowing if the delivery will go successfully; it's too much for him right now. Thank you for coming."

"It is my pleasure, Syd," I say as she begins squeezing my hand so tightly that the circulation ceases to flow. She is in pain but pain of a beautiful nature. She pants, and I wipe her brow and give her a supportive smile. Once the pain subsides she enquires about the mission.

"You don't need to know about that now, Syd; you have more important things to be thinking about."

"Please, Claire, I need the distraction," she says and then encounters another contraction.

"They are coming fast and more intensely, Sydney, it won't be long now," the nurse assures her.

"Please let her be all right," Syd prays.

"It will be fine, everything will be fine," I comfort her.

"What would I do without you, Claire? You are wonderful."

"Hey, you are the one giving birth here. You are the wonderful one creating a miracle."

"Yes, I am, aren't I?" Then another contraction.

"Okay, Sydney, you are doing so well; I can see her head," the nurse exclaims. "Keep pushing, keep pushing."

And with all her might Syd pushes and Rupert comes into the room just in time to see his daughter's head emerging.

"Oh Syd, I am so sorry. I shouldn't have left you; I just panicked." He holds her other hand and she begins to squeeze our hands as hard as she can. Rupert looks at me and mimes "Thank you." I smile back. Then the focus is on Syd as she pushes her little miracle out. A glow surrounds the infant as the nurse holds her up and places her straight away on Syd's bosom to ensure an instant connection.

The little mite looks up at her mum and dad. It is such an intimate moment that I feel as though I am imposing on their personal occasion, so I leave the room and wait in the lounge.

After a time, the nurse comes out and says that Sydney is asking for me to return.

"Oh, she is beautiful," I say, looking at the baby's little peaceful face as she sleeps. Already she has a lot of hair that is the lightest blonde I have ever seen.

"We are going to call her Arianna Claire; Arianna because it means *child of the universe* and Claire because you were here for me when I needed you most."

"Oh, I really am honoured. I don't know what to say."

"Please say that you will be her godmother and help us to guide her in the best possible way through her existence," Rupert says.

Without hesitation I say, "Yes, I would love to, I am honoured."

"Would you like to hold her?" Syd asks.

"Really? I can hold her already, you don't mind?"

"Of course, here you are." Sydney passes her to me.

I hold her close in all of her miraculous beauty and she opens her eyes to see me. "Hello, little Arianna Claire, I will always be here for you should you need me, I promise."

I am feeling very connected to her and I know she will need me to be there for her at some point in her being. She is unique in every way. Her radiating energy glows all around the room. It really is quite astounding. I have witnessed births before, but this is special. I feel that her coming is significant. Syd and Rupert are engrossed in the moment. I walk over and return their gorgeous bundle of joy to them. I give them both a kiss and assure Syd that everything is fine with the mission but that I must return.

"I will be in touch soon, Claire."

"That would be lovely," I say. I know it is a special time for them right now and they need to focus on their new little family. I will be fine; the twinkles are working their magic and I am listening to my inner guide, so nothing can possibly go wrong. I shall return when things progress. I am feeling drawn back to Joy, so I must commence with the undertaking I had abandoned but for the best possible reason.

CHAPTER TWENTY-FOUR
Share the Joy

I am drawn closer to Joy. The scene is a studio. There are glass boxes and vast boards covered in switches for a multitude of applications I presume. Joy is in one of the glass boxes and she is speaking softly into a microphone.

"You are your own power. The power to love is yours when you want it. The power of endless joy is yours should you desire it. We all have the power to heal our hearts and bodies by healing our minds. During our lives we cannot control all of the elements that we are exposed to, all of which influence our development both physically and emotionally along our journey through our lives. On occasions these influences leave debris that grows into disease and illness. But what most people don't recognise is that through our minds we can assist in the healing process of our bodies. The first and most important thing is to be positive. Being positive sends little healing ripples through our bodies. Laughter and joy have been acknowledged to have healing results on patients throughout history. Do you remember hearing the saying 'Laughter is the best medicine'? In this CD we will work through a number of exercises that will assist you in healing your mind, body and spirit. I assure you that your life is going to change for the better now that you have invested your faith in me."

She then takes off her big earphones and leaves the glass booth to join the producer at the control panel. He swivels around in his chair to face her.

"Well, Joy, how are you feeling about that?"

"Yes, it was good, Matt, but there is just something missing that is going to make a difference and I don't know what that is yet."

I know she is listening to the twinkle guide. Her wish will come true easier and quicker because she is listening.

"That can be inconvenient, Joy, but hey, we have to do this thing right from the beginning. So how about calling it a day for today and you can go see if that inspiration finds you."

"Really, Nat, you are great, you know."

"Yes, I know," he says, smiling.

She quickly grabs her bag and blows Matt a kiss on her way out the door.

"I'll chat to you tomorrow," he calls after her.

"Righto," she hollers back.

I follow as she runs through the streets in search of something but possibly not knowing what that something is. She is allowing herself to be guided by her knowledge, trusting that it is leading her towards her answer. She knows her desire is to fill people's hearts full of joy and spread this joy throughout the world to help it heal. She believes in her work and she knows she is ready and committed to putting her all into it. She is ready for the missing piece of her puzzle of success to find her.

Suddenly she stops in her tracks and stares. It takes me a few moments to catch up with her because there were so many people in the street. This is one busy town, and everyone seems to be in such a rush and lacking the knowledge that Joy is being guided with.

When I arrive by her side I see that she is at a newspaper stall. The billboard shows the front page of a newspaper. The headline reads 'Modern day healer cures mum of terminal cancer,' accompanied with a picture of Melody and Irene.

"Hello, I will have one of those papers, please," Joy asks the guy as if she is purchasing the answer to her prayers.

He quickly obliges when he sees her serious intent – he obviously doesn't experience this very often – but when she tells him to keep the change he soon changes his reaction from serious caution to one of sheer joy and says, "Thank you, lady, have a real good day."

She stops for a moment to look back at him and responds, "Yes, I think I will. You have a good day too." Then she puts the paper under her arm and walks at a more contented, slower pace towards a nearby cafe.

When she arrives at the quaint street-side cafe with all of its fine wooden features she orders a mint tea and takes a seat in the corner. She spreads out the paper to read more. Engrossed in the article she doesn't see the timid woman approaching her. She is in her forties and has brown hair cut into an un-styled bob. She doesn't wear make-up and her chosen style of dress is a pair of grey trousers, flat black shoes, a woollen cardigan and a colourful knitted scarf.

"Sorry to bother you . . . but are you Joy Hunter?"

Joy smiles to make the lady feel more at ease. "Yes, I am, and you are?" She asks as she stands up and holds out her hand.

Relieved, the lady replies, "Sally. My name is Sally Manning. I have been to many of your shows and I just wanted to say that I think you are so inspiring."

"Thank you so much for your lovely words, Sally. Can I offer you a tea or coffee?"

"Me? Really? You want to have tea with me?"

"Yes of course. Why not?"

"Well, because I am me, and you are you."

"We are both cut from the same cloth, Sally; now would you like tea or coffee?" she asks, smiling.

"I would love a mint tea please."

"How wonderful! That's exactly what I am having; we even have the same taste."

Sally laughs shyly, and Joy orders another mint tea.

"Oh, I see that you are reading about the mum who got cured from cancer."

"Yes. Isn't it wonderful?"

"It sure is. Do you know that she has young twin boys and that she has just been reunited with the daughter she was forced to give up seventeen years ago?"

"That is amazing." Joy listens attentively.

"Yes, it is and the lady who cured her is actually her aunt in a way . . ."

"Sorry to interrupt but do you know them?" Joy enquires.

"Yes, I do know the family. I grew up with Irene's mum, Joanie. We are still in contact."

"I would really love to get in contact with the healer."

"Yes of course, Joy. I am sure she would love it if you were to get in touch."

Joy rises and gives Sally a hug of gratitude. "Thank you, Sally, I am grateful for your help."

"I will ring Joanie now for you if you wish."

"Oh okay." Joy thinks for a moment. "Well there is no time like the present, so yes go ahead."

Sally takes out her outdated mobile and dials the number. She waits for a moment and then says, "Hello, Joanie, it's Sally here . . . Yes, it has been a while . . . How are you? . . . That's good. The reason I am calling is that I am sitting here with Joy Hunter . . . Yes, Joy Hunter the magnificent stand-up comedian . . . Anyway, she is hoping to chat to Melody . . . oh she is . . . okay I shall tell her. Thanks, Joanie, I will call again in a few days . . . bye."

"She is staying in the local Charleville Inn until tomorrow. Then she is going back to Madison Valley."

"So, I must go there now," Joy says.

They continue to chat and drink their tea and Joy gives Sally her card so that she can contact her to meet again for tea the next time she is in town.

Joy goes back to her beautiful out of town home to pick up a few things to get her through the night. As she walks into her country-style kitchen she is pleasantly surprised to discover Ben in all of his handsomeness standing cutting carrots beside her sink. His usual attire of a smart and expensive suit is now accompanied with a bright pink flowery apron. Joy's arrival startles him.

"Joy, I was hoping to surprise you after your big day in the studio. Is everything okay?"

"Yes, everything is fine, Ben," she says, moving closer to him. "It's perfect actually," she adds and tells him all that happened at the studio and about meeting Sally in the cafe.

He listens to her every word and responds accordingly.

"You are so inspirational, Joy. You just let your gut instinct guide you, didn't you?"

"It has worked for me so far, Ben. Now what are you up to?" She then hugs him, and he returns the hug with a carrot in one hand and a scraper in the other.

"Look at you," she smiles.

"Look at you," he says, dropping both items and lifting Joy up onto the large wooden country-style table where she now sits straddling him. Arms around each other they gaze longingly into one another's eyes. He begins to open the buttons of her silk, slightly ruffled blouse revealing her small pert breasts nestled in a lacy white bra. He starts to caress her neck with tender kisses while also supporting her head with his strong hands. Joy allows her head to drop back into his support and he receives the signal to advance. He swoops her up into his arms and carries her to a nearby bedroom. Gently placing her on the bed he slowly continues to undress her, turned on by every glimpse of her perfectly moisturised skin. She lies in all her natural beauty gazing at him as he continues to undress himself in such a manner that it arouses so much desire in her. Her back arches and she begins to caress her breast with one hand and her area of passion with the other. Ben waits, standing in all of his nakedness to watch his beautiful lady; then he lies alongside her, taking moments to lovingly kiss during the course of their lovemaking. The energies they are creating right now are so strong they could power a whole city for a time. He ensures that he does not rush, and that Joy is receiving as much pleasure throughout as he is. As all beautiful things have to come to an end, their lovemaking finishes with a perfect simultaneous climax. They are in total tranquillity as they remain wrapped in each other's embrace for a few moments without a care in the world; in this moment they are each other's world.

They certainly are a match made in heaven. Their sensual, emotional and physical connection is resilient and now that they have found each other they will both be stronger as they can always rely on each other for support.

After a short time, Joy sits up in the bed.

"So, what was it that you were making for lunch before I so rudely interrupted you?"

"You can interrupt me anytime," he says, kissing her arm. Then unexpectedly he jumps out of bed and quickly puts on his clothes and says, "Right, Joy Hunter, soon to be Mrs Joy Thompson. I shall get you some provisions before you venture off on your mission to entice your healing friend with an offer she can't refuse."

"Oh yes. I had almost forgotten. I was so distracted," she teases as she begins to get dressed herself. "I must take a quick shower."

"Need anyone to scrub your back?"

"Ben, though I would love nothing more than that I must rush today."

"I will save that thought for the future."

"You're on."

In no time she is in her little yellow beetle car on the road to Charleville.

Finally, she reaches the sign 'Welcome to Charleville. The home of Grace.'

Oh, what a lovely welcome! Joy thinks.

Before long she locates the Charleville Inn, a picturesque country-style building with a thatched roof and lots of colourful flowers hanging from baskets and in window boxes. On entering she is in a quaint lobby where there is a pine desk with a young receptionist dressed in a striped shirt and with a made-up face and a funky hair style.

"Can I help you?" she asks.

"Yes, thank you. I would like to book a room here tonight please."

"Sorry, Ma'am. We have a function tonight and we have no rooms available. In fact, I have heard that all the accommodation in the town is booked out."

"Okay. I didn't expect that . . . I shall go and have a coffee and then think what I shall do about accommodation tonight."

"Sorry, Ma'am. We don't do coffee at this time of the evening because the kitchen is closed, but you can have a drink of something else if you want. Go on through those doors there. The lads will be happy to help you."

"Thanks," Joy looks at the receptionist's name badge and adds, "Thanks, Genevieve." Then she makes her way through the wooden doors to the bar area.

She approaches the bar and is fortunate to be served straight away.

"Hello, love, what can I get you?" a young good-looking bar tender asks.

"An orange juice, please."

"Hey, you're that Joy Hunter, aren't you?"

"Yes, I am," she answers.

"You are the second famous person I have served tonight. How cool."

"Really?"

"Yes, I served that healing lady earlier."

That gets Joy's attention. "Is she still here?"

"Yes, for sure. The soirée in the function room is for her for healing people or something."

"Thanks, young man, keep the change.

Joy quickly makes her way towards the function room door where a man is collecting money. A sign states that all funds will go to help children in need all around the world. Joy reaches into her purse and places a number of notes in the tin. I have noted that she is generous when it comes to worthy causes and people.

On entering I observe that the room is not adequately sized for the number of people present, but that doesn't stop Joy from manoeuvring herself right up to the front. She stands and watches Melody, who is sitting on a chair. People approach and hug her and then whisper in her ear. Eyes closed, she lays her hands on their body for a few moments and I can see the healing energy leave her body and enter the recipient's. She is sacrificing herself for others on a huge scale. Melody indicates to Joy to come forward, catching her off guard, but she proceeds to approach. Together they are super energised because they are connected through the twinkles.

Joy's energy will help Melody reinstate her healing energy to a safe level, so she will be able to continue to heal.

Joy whispers in Melody's ear, "Will you help me to heal the world?"

Melody sits back and looks right at Joy as if to study her intention. She then motions for Joy to come closer again and replies, "Yes."

Joy nods and moves back into the crowd.

Still having nowhere organised to stay overnight she awaits Melody's company. When the soirée is over, Melody approaches Joy.

"Thanks for waiting."

"No problem, it's my pleasure," Joy replies.

"As soon as I saw you I knew you were the person I asked the universe for."

"Wow, as soon as I saw your picture on the front of the national newspaper I knew you were the person I asked the universe for also."

In relief they both hug but so many people keep approaching them it makes further discussion impossible.

"Fancy going somewhere else to do this? Are you staying here too?" Melody asks.

"Well, you see there is my dilemma. The whole town is booked out for your function tonight and I was unable to get a room."

"You are welcome to stay in my room," Melody offers. "It is huge and there are two beds. Anyway, you could share some ideas."

"Again, you have answered another of my requests to the universe, thank you."

They leave the bar area together.

I shall leave them now as they put their masterminds together. I will rest tonight and then in the morning I will visit Irene and Lucy.

CHAPTER TWENTY-FIVE
Togetherness

I do not have to venture far to arrive at Irene and Lucy's location. They have been practically inseparable since they were reunited. I am pleased to say that Irene is looking so much healthier and, in less pain, than at any other time we had visited. Lucy, on the other hand, is looking quite pale and sickly. She is snuggled on the same sofa where Irene lay not so long ago, and Irene is sitting by her side.

"Everything will be fine darling; I won't let anything happen to you. I will make sure that you feel better soon. You know what they say about how a mother's love is healing."

"Thanks, Mum, but you know I have never felt that love until now."

"Oh darling." Irene hugs her, not wanting to let her go. "I am sorry that you had to endure those people for so long. Please know that you were always with me in my heart. Always."

"I know, Mum, and we are back together now, and you are getting better. We will have me sorted in no time."

"I must go check on the boys, Lucy. Would you like me to bring you anything?"

Lucy shakes her head and Irene leaves the room and picks up the phone. She waits for a moment and then in a low anxious tone she says, "Hi Mel, there is something seriously wrong with Lucy. She is really unwell. What if she has absorbed some of the darkness that left me? Will you come and heal her? I couldn't bear to lose her . . . you are about to leave? . . . You will? . . . Oh, thank you, Mel. I will see you soon."

"Mum," Lucy calls from the living room.

Irene hurries back to find that Lucy has thrown up on the floor. "Sorry, Mum, it was . . ."

"Ssh, my darling, it will be fine. I can clean it up in no time."

Irene rushes to get a basin and some disinfectant and cloths to clean up the mess. Just as she finishes there is a knock at the door, then Melody lets herself in. She notices immediately what has happened.

"Oh, poor Lucy, are you feeling unwell, love?"

"Yes, I can't stop . . ." Lucy grabs the basin just in time.

"Can I spend some time with you to see if I can help you?"

"Yes please." Lucy drops her head back onto the pillow.

Irene leaves the room with tears flooding from her eyes.

Melody sits for a moment just looking at Lucy. She places her hands on her head, her chest and her abdomen. She sits quietly, projecting her healing love into this beautiful young girl so that she may feel well again.

"You will be fine," Melody assures her. "You need to rest, drink plenty of water and eat something to keep your strength up or you will waste away."

"Really, Aunty Mel, will I be all right?"

"Yes, my love, you will, I assure you," says Melody, giving the girl a hug.

She tucks the blanket around Lucy, who falls asleep almost immediately. Melody strokes her forehead and then goes to the kitchen where Irene stands in floods of tears. Melody wraps her arms around her in a hug.

"Irene love, Lucy is going to be fine. You don't need to worry."

"Really? You're sure?" Irene asks, wiping the tears from her eyes while taking a step back to look into Melody's eyes in search of the truth.

"Yes, I am sure. You will have to get it confirmed but I feel that Lucy is expecting."

In total shock, Irene responds, "Expecting as in having a baby?"

"Yes, Irene love, how do you feel about that?"

After a moment's thought, she says, "I am fine with it. I am so happy that I am well and able to support her through this. Something I didn't receive, but gee, this is a shock."

"Lucy is very lucky to have you, Irene."

"Oh, I just had a funny thought. Imagine what my mum will think when she finds out."

"Yes, she won't like the prospect of becoming a great granny before her time," Melody giggles. "How are you getting along with her now?"

"I am afraid she is not in our lives any longer. She couldn't stop interfering and Lucy and I needed time to re-connect, so I asked her to leave us alone and stop coming around. I haven't heard from her since. I am glad of the break from her dictatorship. I can now think for myself."

"Well done, Irene, but you must remember that forgiveness is a big part of the process of love. Although to be able to forgive fully there must be remorse. You can start by doing some forgiving just for you. Forgiving another is not a gift to them. It is a gift to yourself as you release the toxic energy that it produces."

"You are so wise, Mel. I wish that you had been my mum."

"I am here for you, Irene. Now what are we going to do about young Lucy? I suspect the father is Jay, the lad who helped her find me. He is a handsome, polite lad and they both obviously had a beautiful connection."

"Yes, she has talked about him often; maybe it is time for them to get together again. He lives close by where Lucy grew up, doesn't he?"

"Yes, I think so."

"We are due to go down there soon to help Lucy move on and get the paperwork completed so that I am her main carer and not those horrid people who caused her so much sadness throughout her childhood."

"That's a brave step, Irene."

"Yes, but a step that we all have to take to move forward with ease. Lucy has clarified that she needs closure there and doesn't want to have them as part of her future life, so I will support her in any way that I can. First things first though. I will pop out and get a pregnancy test and we will be guided from then on."

"I will wait here and keep an eye on the boys and Lucy."

"Okay, I won't be long." Irene grabs her bag and rushes out the door.

Melody takes a few minutes to check in on Lucy and the boys who are happily playing in their play room. She then proceeds to make herself a cuppa and wait for Irene's return. While she is doing that she hears someone coming through the front door and thinks, *Wow, she was quick.*

But when Melody turns around she is surprised to discover Joan there, not Irene

"What the hell are you still doing here?" Joan yells.

"Calm down, I am just helping Irene. She called me."

"Called you? I am her mother, not you. If she needs help, then she should be calling me. You can go now; I will sit with the children until she gets back."

"I am sorry, Joanie. I won't be able to do that."

Just at that moment Irene returns.

"Mum, what are you doing here? I told you the other day that we needed a break from you."

"So, you have her as my stand-in replacement, do you?"

"No, it is not like that at all. Lucy is sick, and I called Melody to . . ."

"To heal her? You are her mother you know."

"Yes, and the failure to be a mother to her hasn't helped."

"What's that you have there?" Joan asks and grab's the chemist's bag out of Irene's hands to reveal the contents.

"Oh Irene, are you?" Then she looks from one woman to the other and realisation dawns. "Oh no, no way, not again. I am not going to be a great granny. I am too young."

The disturbance has awakened Lucy and she enters the kitchen.

"Mum, what's going on?" she asks, rubbing her tired eyes.

"Come here, darling." Irene holds out her arms to shield her daughter from her grandmother's venom. "Your Nan is just leaving."

"Blooming sure I am leaving. I am not going through all of that again. This is entirely your fault," Joan screams at Melody as she departs. The residue of her negative toxic energy takes a moment to follow her.

"Let's all go into the living room and I will make us all a cup of tea." Melody encourages them to move to a different room to get away from the polluted atmosphere that surrounds them. She shuffles in her bag and pulls out an incense stick and lights it. "This should restore harmony," she says and swooshes it around the room.

"Where's Lucy?"

"She has gone to do the test."

"How are you feeling?"

"I am sad that my mum thinks the way she does, but I am happy to be here for Lucy as she will need all of the loving support she can get."

'I'm scared," says Lucy in a small voice, returning to the room.

"Don't worry, my darling. We will get through this together," Irene says, comforting her daughter, bringing her over to sit on the sofa.

"Now how do you feel about making contact with Jay?" Melody asks.

"Do you think he would want to know?" Lucy asks innocently.

"I am sure he would, love, and I know that you miss him, so maybe it is meant to be."

"Mm... I don't know."

"Becoming a young mum is all too often portrayed to be a negative experience but there are very many young girls who have babies and who love them so much and take care of them so well. I believe you are one of those special girls just like I would have been if I had been given the choice," Irene explains.

Lucy appears comforted by those words. "Okay, I will text him."

Hi Jay coming down on Fri, fancy catchin up?

Almost instantly she receives a reply.

Cool let's meet at Goody's cafe at 1.

"Now it feels real," Lucy says.

"It will all work out fine. Every life is a beautiful gift. This is a celebration. Now who is for cake?" Melody energises the room with her dazzling spirit.

I think it is beautiful that these three have each other. They are drawn to each other and I imagine the twinkles have been at work making this wish come true. Irene has now fulfilled her wish and I suspect it shall not be long before Lucy's wish is totally fulfilled also.

Melody and Joy are also progressing towards the fulfilment of their wishes, but I don't know if Jade is in the right time and place to receive hers. However now is not the time for me to find out as Syd has messaged me.

CHAPTER TWENTY-SIX
Love Letter

I begin to make my way back to the Vortex. Jade has been playing on my mind for a time now. I feel that she needs assistance and so I take a moment to send her some loving energy in the hope it will comfort her until I return. I do this by hugging my arms tightly around my chest and body, dropping my head backwards, seeking my thoughts and energy deep within, and absorbing every little molecule of goodness that I can muster. Then I stretch my arms wide open, releasing it into the sky to find its recipient. It is beautiful as it floats gracefully past and then quickly disappears travelling on a different frequency than I am occupying at present. I hope it is enough to keep her above emotional subsistence level for now.

Moving closer to my intended location I am stunned when I catch a glimpse of someone there already. It is as if they are waiting for someone. Many thoughts enter my head, but I choose to keep going forward. When I get closer I see that it is Jayden. I am caught off guard to discover that I will not be travelling the Vortex alone, but I suppose it is more practical to have two entities return at once. He does give me the shivers though. There is something about him that I don't trust.

"Well my job here is complete," he exclaims.

"That's nice," I reply with my head lowered.

"You're not a very confident person, are you?" he asks bluntly.

I don't answer because I feel that I don't need to defend my character to him.

He continues, "I have to admit that I am quite surprised at Syd's choice of replacement but in a good way. You know the history around here between Visitors and Wish Givers, don't you?"

I look at him horrified at his implied reference to me and him. No way.

"I will whip you into shape in no time and we will make just as good a team I reckon."

I am hoping the speed at which I am walking on ahead of him down the long corridor indicates that I am not interested in pursuing any type of relationship with him. I don't trust him.

He calls after me, "See you around then. I hope you like the little surprise that I left you with down below."

Even though I would like to confront him about what surprise he is referring to, my desire to get as far away as possible outweighs my curiosity so I keep walking.

I soon arrive at Rupert and Syd's quarters and as I knock Syd appears, so suddenly that I knock my clenched fist on her nose. It is quite embarrassing but to my relief she thinks it is funny.

"Come in, come in." She seems so happy.

"Thank you, I will be so happy to," I say as if I have reached my sanctuary.

"Everything all right, Claire? You seem a little on edge."

"Everything is fine; I just shared the Vortex back with Jayden."

Syd turns to Rupert and says, "See I told you they should not have travelled together."

"Sorry. Hello, Claire, good to see you by the way."

"Hello, Boss, please don't worry. It is fine, really."

"Would you like something to drink?" Syd offers.

"Yes, that would be lovely. Whatever you are having, please."

"Excellent. Won't be long," she calls as she dashes over to the kitchen.

Rupert rises with Arianna. Her golden hair has grown and is now held together with an adorable pink bow on the top of her head. "Now all done," Rupert proudly exclaims. "I must get to work, so may I?" he asks as he passes her to me.

"Oh yes, my pleasure." I look down at Arianna and she smiles the biggest smile ever at me. This baby seems to be so happy and content.

Rupert quickly grabs his jacket and briefcase, gives Arianna a kiss on the head, and then dashes to the kitchen to give an unsuspecting Syd a kiss before leaving in a flash.

"Left you holding the baby," Syd jokes as she returns.

"I don't mind at all," I say, running my finger along Arianna's cheek.

"Have a seat, Claire, make yourself comfortable."

I take a cosy seat and discover that Arianna has fallen asleep in my arms; such a peaceful, graceful moment to treasure. I keep looking at her, and I inhale her beauty.

"Oh, is she asleep? Do you mind if I place her in her basket? She will sleep soundly there and for longer."

I reluctantly pass her back to Syd.

"She is gorgeous, Syd, and so happy."

"We are so lucky. I have to pinch myself sometimes because she is so beautiful. She is so good, and she never ever cries."

"Perfect," I smile.

"How have you been, Claire?" Syd asks, changing her tone.

"I have been good, busy but so good."

"What about Joe? Has he sensed your presence since?"

Emotions come to the surface and I start to cry. Tears flow from my eyes and I cannot stop them.

"Oh Claire, I really didn't mean to make you cry but now that you are just let it out, don't try to stop it. You must release this pent-up emotion."

After a few moments I blow my nose and compose myself enough to utter a few words.

"I love him, Syd, and it cannot be." Then the tears flow again.

Hugging me, she consoles, "And he loves you too, Claire. Anything is possible. Just look at my happiness. You have just got to wish and believe it is possible."

Suddenly she jumps up and runs to a high cupboard and pulls down a small colourful box. She brings it over to where I am sitting and sits close to me.

Looking deep into my eyes she says, "Claire, when we first encountered Joe he left you a letter, but you were in dismay and I took it so that I could give it to you when the moment was right. I believe this is the right moment."

I grab the tattered looking envelope and hold it to my heart. I know that whatever words are written on these pages are going to hurt my heart further, but I need the comfort of them, so I open the envelope. I take out the two letters that match the envelope in their floral design. I remember that these pages used to be perfumed and hold them to my nose. They still hold the fragrance and it brings my thoughts right back to that time. I open the newer letter and read...

Dear Claire,

I wrote this letter for you many years ago and even though it is now reaching you too late to keep you in my life I hope that you receive it with all of the never-ending loving intention in which I wrote it for you when I was thirteen.

Forever yours,

Joe.x

I allow the emotion of these words to guide me and I hand it to Syd to read.

"*My lovely Claire with the loving eyes and the beautiful hair, I want you to know how much I care. Even though we are only thirteen, I want to marry you in Gretna Green. So, let's say goodbye to our family, then at last we can live happily.*"

"He proposed. Does that mean that he proposed?"

"Yes, I believe it does," Syd answers through floods of tears.

"Please, Syd. I need to distract my thoughts because it pains me to think about this. Can we talk about the assignments?"

"You are going to have to deal with it all sooner or later."

"Yes, I know, Syd, but later when the best path to healing reveals itself."

"Okay, Claire, maybe I should not have shown it yet."

"No, it's fine. I just need to allow it to sink in without my full thoughts being consumed by it all as the pain of this revelation aches my heart."

"Right you are then. I will do my best. So, come on and fill me in. I have been so off the ball with the arrival of Arianna, but Rupert informs me that you are taking care of things really well and everything is running smoothly."

"Well, everything is coming together, Syd, and I am learning so much and connecting with my inner guide more, which is refreshing as I am more used to leaving my entity than going within."

"Come on then, what is the run down?"

"I have just checked up on Lucy. She has been reconnected with her mum, who is of course Irene. She is going to let her adopted parents know that she would like nothing more to do with them, but she has also discovered she is pregnant."

"Teenage pregnancies usually bring much needed direction for those involved. I hope this is the case here. I am so happy that this connection has occurred under your watchful eye, Claire."

"Yes. Joy and Melody have also linked up. They are about to join forces to bring to the world joyful healing. They are inspirational and so connected."

"Yes, these ladies will make a difference. I am proud that they found each other through our twinkles."

"I have not been called to Jade for a while but when I was coming here I felt a really magnified beckoning from her spirit hollering for assistance, so I stopped along the way and sent her some loving energy. I do hope that she is okay."

"Yes, I do too. We all know that the Visitor comes for a reason. It may not be transparently clear and so I suspect she will need all of the loving energy she can get right now. You must return there first."

"Okay I will. Thank you for the guidance."

"You are welcome and please know that I am not trying to push you."

"Not at all. I am grateful for your priceless input."

"Oh, you are welcome. So, did you have any trouble recalling the twinkle?"

"I never knew that I was to do that."

"Did Jayden not pass on the message?"

"No, he didn't, Syd. What should I do?"

"That is the bugger. He always tries to stir things up. It is important that the twinkle returns, or it will have an adverse effect on the poor unfortunate individuals who come across it."

"I will go back then and try to locate it."

"Here, take this scanner. If you scan the area you will be able to detect if it is close by. Sorry, Claire. We should have known not to trust Jayden. He has messed around with things in the past too."

"Really? I had a feeling that was the case. I shall do my best to bring the twinkle home safe and sound."

"I shall try to connect with you soon."

We hug, and I depart. This time I am watching out for Jayden as I make my way to the departure lounge, but he is nowhere to be seen. Maybe it is for the best that I didn't stumble across him. Even though I am not an aggressive person I feel fire in my belly when I think that he has interfered with my first mission.

I am fast-tracked to the Vortex and back on the land of physicality in no time. I have some catching up to do.

CHAPTER TWENTY-SEVEN
Enlightenment

When I reach Jade again she is in her bed and I see a new lock attached to the door. Things certainly have deteriorated. This loss has had devastating consequences. Why have I not been drawn to her earlier? Then I recall that Jayden has also been visiting Jade and this could possibly have something to do with it.

I also suspect this may be something Jade has to endure in order to build the foundations for true love to reach her. Her phone is ringing beside her and she doesn't even flinch. Numerous missed calls are registered on the screen. Then the house phone rings and is answered. I can hear footsteps coming up the stairs and a knock at the bedroom door.

"Mum," the voice calls. "Mum, it is Aunty Carrie on the phone, she wants to talk to you."

Jade responds to this call. She slithers out of bed and unlocks the door, opens it a crack and puts her hand out to grab the phone.

"Thanks, love," she says in a low voice. Then she closes and locks the door again. Snuggling herself back into bed she holds the phone to her ear.

"Hello, yes not good, sis . . . I can't, I have tried . . . no, I haven't taken any pills; just some for a headache . . . no, I haven't been to the doctor since it happened . . . I know that you know what I am going through. Any tips on how to get through it? I am not doing so well . . . No, I didn't get the parcel . . . okay, I will check and watch it . . . yes, you can call me later . . . yes, I will do it now . . . chat to you then, bye."

She gets out of bed and goes down the stairs to a large bunch of unopened mail. She goes through it until she finds a brown parcel with an Australian postmark. She goes and grabs her laptop from the office and heads back up to her room.

When she takes out a DVD I am taken aback. The heading is *Heal Your Heart and Feel the Joy* and there is a picture of Joy on the front cover. I am amazed at how everything connects and how all of my ladies have unknowingly encountered each other on their journey to fulfilling wishes.

Straight away Jade places the CD in the disk drive. An array of colours, music and energy is immediately released from the screen. Then I hear a voice that is also familiar. It is Melody's voice. She has joined Joy in her quest. I watch as she directs Jade to place her hands on her heart, one on top of the other.

"Imagine the energy of your pain. Imagine that it is physical and that with your loving hands you are able to draw that pain from your heart. When you feel your hands are full of pain, close your hands over. Be sure not to spill any, now throw that pain right out of the window. Continue this process for a few times. Then we are left with a heart that is a little vulnerable and in need of love to help it heal. You have access to the loving energy that you need to heal your heart."

"Where?" Jade asks.

"I hear you ask where," Melody continues. "Close your eyes. Think of your beautiful self and only your beautiful self. You are your best friend. You have so much healing energy within you, locked away from use. Your thoughts hold the key to unlocking this treasure chest. So, we will now go in search of it."

Jade is relaxed on the bed and listening to every word Melody is saying and I am so happy that she is embracing this.

"We will start by picking up the key in your mind. It is there. It is the lightness. Pick it up. Once you have it we will make our way down through your face. Past your beautiful eyes that bring you so much to see, past your nose that smells the aromas around you, past your mouth that you use to taste the foods of life, we will travel down your neck that is strong enough to hold your head high. Then down to the chest where the treasure chest resides tucked away safely behind your ribcage. See how your heart is alive and pumping. Within your heart is the most powerful healing energy that far surpasses any alternative. This is your gift to yourself should you choose to open it. I say open the treasure. You have nothing to lose. Fear will subside, sadness will ease, and love will flow to the surface. The more love you feel the more love is produced because your supply is endless. See the lightness of this elixir shine through the cracks. Do you want to feel the pleasures it can provide you with? Then choose to open your heart to YOUR love. Take your key and open it. Do you feel the lightness ripple through your body like a wave of comfort?"

Jade shivers from the effects. A small smile appears on her face and my heart sings for her.

"Put your key aside for now. Capture some of this healing energy in your hands. Physically hold it there. Do you feel its power? It is intense; feel it. Now place your hands on your heart, releasing this ball of love to surround your heart and heal the wounds that have been left behind. Feel it doing its work. Feel the comfort in the knowing that your heart is being protected from harm and that healing has commenced."

Jade looks so much more relaxed and at ease with herself. Her posture is not as rigid as before. She is feeling the benefits already.

"Now pick up that key. You are going to lock our treasure chest for now and return the key to its safe place. The treasure chest is locked, and you are working your way back up your neck. It is strong but not as rigid as it once was when you travelled past it previously. You now work your way past your mouth. It will now be able to taste the fruits of life so much more pleasantly. You now work your way past your nose. It now has the ability to smell the aromas life has to offer so much more satisfyingly. Your eyes are next, and they now have the ability to see the goodness that is all around. You are back in your mind now. This is where you will place your key. You will always have the comfort of knowing that it will be there waiting for you anytime you should need to access it. Before you open your eyes, I would like you to be aware of your body for a moment. Does it feel lighter than before? Does it feel more healed? How about your heart? Does it feel protected? You can open your eyes now. Open the curtains on your life and let the brightness in. Go to your closest window, take three deep breaths, filling your lungs to capacity, and exhale slowly. When you are done go and have a shower and wash off any residue of the toxic energy you released that may still be on your body. Let it go down the plug hole where it belongs. That is the end of part one of our healing. In part two Joy will show you that once your heart is feeling healed it is safe to leave your treasure chest open and share your love with those around you."

Jade presses pause on the computer and gets out of bed. She rushes over and opens the curtains and breathes deeply. She allows her lungs to be filled to capacity and then she exhales, repeating this a few times. She sighs and feels a little dizzy. Then she goes over to the long free-standing mirror that is in the corner. She takes one look at herself and says, "Right, let's get you in some sort of shape."

She quickly grabs some towels and heads for the shower. After spending some time in the bathroom, she returns to the room as she hears the telephone ringing. She sees that it is her sister again.

"Hi sis, yes, it is really good. I feel much better thank you . . . yes, I know that, but I am enjoying the new feeling. . .Oh you have really . . . where is it? . . . Oh, I don't know. I can't leave the kids. So, Mum says that she will take care of them over the weekend . . . Yes, I do want to heal my heart for good . . . love myself? . . . Yes, I hear you. Okay I will go, thank you . . . No, I will drive. I am fine . . . Yes, I have a pen."

She scribbles a name and address on the back of the empty package.

"Yes, I will leave soon. Thank you for my wakeup call. I won't ever forget this . . . I love you."

I look at the piece of paper and it reads 'Angela, House of Peacefulness, Harlem Peak.' Her sister is really looking out for her. Jade packs up the DVD and as she does a flyer falls out of the cover. It reads 'Heal Your Heart is on tour and we have tickets to give away. Send us your details and a little note telling us how we have helped you heal your heart and you could be in for a chance to meet the ladies in person at one of their performances.'

Jade drops to her knees and starts pushing buttons on her computer. I peer over her shoulder and see that she is on the Heal Your Heart website entering the competition straight away. She simply writes, *My heart was asleep and now it has awoken. Thank you, ladies.*

So simple and yet so powerful.

She gets dressed, packs a few essentials in a bag and makes her way down the stairs. She is met at the foot of the stairs by an older woman and signs indicate that she is her mother. They look quite similar and have a warm hug.

"Thanks, Mum, I know that I need to do this."

"Take as long as you need, love. I will make sure that the kids are fine. You just get yourself back in shape."

"I will, Mum. Don't worry."

"What do you want me to tell the kids when they ask?"

"I will chat to them before I go."

They both proceed to the kitchen where the girls are.

"Yay, Mum's up," the little girl cheers.

Smiling, Jade holds out her arms to give her girls a big hug and they go to her. "Girls, I am going away for a few days to see a friend and get better. Nanny is going to stay with you here so that you can still be at home. So be good girls."

"Yes, Mum," they say in unison.

"Right. I better go, or it will be dark when I get there."

"Take care driving, love. We will be fine here. So, don't worry. We're going to have a Chinese takeaway tonight and get a movie."

"Yay," the girls cheer again.

Jade makes her way out of the door and gets into her car. It is a small metallic blue car that doesn't have many miles on the clock. She puts down the window and waves goodbye.

"Bye, Mum, I love you," her youngest shouts.

"Bye, Mum," her eldest hollers while hugging her nanny. "Mum will be all right, won't she, Nanny?"

"Yes, love. She just needs a few days to herself. Lots of people feel sad like your mum but when they make themselves better they will be very much happier people afterwards."

Jade is really loved at the highest level. She must open her heart and accept that this love is genuine and unconditional and that she is surrounded by it always.

Catching up with Jade I see that she has pulled into the service station to fill up for her long journey.

She runs in to pay for her fuel and grab a few supplies for the trip. When she comes out of the store and gets into her car she is shocked to find Sean sitting in the passenger side.

"Sean, you scared the life out of me. What are you doing?"

"Jade, we need to talk."

"Sean, I can't right now. I have to go somewhere."

"When then?"

"When I get back."

"When will that be?"

"In a few days."

"A few days. Where are you going?"

"I am going to stay with a friend for a few days. I need to get out of town and get things in perspective."

"Am I part of your perspective?"

Jade looks to the floor.

"I take that as a no."

"It's not that, Sean. I am not in the right place emotionally to give you any answers."

"It was my baby too, Jade."

"I know it was but it's not as if we were in a full-on relationship, Sean."

"Well, it meant something to me, even if it didn't mean anything to you."

"Ah, don't be like that. I didn't mean it that way."

"There is no other way to mean it."

"Please, Sean. I need to get going or it is going to be dark when I get there."

"Dark? Why? Where are you going?"

"Listen, I will call you when I get back."

He gets out of the car without saying another word.

Jade puts her head in her hands and then pulls her fingers through her hair. Looking in the rear-view mirror she says to herself, "Focus, focus, Jade, start your journey."

She starts the engine and spins off out of the forecourt and heads south. Along the way she listens to the *Heal Your Heart* CD. Joy's joyous voice projects from the speakers, beaming positivity into Jade's heart and mind.

"Now that you have experienced part one with the wonderful Melody I will share with you part two. It is all about discovering your inner power, how you can make yourself joyous and in doing so how to help our world to be a happier place. It all starts with you.

If you do not love yourself, how can you expect anyone else to love you in return?"

Jade presses the pause button. She pulls onto the side of the road. It is as if she has just had a moment of significant shift in consciousness.

"So that is what it is. I need to love me first. If I don't love me how can I expect anyone else to love me? That's it; that's what has been going wrong all along."

She plays the CD again and gets back on the road.

Joy's voice continues. "When we love ourselves, we create joy for ourselves and those that are closest to us will be joyous also because they care for us and want us to be joyful. They also pick up on our frequency of joy that feeds them joyous energy that will help them be happy. When we are joyous people will want to be with us more because it is like a magnet and has a positive effect on the lives of those it touches. Prepare yourself so that from this moment forward there will be positive changes coming into your life. Keep yourself open and aware of the signs."

Then something happens that startles me. The song 'Be the change' rings from the speakers. It is the song that Lucy's past influence sang when we encountered him at the beginning of our mission. Jade sings along with the words at the top of her voice.

We must, we must be the change we want to see in the world. When our hearts sing, it is a magical thing. We must be the change, no matter how strange. We must be the change we want to see in the world tonight. Share the joy from your heart; it is a great way to start. It will shine like a star and reach everyone afar. We must be the change we want to see in the world. This love is all healing. Oh, what a beautiful feeling. We all have the right to endure, so don't let yourself be so unsure, and be the change you need to be in the world. If we start from today, we are one step closer to being okay. Let's heal the world with our joyous love. Let's be the change we want to see in the world.

Oh, what a release! She presses the button to replay it and I join in. Never before have I expressed myself in this way, but it feels good.

In what seems like a blink we arrive at a town. It is so picturesque. The feeling is different here. Your ears pop and you know that you are on a different level of existence.

It is sunset and that adds to the magic of the moment. Jade gets out of the car and looks to the distance absorbing the natural energy provided by the magical display. It is revitalising to the core. She takes a deep breath and then exhales slowly. The moment is soon disturbed by a car pulling up alongside hers and a man getting out of it.

"Oh goodness," she says slowly. "Sean, did you follow me the whole way?"

"I just wanted to make sure that you were all right, Jade. Please listen to me for one moment. You can at least give me that. I promise I won't bother you again once you have heard me out. You can't go making life-changing decisions without first hearing what I have to say."

She holds her head in her hands. "Okay, okay, just say what you have to and then please leave me as I need time to work things out."

"Jade, what we had together may have not been ideal, but we had a connection. When we made love that night it was something more than just a physical romp; it was a deep spiritual connection too. I know you felt that too, Jade, but you won't allow yourself to admit it. We have something to build a relationship on, Jade, and I promise to try my best to make you happy if you would only give me a chance. That's all I have to say."

She doesn't respond and so he walks over to his flashy company car and drives off.

In hearing the car quickly driving off, a lady comes running out of the house and puts her arms around Jade.

"Come on, love, let's get you inside," she says comfortingly, grabbing hold of Jade's bag. Jade can only conjure up a fake smile as she is still dazed by what she has heard.

They walk into the house and stop in the hallway.

"How are you, love?"

"Err, I am fine, thank you," Jade says. Then, snapping herself out of her daze, she says, "Well, actually I am not fine. I feel that I need guidance. Can you help me?"

"My dear, I shall show you how to help yourself," Angela explains, directing Jade into a magnificent country-style kitchen. "Now let's have tea."

In no time at all Jade has made herself at home and she and Angela are snuggled up on cosy armchairs in the comfort of the homely lounge room. There is no TV or other digital distractions.

Angela appears to be quite knowledgeable about Jade's situation and so I gather that Jade has updated her.

"Jade, I know one thing for certain and it is that everything happens for a reason. We need to endure some things in life to help us move forward in our own power. Maybe the universe is trying to get you to look at the bigger picture. Think of your life outside of your physicality. When we have wished for something to come to us the universe does everything in its power to bring to us the fulfilment of that wish. Usually when things start happening it is because we have wished for something and the powers that be do all that they can to work for our higher good. If we are navigating down the wrong path, we will feel like we keep hitting brick walls. Your spirit wants to guide you and shine bright but you are feeling fear and so you are preventing it from reaching you. It is okay for you to feel fear about evolving. Even if you suppress it that doesn't mean that it goes away. It just means that you are hiding from your true self. Things will change for the better as soon as you embrace yourself. Honour your feelings."

"I know you are right, Angela. That is why I am here, so that I can learn how to face the fears I hold within. I have often wished to be loved you know."

"There you are. You have to first love yourself; it is a tough one to understand at first but when you experience the instant results of truly loving, honouring and respecting yourself, you will be astounded."

"I am looking forward to it. Thank you, Angela. I really appreciate your guidance."

"It's my pleasure, lovely. I think we should tuck ourselves in for tonight and begin the day with a morning meditation and then a walk on the mountains. Sound good?"

"Yes, for sure, sounds good."

Then they both ascend the stairs to their rooms.

In the morning Jade awakens to the sound of tranquil music coming from the kitchen area. She gets ready in her leggings and comfortable top in preparation for her meditation.

"Good morning, Jade, how did you sleep?" Angela asks brightly.

"I slept really well, thank you, better than I have done in a long time."

"I am happy to hear that, love. Coffee or juice?"

"Juice please."

They sit at the big oak table in silence, Angela thinking about the possibilities of personal advancement this day can bring to Jade, and Jade in expectation of the change this day is likely to produce. It creates captivating energy, something to build upon.

Angela rises and makes her way to a small cosy room where two mats have been placed in the middle of the room, one in front of the other. She kneels on one and Jade kneels on the other.

"Now see how you knew to follow me and what my intentions were?"

"Yes, I suppose I did, didn't I?" Jade responds.

"Well, that is the type of awareness I want you to harness today. It is when we utilise our intuitive awareness that we navigate accurately."

"Oh okay."

"Don't think too much into it or the thoughts will distract. It is our natural ability to manoeuvre in the power of our inner guide. We are born with this ability but for some reason, as we grow, many of us lose touch with this connection. I want you to reconnect. It will change your life."

"Oh, I feel shivers," Jade says, rubbing her arms.

"That's your guide telling you that this is an exciting revelation for you."

Jade absorbs that thought.

"Now Jade, I want you to make yourself comfortable. Close your eyes and empty your mind of all the junk left behind on your travels thus far. This moment is when your new beginning starts. Have you ever opened up your heart chakra before?"

"You mean my treasure chest of love?"

"Yes, that's it."

"I did it for the first time yesterday and that's why I am here today."

"See, it is already changing your life. The effect of this is priceless. You will be able to withstand any challenge you face because you can now heal yourself through the heart."

They sit in silence for a time.

"My heart is now open, Angela."

"Now let's return to the mind and create a room. First we are going to request the energy of your little lost angel to visit."

Tears come from Jade's eyes. "Hello little one, I so wish that you had stayed . . . Yes, I know I wasn't ready . . . you did come for a reason, I know that . . . oh you will return, thank you . . . I love you . . . Yes, goodbye. I will meet you again soon then."

"Now Jade, that is very intense for your first experience. Take a moment to absorb it."

Taking some deep breaths, she responds, "I am ready, Angela."

"Now I would like you to summon your past self. Be sure to say thank you for all of the lessons you have learned and then say goodbye because you now choose to move forward in the power of your new enlightened self and no longer require accessing the energy your former self holds. Be sure to part on good terms."

After a long period of silence Jade says, "I have said goodbye and am in my room alone."

"Now it is time to turn off the light and lock the door until you need to access it again. When you are ready you can open your eyes."

Jade opens her eyes and Angela gives her a big hug. Tears pour from Jade's eyes.

"Just let them flow, love. They need release."

"Thank you, Angela. That was an extraordinary experience. I feel lighter."

"It is a tough thing to do at first. You did really well."

"Thanks, Angela."

"Now let's get some breakfast. We're having porridge. Is that good for you?"

"Yes great."

Over breakfast they talk about Jade.

"You do know that you were guided here for a reason, don't you, Jade?"

"Yes, I feel that, Angela. It is kind of scary though, the thought of changing everything I have known."

"Yes sure, but you are not living true to your own self and so you are being guided to let go of the way you have done things and let in wonderful new things into your life."

"It sounds so simple when you say it like that."

"Yes, it is easier said than done but the rewards are worth it. As you now have the ability to think more consciously and are more aware of the signs the universe is sending to you, it won't be long before you experience this knowing."

"What's the knowing?"

"You will know when you experience it. It is the feeling of true magic that you won't believe is possible unless you experience it firsthand."

"Oh, I can't wait to experience it."

"So how do you feel about being here so far?"

"Angela, I can't explain it. Coming here is life-changing and in such a short space of time. I cannot believe how for the first time in my life I have clarity. I looked in the mirror this morning and actually liked the person looking back at me. Life seems brighter. Why I didn't do this sooner I don't know, or why everyone doesn't do it."

"That's because you have to be at the specific stage in life where you are ready to let the light in and open your heart to yourself."

"I am so grateful to have been guided to you and to the Heal Your Heart program. It has changed my life."

"Well, on that fabulous note shall we get our hiking boots on and climb to another beautiful summit?"

"I don't know if I am fit enough and I don't have any boots."

"Don't you worry, love. I have a spare pair for you and I promise it will be tough but just like the mountainous inner challenge that you have endured and triumphed over, you will feel equally fulfilled when you reach the top."

"Okay I'll do it,"

All suited and booted they embark on their journey.

"Why are we leaving so early, Angela?"

"Because it will take us a few hours and it is best to get to it before the day is on, don't you think?"

Jade smiles, unconvinced and cold.

She follows Angela, the expression on her face showing that she is feeling every step of the ascent.

"You okay there, Jade love?" Angela shouts behind her.

"Yes okay," Jade replies unconvincingly.

"We will go for another fifteen minutes and then take a break for a snack."

"Righto."

They stop on a ledge and there is a lovely, tantalising view. The sun has not long risen, and it is beaming heavenly light through the fluffy clouds.

Handing Jade a chocolate bar and a bottle of water, Angela enquires, "So how are you feeling?"

"Well, to be honest I don't think hiking is my thing."

"Really, why not?"

"Well, it's just that it is not what I am used to, and it is quite tough."

"Well Jade, my love, that is because you are making yourself perceive it to be that way. Before we even left the house of peacefulness you had your mind made up that you would not enjoy this hike. It was written all over your face. Now for the second half of the ascent I want to look at it as an adventure. Look at the beauty that surrounds you, not just the tough road ahead. Absorb the smells, the sights, and the sounds and you will realise that you are experiencing one of the most wonderful adventures ever. It is all to do with your perception."

"I will try, Angela, but I can't promise miracles."

"I can," Angela whispers.

Soon I see that Jade's face shows no pain and her eyes beam with joy at the beauty she is absorbing with every stride. Excitement fills her, and I see for the first time her energy glowing fully. Enlightenment has occurred; there is no turning back now for Jade. She will never see things as she did before.

In no time at all they are at the summit.

In a moment of sparkling realisation, she shouts, "Angela, I have to go. I know what it is that I need to do. Thank you, thank you, thank you!"

She runs over and kisses Angela and begins her descent towards the house. Angela stands there knowing that there is no point in trying to stop her because she is fuelled with passion right now and has something that she has been guided to do.

In half the time that it took her to ascend Jade comes down. Taking only her handbag she runs through the house and out the front door. She hops into her car and speeds off in a northerly direction. What previously took her four hours to drive now takes only two and a half to return. I am not surprised at all. She pulls up outside the pub and gets out of the car with such a determination that everyone who sees her takes notice. It is not long after midday and people are having their lunch in the bar. She stands scanning the area for a moment but who she is looking for is obviously not there. She looks slightly deflated. Then she sees him in a shirt, fancy trousers and a tie. Sean stops in his tracks when he sees her standing there. He does look funny with the two pint glasses of orange juice that he is holding stretched out. One of his mates comes to take them off him.

Jade begins walking to him and he walks to her so that they meet in the middle.

"Does this mean . . .?"

She looks into his eyes and says, "Yes, yes, Sean Patterson, I will marry you."

He smiles from ear to ear and then kisses her with all of his love. When they finally pull apart he says, "Oh wait here, don't move." He runs to the table at which he has his coat, lifts it and returns to Jade.

He gets down on his knee and holds out a little square red satin box.

"Jade Priestly, will you do me the honour of becoming my wife?"

He opens the box to reveal a big sapphire ring surrounded by a circle of diamonds set on a white gold band. A tear comes to my eye. Jade nods as she cannot get any words out; the emotion has overwhelmed her. He takes the ring out of the box and places it on her finger; it fits perfectly. They hug tightly and the captivated audience that has gathered are clapping and cheering. Sean lifts Jade up into his arms in a cradled position. He makes his way to the door to leave the bar with his new fiancée in his arms. Just as they are about to leave, it is as if the universe at that very moment sent Justin through the door. The whole bar goes quiet in anticipation of what might happen.

"Oh, for real you have chosen him over me. Well, I hope that you will have a lovely life together." With that Justin turns around and storms out of the door he has just entered.

Jade and Sean look at each other and giggle. They jump into his car and drive to her house where her mum is delighted to share their joyous news. The girls are also very excited; they have known Sean as a family friend for many years.

CHAPTER TWENTY-EIGHT
Recall

The moment has come for me to visit each of the ladies and recall their twinkles. This mission is now at the stage where it has run out of the precious commodity of time. I cannot allow myself to go past my allocated timeframe, especially as it is my first undertaking as the Wish Giver.

It concerns me deeply that I have not yet found Irene's twinkle. I do not know if Jayden has tampered with it in order to sabotage my first mission. After delivering its wish for Irene it must have been drained and needs recharging. I will conjure up all my faith in the belief that everything is happening for the best reasons possible.

Refocusing, I pull myself back to the task in hand which is to recall the twinkles of Lucy, Melody, Joy and Jade. I wait to see where I am guided first. I am surprised; it is back to Jade.

JADE

Back in the comfort of her home, Jade is beaming joy. She calls out from her kitchen, "Anyone for lemonade?"

"Yes please," a chorus of voices replies.

She prepares four glasses with homemade lemonade. The sun is shining, beaming through the open back door. Sean comes walking through it, grabbing Jade from behind and kissing her neck playfully.

"Stop, Sean, you will make me spill these," she complains.

"Come here," he whisks her around to face him. "I love you, Jade," he declares and kisses her.

"Huh hmm," a small voice tries to grab their attention from the doorway. "Where's our lemonade?"

Laughing, Sean says, "Oh sorry, precious, it is coming now." He grabs three lemonades, smiles at Jade, and follows her back to the yard.

Jade's phone rings.

"I'll be with you guys in just a minute," she calls after them.

"Hello, what, sorry, didn't catch that . . . really? I have one of the tickets? Yes of course I would love to come . . . this weekend? Yes, that's good for me . . . see you then, thank you. Bye."

Sparks are flying from her and she runs upstairs to her room. The Jade we witnessed hiding from the world under her blankets is no more. She is now allowing the light of life to find her and so wonderful things are coming into her life.

She stands and looks out the window at her beautiful girls and loving fiancé.

"Thank you, universe. Thank you for turning things around for me. My life is perfect, and I am grateful."

She stops to look at herself in the mirror and say, "I love you too."

At that moment a dazzling light appears from nowhere. It projects powerful energy all around the room and then it assumes the form I am familiar with. It is the shiny round sphere that is the beautiful twinkle. I open the holding vessel, summoning it to return to its rightful place to recharge and harness its energy again.

Jade shivers as she picks up on the beaming energy that is blasting her way. She has a quick scan around the room but sees nothing, so she leaves. My mission with Jade is now complete. I wish her well in her future. It certainly looks bright from where I am standing.

JOY

I am summoned to Joy. She is at the set of a television talk show. There is a large audience and the host of the show is a dynamic lady who exudes energy. She is so vibrant and every word she says is from the heart and I can sense that many people trust her. The name Lori dominates the background and so I assume this is her stage name.

"Ladies and gentlemen, welcome to our show Joy Thompson."

The audience all stand up and clap as Joy walks across the stage to meet Lori. They greet each other and take their seats. The audience stops applauding.

"Wow, what a welcome, Joy!" Lori acknowledges.

"Yes, Lori, it is amazing." Joy smiles and thanks the audience.

"Joy, you have made it your life's mission to live up to your namesake by promising to share your loving joy with the world."

"Yes, Lori, I sure have. Joy for me brings magic into our lives. Joy is one of the buds that flourish from the root of love within us. When we allow our joy to blossom it can enchant the hearts of those who encounter it. I truly believe that this beautiful energy can even penetrate negative energies when we flower enough joyous buds. I am here to ask people to allow their buds to blossom and help us replace some of the negatives in our world with the beauty we have been gifted with by Mother Nature. Let's all promise to take time out of every day to smell the roses. Let's be the change we want to see in the world."

The audience are applauding. Lori rises to her feet and Joy is humbled but glowing because she has now reached a pinnacle in her pursuit of spreading the message of joy with as many people as she can reach.

Then the twinkle begins to rise. The energy in the studio is already dynamic. When the twinkle rises it creates a radiating glow that electrifies anyone in the vicinity. A lot of people are going to feel this energy right now. I prepare the holding vessel to receive the twinkle safely to its rightful place.

I watch as the ripples of the energy pulsate through every person in the room. This is a moment that many of them will not forget. I look at Lori and she stands with a smile on her face. She whispers to Joy, "I have had a wish come true also. Enjoy the goodness that is to come your way," she says knowingly, and Joy responds with an unknowing reaction.

She may not recognise the signal of wish receiving but she is aware that her wishes have manifested, and she is grateful for all of her blessings. She can only shine from now on.

Joy's twinkle has completed its work here and so I must move on.

I wait a moment to receive the summoning. It is Lucy whom I shall visit next.

LUCY

We return to the house where we first encountered Lucy. We are in a formal room with a large mahogany table dominating the central space. Lucy's adoptive parents are present, and Lucy and Irene are seated at the opposite side if the table. They hold hands tightly under the table symbolic of the support they give each other through this awkward time.

"So, Irene, you expect us to sign papers giving custody of Lucy over to you?" her father asks.

"Well yes of course, why not?"

"Because, dear lady, she has been under our care for sixteen years and we are not going to hand her over like that just because she has decided on a whim to find you."

"She never loved me one day of my life," Lucy says frankly.

"How dare you say that? Elizabeth has loved you as her own since the day you came into our lives."

"She has a funny way of showing it," Lucy snaps back.

Irene squeezes Lucy's hand under the table in an attempt to calm her down.

"Can I say something here?" Irene speaks up.

"I suppose if you have to," the man grunts.

"Henry and Elizabeth, I have lived half of my life without my child because my mother gave her to you. Now that she is seventeen and old enough to make her own choices she has decided that she wants to be in my life. I want to connect with her and make up for the years we have lost. Even if you don't sign the papers we are still going to be a big part of each other's lives, whether you agree to it or not."

"I understand that, Irene, but wanting to cut us out of her life altogether, well, that is preposterous; I won't have it." Henry exclaims.

"I'm pregnant and your rivals next door, well, their son is the dad. Do you still want me around now?" Lucy explodes.

"What? You stupid girl. You did this on purpose. This is most inconvenient. You most certainly cannot be out and about parading yourself now. You will have to stay here and when the baby is born and when suitable parents are chosen you can go wherever you please." He stands up and begins pacing the floor alongside the table while his wife sits attentively in her seat.

Irene stands up. "You will do no such thing, Henry. Lucy is not going through what I went through. I will make sure of that if it is the last thing I do." Then she sits down and hugs Lucy.

Just at that moment the double doors open and in bursts a woman.

"Aunty Gina!" Lucy runs to her to receive a loving hug.

"I have been listening, Henry, and I know that you are my brother and I am Lucy's aunty, but I cannot let you do this to her. If you do not sign those papers now I will report you both for threatening to imprison Lucy and other things that I might remember when I get to the station, do you know what I mean?"

"You wouldn't," he blasts at Gina.

"Try me," she retaliates.

"Right. Have it your way, Irene, but you needn't think that she is going to get her sinful little hands on my estate. I shall be signing you out of my will."

"I don't want your money; I just want my freedom. "Anyway, once you sign those papers you no longer have any connection to me, so we can move on and forget that we ever met."

Everyone in the room looks at each other.

"What?" Lucy asks suspiciously. "What's wrong? Why are you all looking at me like that?"

"I will tell her," Irene says.

She sits Lucy down and begins, "Lucy, my darling, your dad is still your dad."

"What? I don't understand. How can that be?"

"Well, almost seventeen years ago I was working part time for your dad and we had a fling. I ended up pregnant. My mother wouldn't let me keep you and papers were signed and you were taken away before I knew it. I never knew where to get you, but I never gave up hope that someday I would find you."

"Yes, and I gave your mum ten thousand dollars for your pain."

"What, you gave my mother money?" Irene asks in shock.

"Yes, did she not tell you?"

"No, she never did. That woman never ceases to amaze me."

"Did she tell you that we said you could visit as an aunty anytime?"

"Now you are kidding me! The physical pain of the separation was so intense that I couldn't even eat. I ended up in hospital with malnutrition. And all of that time I could have been cured by one visit, one hug, one kiss. All of this was possible, and she just watched me suffer, letting on that she was the best mother ever. I can't believe it." Irene sits down.

"Here." Henry scribbles his name on a few sheets of paper and hands them to Irene. "You have suffered enough and, to be honest, so have we. Now if you don't mind I have other things to attend to."

He gets up and leaves the room closely followed by Elizabeth.

Lucy jumps up. "I don't ever have to see them again," she says joyously.

I see the twinkle begin to surface. I prepare the holding vessel. The energy sparks towards each of the three ladies in the room, filling each with a spark of magic to add to their day.

"I am still your aunty remember, and you can't get rid of me too easily. So, I want you to keep in close contact with me, my gorgeous niece."

"Yes of course I will," Lucy replies.

It is now time for me to move forward and so I focus on my pending work. I am still at the same location, but my focus now is with Irene. How can this be? I suppose I should not ask questions as all will be revealed to me.

IRENE

They are now leaving the country estate in their small city car that looks to be of a miniature scale in comparison to the grandeur of the house and its driveway. Reaching the gates, they see Norm.

"Hello Ma'am and young Lucy."

"Hello, Norm," Lucy replies.

"Hello," says Irene.

"Norm, thanks for letting me get ahead that day."

"Oh, young Lucy, I don't know what you are talking about." He smiles. "You see it's my hip, it is not like it used to be."

Lucy smiles in gratitude. "This is my real mum, Norm, I found her."

"Well that is lovely," he says, holding out his hand to shake Irene's. "Lovely to meet you, lady. You have a lovely daughter here."

"Yes, I know," Irene says, looking at Lucy.

"Well, I will open the gates for you, have a lovely day."

"Bye, Norm," they both say in unison.

They drive up the road Lucy used as her escape route. Even the skid marks from Jay's tyres are still there and she reminisces about the adventure they had together.

"Ok, so where are you to meet Jay?"

"Goody's Cafe at one o'clock."

"Well, it is nearly that now. So, is it okay if I drop you off and go get a few things from the shop over there?"

"Do you not want to meet him?"

"Yes, of course I do, darling, but I want to give you half an hour on your own to reconnect before I butt in."

"Yes, that's cool."

Irene pulls up outside Goody's Cafe. "Here darling, here is some money just in case you need it."

"See you soon then, Mum,"

"Yes love, won't be long."

I can see it is hard for Irene to leave her, but she knows that this is something Lucy must do on her own. She watches Lucy enter the cafe and take a seat beside Jay. He stands up to greet her and gives her a hug and a kiss. Irene is relieved to see this and so she decides to pop into the store next door.

She is trying on a nice dress that has a cream bodice with sequins embedded into it. The corresponding skirt is knee length and flowing. The dress is perfect for Irene and she knows it as she admires herself in the mirror. I realise that it has probably been a long time since she did this. The dress colour suits her hair and skin tone. She looks at the price tag in horror.

"Ah well, it wasn't meant to be," she declares.

Suddenly her demeanour changes and she dashes out of the changing room and out of the shop wearing the dress. The shop assistant cannot believe her eyes and sounds the alarm. Irene seems to be making her way quite dangerously through the traffic to get to Goody's Cafe. When she arrives, Lucy is in floods of tears.

"Oh, Lucy honey, what is wrong?"

"Mum, it was terrible. He said that he can't do it because his parents wouldn't fund his college or anything if he told them because they don't like my dad. Oh Mum, I am so happy that you are here."

"Oh Lucy, I should not have left your side. I am so sorry. But love, please know that he is just reacting out of shock and fear. Give him time to absorb it."

"Can we go home?" Lucy pleads.

"Yes of course we can, darling. I will always be here for you. You can rely on me."

"Thank you, Mum, I really need you now."

Just at that moment the twinkle begins to rise. This is such a relief for me as I had obviously misinterpreted the completion of Irene's twinkle. It rises up and in a flash of sheer magnificence it sprays everyone with its powerful rays of energy. They all stop what they are doing as if frozen in that moment. Then when the twinkle returns to the holding vessel they get back to what it was they were doing but with a renewed lease of energy.

"Mum, what are you wearing?" Lucy asks. "It's lovely on you."

"Oh, my goodness yes, the dress, I must get it back to the shop."

Just as she says that the police walk into the cafe. Irene exclaims, "Sorry, officers. I am on my way back to the store now. My daughter needed me."

"Save it for the statement, lady," one of the policemen responds.

They proceed to escort Irene back to the store. She is hugging Lucy tightly as they are paraded across the street. When they get into the shop the shop assistant is waiting.

"Is this the lady and the dress in question?"

"Yes, officer," she says and then she recognises Lucy.

"Lucy are you okay?" she asks.

Irene and Lucy release each other and dust themselves off.

"Yes, I am fine. How are you, Francis?"

"Well, I will be all the better when I get to the bottom of why this lady ran out of the shop wearing one of our most expensive dresses."

Irene speaks up. "I am sorry. I just knew that something was wrong with Lucy and in a moment of panic I didn't even consider the dress. Call it a mother's intuition."

The assistant looks confused and glances at Lucy for an explanation.

"Francis, this is my mum. I discovered that I was adopted, and I found her."

The shop assistant seems to be more relaxed now and says to the policemen, "Thank you, officers, I am sure that I can get the misunderstanding sorted out from here."

The policemen leave, and Francis turns to Irene and Lucy.

"Oh my, that is amazing, Lucy. You must have been shocked to find that out."

"Yes, I was for sure but now that I am with my mum I am super happy."

"That is wonderful, Lucy." Francis turns to Irene. "Can I have the dress back now, please? I need to check it for damage or I might get in trouble with my boss."

"Yes of course." Irene makes her way to the changing rooms leaving the girls to catch up.

In there she is guided towards her bag. She opens up a side zip pocket and discovers a gold card with her mum's name on it.

"Oh wow, I am meant to have this dress," she whispers. "Why should I not? She sold my happiness all those years ago."

Bursting from the dressing room she returns to the counter.

"I will take the dress," she announces to the surprise of both Lucy and Francis.

"If you are sure, Irene."

"Yes, I am sure and Lucy, I want you to choose something for yourself too."

"Wow Mum, really?"

"Really, anything that you want."

"Oh cool. I am going to get a bonus today," Francis says happily.

Just then Lucy's phone beeps. She reaches into her bag and reads the message.

I am sorry please forgive me luv Jay. x

I know that all will be well here, so I choose to move forward. Finally, I am drawn to Melody.

CHAPTER TWENTY-NINE
Final Twinkle

MELODY

I have travelled through a short time warp to get to this glitzy bright time location. Signs are neon and the power that is projected onto this street in one night alone would probably serve the needs of a small country for a week. Everything is on a huge scale. I am drawn to one of the illuminated buildings. Inside everything is dazzling. The diamonds the ladies' showcase are huge. This is the place to be if you want to live it up in the big time. That is why I am trying hard to comprehend why Melody is here.

I navigate toward an elevator and am brought to the 32nd floor. I walk along the hallway to a room where I believe Melody's energy was.

Entering the room, I discover that it is not your average hotel room; it is bigger than many people's houses. Every detail is of the highest quality and the design theme for the room is French romantic. The atmosphere she has created is much more calming than the fully charged super energies that are running at full speed a few floors below. Even the shutters on the windows are closed in an attempt to dim the neon lights that invade every area of vision.

Melody and Joy are sitting in the lounge area in white robes with towels on their heads and painting their nails.

"Joy, we are healing the hearts of the world. I want to say thank you for giving me the opportunity to do this."

"Are you kidding me, Melody? It is my pleasure and I should be thanking you."

"Yes, but you are a global starlet now. You don't need me dragging along behind you."

"Now stop right there, Melody. If it were not for your miraculous healing abilities I would not have attracted the interest of the media top guns and just remember they wanted, you too."

"Yes well, that's not within my comfort zone."

"Well, you are about to put on a very spectacular sparkling full-length gown and address thousands of people in a sold-out show and that doesn't make you nervous?"

"No not really, because I know they are here because they need my help and if I can help thousands of people heal at one time, well that is why I exist. I cannot fear that."

"You are so true to your calling, Melody, it inspires me so much."

There is a knock on the door and in come a fleet of people with bags and clothes. This show is going to be a mega event.

"Are these guys for us?" Melody stands in amazement.

"Yes, they certainly are. Have a seat and enjoy the transformation," Joy says with confidence.

The make-up artists work on Joy first while the hair stylists do magic with Melody's curly mop. In no time at all Melody is being transformed before my eyes. Joy looks over at Melody in astonishment.

"Wow Mel, you look fabulous."

"So, do you," she replies.

"Time for the dresses I think," Joy announces.

The ladies go into two adjacent rooms. They are closely followed by clothes designers carrying long dresses.

The transformation is complete. Joy is the first to emerge from her room. In all of her beauty she shines brighter than on any previous occasion. Her dress has gold sequins from head to toe, little cap sleeves and a v-neckline. She dazzles.

Melody has been totally transformed from a non-make-up wearing free spirit into a radiant goddess who will grasp the attention of the crowd because of her sheer gorgeousness. So, when she opens her heart to gleam the magnificence of her healing love she is bound to be classed as a goddess of the time. This butterfly has emerged from her cocoon and is now ready to spread her beautiful wings far and wide. Her dress is silver sequinned.

The transformation team gasp when they behold the ladies.

"Wow, you guys are going to bowl them over looking this good," one of the dark -skinned hair stylists declares.

Then a production guy comes busting into the room.

"Right, ladies, we need to get you moving." Taken aback he says, "Whoa, you guys look amazing."

"Thanks, Bill, we are ready when you are," Joy replies.

The atmosphere in the large room is one of peace and calmness. It is nothing like the crazy world outside its double doors. The venue is filled to capacity. The chairs are roomy to ensure maximum comfort, and everyone is occupied. The ladies are introduced onto the stage. Everyone rises to clap for them.

Joy speaks first. Her voice is enchanting.

"Hello, ladies and gentlemen, thank you so much for joining us today. Melody and I are humbled by your presence and we assure you that today is going to be a significant day in moving forward to your future in your joyous power. Please read your program so that you understand how we intend to conduct this evening. However, please know that this is only a guide of our intentions. We will embrace the natural flow of the evening. I will hand you over to Melody now so that we can begin by creating some loving healing energy for us all to absorb throughout tonight. Thank you."

The audience applauds, and Melody comes forward. She is softly spoken and engaging.

"Hello, everyone. Please make yourselves comfortable and close your eyes if you wish to. We have all come here tonight for different reasons. Some of us need to heal a physical ailment, some of us an emotional one. Some of us are just curious and want to see what happens. But one thing we all have in common is that we have the power to create healing love. It is one of the unique qualities that we are born with but because it is tucked away deep down inside it is not accessed enough. When we unlock our treasure chest of love good things happen. Sharing love and the power that this creates is so underestimated in our ever-changing world. Each time we display love we heal ourselves and the world a little bit more. The loving energy that we have the potential of creating is truly substantial. Let's join together tonight to create immense healing for ourselves and for those in the world who have locked their chest because of fear and ignorance. To change the world, we need not fight wars; we only need to share more love. Love conquers all. Here in this room tonight we are in our safe place; we are in our loving cocoon. We will all heal together. When we leave this room tonight and emerge into the bright busy world beyond, bring as much of that healing love that you can and share it with anyone you can, be it through physical communication, or sending thoughts to another through your inner self in a moment of silence, any way that resonates with you. Share the love. Feel the joy and heal our world. Why? Because we can!"

"Thank you, Melody. I am feeling the energy already. This is going to be a miraculous night I can feel it. Melody will be guiding us all through her renowned meditation shortly which I am sure everyone is looking forward to. For those of you who are not familiar with this healing meditation it is on our Heal Your Heart

DVD and CD which will be available for sale tonight. Please remember that all profits go towards our charity which provides the orphans of the world with a loving life."

Everyone applauds this.

"Thank you, we are proud of the work we do but we cannot do it without your support and so we are grateful."

Everyone applauds again.

"Now is there anyone here tonight whose life has been changed because of our vision?"

Most of the people raise their hands. Joy chooses a lady from the audience and one of the crew escorts her to the stage. I am caught in a serendipitous moment when I realise it is Jade. She hugs Joy and Melody very emotionally and then is guided to a seat on the stage opposite them.

"Oh, I can't believe I am meeting you ladies; you have changed my life," she says. Her hands are trembling and tears well in her eyes.

"Oh love, you have been through it, haven't you?" Melody comforts Jade and moves her chair towards her to hold her hand and give her support.

"Yes, everything was going wrong. I was neglecting my kids, having unhealthy relationships and then I had a miscarriage. My life was falling down around me, and my sister sent me your CD and it woke me up. I am now living again instead of just surviving."

The room explodes in applause for Jade. I can see that she is humbled by this.

"We are so happy that we could guide you, but you did it yourself, Jade. You are the one you should be thanking. Please say it, Jade. Please say to yourself, thank you."

"Thank you, Jade, I love you," she says.

"I feel shivers, thank you for sharing yourself with us."

Jade is then escorted back stage by one of the crew.

"Here is a pass for the after gathering for you and your friend," the crew guy explains.

The joy in Jade's eyes says it all and she returns to her seat.

The girls continue with their show and even I am astounded by this energising experience. I watch the crowd's reaction and by chance I come across Irene and Lucy. Lucy is glowing, and she is developing a small bump. I wonder at the realisation that with all of the ladies here together so close the combined energies that they will create through me are beyond anything any of us can comprehend. Tonight, we are going to experience a shift in consciousness on a great scale.

"We will finish off now by each of us holding hands, closing our eyes and sharing a little of our love with the world," Joy explains.

Joy and Melody go down to join the crowd. Joy holds Melody's hand, Melody holds Lucy's hand, Lucy holds Irene's hand, Irene holds Jade's hand and I am barely able to remain standing with the beams of power that are being created. Every single person feels this as they stand with their eyes closed, projecting a little piece of them with the world. This is something that no money can buy.

I look at the ladies. They create the beginning of this chain of connection and I wonder if they know they are connected in a way other than their physical connection in this moment. Joy certainly must be subconsciously aware as she chose Jade out of all of the possible candidates who raised a hand.

I watch as the twinkle rises from beyond Melody. Its duty has now been fulfilled and it is ready to return to the holding vessel. These three elements combined in this moment in time have increased the capabilities of the mass of healing energy projected and the vastness of the area it reaches.

After a few more powerful minutes Melody guides everyone out of this state and back to full awareness.

"Giving feels good, doesn't it?" Joy says.

Melody continues. "Thank you for taking the time and energy to join us tonight. Healing for each person here has progressed. We love to hear how we may have made a difference in your life, so please jump online and share with us your story. We hope to connect again soon."

The doors open to the outside and the energy is released to work its magic and heal.

Beyond the doors is a casino. Gamblers swarm upon this place to play games and quite often lose money.

"That's it. I am finished with gambling," a man exclaims from a poker table.

"Yes, me too," another man exclaims and another and another. Soon the casino is empty. These people have obviously received enough healing power to quit their spirit damaging habit.

I must move on, but I am happy to have witnessed this. I move to observe the ladies for one final time. They are upstairs in the exquisite room that Joy and Melody prepared for the show. They stand together in a circle with glasses of champagne and an orange juice for Lucy who is standing hand in hand with Jay. Young love is special. He certainly seems smitten by her as he stands close protecting their little bump.

"I feel as if we have all met before, but I know that we haven't. So, it is strange," Jade shares.

"I feel the same way," Irene contributes.

"I think we all do and that is why we were drawn to each other. I feel a deep connection and would like to suggest that we all keep in contact. I love the energy we create," Melody says.

It is time for me to go back to the Waiting Zone and return these precious commodities to dispatch where they can be de-spirited and re-energised.

I have learned so much that I didn't expect to learn about myself. I still have lots of personal work to do before I reach full enlightenment, but I know what I need to do and hopefully someday soon I will be able to commence the healing process my spirit needs to move forward. I am grateful for the distraction that this mission has provided. It has connected me back to my painful past and led me to reconnect with Joe. I am happy to have had that beautiful correlation with Joe through Melody and although she generously offered that I use her body as a vehicle to instigate a relationship with Joe whenever I want, I am refraining because it is too painful when we are apart. Also, although it felt loving I don't want to get used to connecting with Joe through someone else.

CHAPTER THIRTY
Return

As I am about to depart my heart flutters with the realisation that Joe has just walked into the room. He doesn't acknowledge my presence. Maybe he has moved on and is no longer connected to my entity; maybe through the ladies he has been healed of his broken heart. I am powerless to mend it, so I accept the non-recognition as fate.

However, my heart is not healed, and I feel such sadness that our love cannot be, but through this sadness I also have faith that our time will come again. I get the urge to say goodbye before I leave and so I move beside him and kiss him on the cheek and whisper, "Goodbye, Joe. I will always love you." I watch Melody smile as she knows what I have done. I turn and walk out of the room holding my hands on my heart in the hope of healing this pain. But this is not going to happen for a time because pain is part of the process of healing.

On my way down, I hear the door close. I look around to see Joe standing there.

"Claire," he calls.

"Joe," my heart sings and I run to him.

Although he cannot physically see me he can sense my presence and hear my thoughts. *So why so hostile in the room,* I wonder.

"Sorry, Joe. I couldn't leave without saying goodbye."

"Goodbye is not all you said, Claire; you said that you love me."

I immediately reply, "Yes, I did, and I do."

"Well then, why have you promised your love to another?'

"What? What are you talking about? You are the only person I have ever loved."

"That's not what your promised love Jayden told me. He said that you and he are destined to be together and that you are promised to him as the Wish Giver."

So that's what Jayden was talking about!

"Jayden is deluded, Joe. There is no way in this universe that Jayden and I would ever be together." Joe's expression and demeanour change. "Well, what is he playing at? Right, there's nothing more for it. I have to leave this earth and join you where you are. It is the only way we can be together."

"No way, Joe. Your life is too precious."

"But it is not fulfilled if I don't have you and now you will be leaving me again."

"I will connect with you, Joe, I promise, and then when your natural life cycle is over I will await your coming."

"It's not enough, Claire," he says, wanting to hold me like he did that night at Melody's house. With the realisation that he cannot, a tear trickles down his cheek and he drops to his knees on the floor. I drop beside him and wrap my tiny frame around his manly body.

"You can do it, Joe," I say comfortingly.

"Yes, I know I can, but I am tired of missing you and I don't want to do it anymore."

We just sit in the moment, both of us ready to surrender to the hopelessness of our unique scenario.

Suddenly I feel a presence and when I look, to my surprise I see feet before me. It is Rupert standing in all of his power.

"Come with me," he says. "Both of you."

I am confused but we both comply. Even though Rupert doesn't have as big a build as Joe, he makes up for this with his authority. I do believe we have broken a universal rule by engaging with each other. I cannot sense where this is leading, and I am not comfortable with that. I quickly glimpse to ensure that I have the twinkles. That is at least one less thing to worry about right now. I have successfully completed my mission; that is bound to be credited in my favour.

Rupert has fast tracked us to his office. He sits at his desk.

"Take a seat," he instructs us. We look at each other with a slight smirk hoping that Rupert is not a witness to it. This experience is like being brought to the head teacher's office for being naughty.

"Now I know what has been happening between you two. Claire, I have to admit that I am surprised at your behaviour. Being distracted from the mission at this point was very bad. In fact, it might have led to a young girl becoming pregnant. It just so happens that it is all working out successfully, but it could have been quite different should she not have reunited with her mother successfully."

"Yes, Boss, I understand. I am sorry," I say contritely.

"Joe, you are a handsome man who I am sure has had many opportunities to move on to a more normal relationship and have a family. Why are you sacrificing so much for something that you cannot have?"

"It's like this, Boss. We are destined to be together. I have no interest in being with anyone else. It just doesn't feel right when my heart is and always will be only with Claire. I feel as though we belong together, as if we have been connected forever and will be connected forevermore."

"Yes, well you have been. In your last lifetime you were married. Claire was the husband and you were the wife. You never had children as that gift was never sent to you. It was your love for each other that kept you alive until you were both in your nineties, something unheard of in those days. Your spirits were due to separate in this lifetime so that they could evolve individually but your connection is so strong that you cannot."

"What now for us?" Joe asks.

"This has caused much angst here for a time as I have had to have a discussion with the higher powers about your unique situation."

"Are they disappointed with my behaviour?" I ask with tears in my eyes.

"It is not that we are disappointed, Claire. It is that the issue needs to be resolved for the wellbeing of everyone involved."

"I understand."

"We have come to a solution that we feel is best for everyone," he informs us.

Joe and I sit in nervous anticipation. *What is to become of us?* I wonder.

"Joe, you love Claire with all your heart?"

"Yes, I do."

"Claire, you love Joe, don't you?"

"Oh yes, Boss. He is the missing piece of my puzzle."

"Your love in this lifetime has always been forbidden and yet it was only natural for you both to connect so early as your spirits have been inseparable for so long. We have decided that we cannot be the force that keeps you apart this lifetime."

My heart rejoices at this prospect as it was never an option before and now it is. How can this be? I am shocked to hear these words. Does this mean that Joe is staying here in the Waiting Zone?

"Now I know all sorts of things are going through your heads right now and so I want to explain the process because it is quite complex."

"Yes, Boss."

"We are not in the business of taking people out of their bodies and bringing them here. Joe, you have awareness second to none. Your connection with Claire is unique and so it has to be dealt with uniquely and that's why you are here. You will not be staying here. You will be returning to your body shortly. I am sure that your family and friends are getting very worried by now and so I will make this brief. When you return you will not remember being here in the Waiting Zone. But you will have an awareness that Claire is coming to you. Claire cannot take her previous physicality, but she will engage you and we hope that you will be aware enough to realise that Claire is the spirit inside or she will end up living the rest of her renewed time in another form. Will you be able to deal with that?"

"So, I will return to my body and Claire will be coming to stay with me on Earth forever just in a different form?"

"Yes, that is it exactly."

"That is of course if Claire wants to." Joe looks to me anxiously.

"Yes of course; this is what I want," I reply with conviction.

Then let's not waste any further time. Joe, I will leave you in the hands of my trustworthy assistant Joyce. She will escort you to dispatch and leave you in the very capable hands of Harry who will ensure your safe return."

Joe gets up, hugs me, and goes with Joyce.

"Sit down, Claire."

We both sit down, and Sydney enters the room to join us. She sits beside Rupert and passes Arianna to him. She looks deep into my eyes.

"Claire, you know that I love you like a sister. I know that you do love Joe, but I sense your anxiety about the prospect of returning to physicality full time."

"You know me so well, Syd. To be honest, I don't mind where I am and to be with Joe is a total bonus because I do truly love him. However, I know that he was brought back to me because I started to love myself again. Being the Wish Giver has brought me out of my introverted shell. I felt alive inside. I don't know if I can be the same person without continuing my purpose."

Syd listens attentively and looks to Rupert. He gives a nod of approval of her thoughts.

"Claire, what if you could have it all? Would you still want to go then?"

"What? How is that possible?"

"We can make it happen. But do you want to? Listen to your heart."

I close my eyes. I search deep down. Nothing; I feel nothing. I open my eyes and see Rupert. My heart awakens. He is pacing the room with baby Arianna who is getting bigger every time I see her. The loving connection is so strong between them as she giggles at every silly face her daddy makes. I want this for myself and I want that for Joe. Clarity has hit me like a rocket. I no longer need to shield my heart from the pain for it will soon be rejoicing in a deep loving connection that is destined for me in the now.

"Yes, I do want to go. I really do," I say.

Syd jumps up and runs around the table and hugs me.

"Oh Claire, I am so happy for you. Let the love in, it will grow."

Arianna becomes a little unsettled and so Syd takes her for a sleep and Rupert resumes his seat.

"How is this all going to work, Boss?"

"You are in a very fortunate position, Claire. It is because you were in an unjust situation so young in life that we have come to the decision to allow you this grace. When a soul on Earth is moving ahead in a damaging way we have the power of intervention, allowing that spirit to return to the tranquillity of serenity and their body to be inhabited by an entity who has earned replacement. For the physical body it is as though they are reborn again. This does not happen often, but you have earned this merit."

"How will Joe know that it is me? What if he rejects me?"

"Well that is a chance you will have to take, Claire. Nothing is guaranteed."

I hang my head. *Do I want to take this risk? If he rejects me, I will be living in another form with no physical or emotional connection to anyone on the planet . . . It is worth the chance!* I decide.

"When are we ready to do this?"

"It has to happen pretty soon as our window of opportunity is closing."

"May I go and say goodbye to Syd and Arianna?"

"Yes. I will make the necessary arrangements and call when the proceedings are ready to take place.

"Thanks, Boss," I say and then I leave. To be honest it is nice to get a few moments for isolated thoughts. I had never considered the possibility of being with Joe in physicality again and so I need the reality of the prospect of it all to sink in. Syd will help me see things more clearly.

I go to knock on the door and again she beats me to it and opens it before my hand meets the door.

In a very quiet voice she says, "Come in, come in."

I laugh to myself as I know that she loves Arianna so much, but she treasures the tranquil moments that follow a tired baby's unsettled time. I tiptoe behind her. She turns around, giggling at the sight of my silliness.

"Don't, Claire. You will make me laugh and I will wake her," she says quietly with the biggest smile on her face.

I will miss Syd. We have a beautiful bond. Even if we haven't known each other for long we both feel the connection which we know only comes from previous connection on our spiritual journeys.

Syd gets us some drinks and we relax in the lounge room.

"I am going to miss you, Claire."

"I will miss you more," I reply.

"Are you happy that you will still get to be Wish Giver on Earth?"

"Yes I am. How is that going to work?"

"Well, I had a word with Rupert and he talked with the powers that be and they concluded that because you are gifted with the ability to transcend your energy through different dimensions you will be able to carry on the work of the Wish Giver on any realm including Earth. So at least we will be able to catch up regularly which makes me feel a little better about you going. I like to think that you will be an Earth angel.

"An Earth angel? I like that. I will miss not being able to be a big part of Arianna's life."

"Well, I was thinking about that also. You see, because she has been born here she will always have the choice to explore the option of becoming human, so if you are on Earth you will be there for her when I cannot. That is such a comfort for me and I do not fear the prospect so much now."

"You have thought of it all, Syd."

"Yes, I have, Claire; I have to make sure you are safe and happy."

"Thank you for caring."

"Thank you for being wonderful." We have a special moment of happy silence that speaks volumes about our friendship. "Oh, I am so excited that you and Joe are finally going to get together."

"I am afraid to feel excited, Syd. If I put all of my hopes into it and if it doesn't come to fruition, I don't know what I will do."

"Oh Claire, relax. What can go wrong now?"

"What if he doesn't recognise me there? Rupert said that there is a chance of that happening."

"Claire, you will convince him; I know you will."

The phone rings and I sit rigid. Syd gets up to answer it.

"Hello, yes Roo, she is here . . . you're ready already? We haven't really said goodbye properly . . . yes, I know that we can connect whenever we want . . . yes, she is happy about it . . . yes, she will be with you now."

Syd hangs up the phone and opens her arms to embrace me. We both hug for a long time and then I say, "I must get going then."

"I would walk you down, but Arianna is asleep, and I can't leave her."

"I wouldn't expect you to, Syd. Good bye, my friend."

"We will see each other soon, Claire. Call me if you need me. I am always here for you." I know that she means this. That is displayed by the glow that surrounds her.

Arianna begins to cry, and Syd quickly blows a kiss and then goes to see to her beautiful baby's needs.

CHAPTER THIRTY-ONE
Detained

I begin my journey and try to arrange my thoughts in preparation for the next stage of my being. On the way to dispatch I meet Jayden.

"So, my lovely, you are leaving me for a mortal?" he says accusingly.

I decide not to answer because I don't need to justify myself to him.

"So, you won't even give me the grace of an explanation."

"Jayden, I do not have to explain myself to you. I should be really cross with you actually. You tried to sabotage everything."

"You were meant for me," he says in a desperate tone. "You have no right being with this person." Then his eyes change, and he grabs my arm and begins to pull me. I am helpless against his strength and determination. He drags me down the hall way and in through a door. It is dark, and I cannot see where I am. He blindfolds me and ties my hands and feet, shoves me onto a chair and then closes the door. I feel so helpless. I need to get out of here or I will miss the window of opportunity. I begin to cry, and tears soak the blindfold. I don't hear him, so I call for help. The door opens giving me hope that I will be rescued in time to make my deadline.

"Shut up," snarls Jayden. Not a rescuer. Him! He kisses me roughly. I want to be sick. He pulls the blindfold down over my mouth. I can taste my tears. I catch a quick glimpse of the compact storeroom I am in before he leaves again and locks the door behind him, leaving me in darkness.

What can I do? I feel as though I am smothering, and I cannot think clearly. How has it all come to this? My thoughts wander towards Joe. I fear that I may miss the chance of us being together. Why is the universe making it too hard for us to be together? Is it because we are just not supposed to connect in this lifetime? I decide to use my energy to see what Joe is doing. I am brought to a hospital and there he is lying with all sorts of machines attached to him. Irene is by his side.

"Joe, please don't leave me. You are my only brother. I need you," she wails.

I realise that Joe is awaiting my coming. He has had plenty of time to return to full consciousness and I just know that he is refusing to until I come to him. There is now so much at stake that I have to do something. I return to the darkness in search of an answer.

As I sit in helplessness for what feels like a long time my heart begins to glow. My inner guide knows that I have calmed down enough to follow guidance. I await instruction. *Connect with Syd.* Yes of course, she will be worried by now. Why did I not think of this sooner?

Syd, can you hear me? I call with my thoughts. There is no answer. I keep trying.

Claire, is that you? To my relief I finally get a reply. There is hope.

Yes Syd, it is me, I need your help.

Claire, you need to be here. Harry is waiting for you. Time is running out, she explains anxiously.

Jayden is holding me captive, Syd. I am in a dark storeroom.

Where? I need to know where? she calls anxiously but in control.

I don't know, Syd. I can't see anything. Then I remember the statuette I saw when he pulled my blindfold down. *There is a statue of Cupid on a table near the door.*

She does not reply. Has she not heard me? I feel helpless again. Nothing happens. I need to transcend. My whole future happiness depends on this moment. I so want to begin my life with Joe. I want us to have a nice house and lots of children and write poetry together and go on seaside holidays and be grateful for the beauty of nature and life itself. I want to finally feel grateful to be alive in my body and that opportunity is about to be taken away from me because of a crazy man's deluded fantasy. My thoughts cry *Please! Someone help me!*

There is a scuffling outside the door and I brace myself for another encounter with Jayden. I don't care to imagine what he is capable of, so I ready myself for an escape attempt. The door knob begins to turn and as soon as the door opens I kick as hard as I can with my bound legs. Jayden goes flying and hits his head on the Cupid statue. He is lying dazed on the floor, so I take my chance. I bounce my chair closer to the door, then bounce around so I will be in position to use my bound hands to grab the handle. But I turn to find Jayden blocking my exit. I can't believe it. There is no hope now.

"Where do you think you are going?" he says in the creepiest voice I have ever heard and slams and locks the door.

"Claire are you in there, Claire?" Syd's call from outside in the hall is followed by desperate knocking on the storeroom door.

I mumble through the gag.

"I hear you, Claire, brace yourself. We have to bust the door open."

Jayden and he arms himself with a large vase. I mumble a warning. Did she hear me? The door busts open and Jayden launches himself at Syd with the vase. She sidesteps, and he falls through the doorway. The vase smashes on the floor and Rupert is there to intercept Jayden before he causes any further damage.

"I always knew you were trouble," Rupert says, leading him away by the collar.

"Oh Claire, are you okay?" Syd asks while untying the piece of cloth around my mouth.

"Yes," I sob through my tears of relief. "How can I ever thank you?"

She unties my wrists and ankles and helps me to stand.

"Did he hurt you?"

"No but it was horrible, Syd," I shudder and hug her as if I will never let her go.

"You are safe now," she comforts me. "I'm sorry to rush you but we have to get going, Claire. I hope we can make it in time."

Holding hands, we run as fast as our legs can carry us to dispatch where Harry is waiting.

"Well thank goodness, young lady, we may just get you there," he reassures us.

Syd quickly says, "Go! Run, Claire, and good luck."

I am fast tracked through dispatch with no time to adjust my mindset but there will be time for that when I arrive. I just need to get there. Will I transfer in time? I shut my eyes and wish.

I open my eyes to realise that the process of transcending has occurred. I am in a place with white walls. A hospital. A nurse is beside me holding my hand.

"That's it, love. Come on, you can do it," she coaxes me to consciousness.

"I need to see Joe," I whisper.

"Joe who, love?" the nurse asks.

"Joe Harvey is he here too?"

"The coma victim? Yes, I am also nursing him. Do you know him?"

"Yes, and I love him," I declare.

She smiles and says, "Come on, love, let's go see him. Maybe you are the answer we need."

In no time at all I am in Joe's room. The nurse steers my wheelchair to his bedside and I take a hold of his hand.

"Joe, can you hear me?" I ask softly. His hand in mine send's ripples of feelings through my entire body. His hand squeezes mine and I know that he is coming around. The nurse sees this and excitedly calls the other nurse to witness the miracle of his awakening. It is not long before he talks.

"Claire, is that you? Have you finally come?"

"Yes, Joe, it is me."

"But I thought her name was Carol. That's what it said on her documents," says one of the nurses, sounding confused.

"I don't think that matters at the moment," replies her colleague.

Joe opens his eyes and lifts his head to look at me. Instantly his expression changes and he pulls his hand from mine. My fears are realised. I remember I look different and he does not know it is me inside this other body. Everything I have done has been for nothing.

I ask to go to the bathroom, so I can see my new physical appearance. My heart is heavy because of his rejection and I realise I wasn't given sufficient time to consider the possibility of that. That was probably part of the transition process, but I had to come so quickly that I did not have time to brace myself for the worst-case scenario.

I shall not give up though. I have some healing to do before I go full swing into a relationship with Joe anyway. The encounter with Jayden has shocked me and I can still feel the aftermath of the incident rippling through my spirit. I will be kind to myself for a few days and then I will come back.

We arrive at the bathroom and I have not heard one word the nurse has said along the way as I was deeply immersed in my own thoughts.

"Thank you. I can walk from here," I say.

"Right love, ring the buzzer when you are ready, and I will come for you," she says helpfully.

I smile and enter the bathroom. There is a large mirror situated above the sink. I am nervous and try to hold off seeing my full appearance. I keep in mind that my new body has not been through a good time of late and that is why it has become available for me to occupy. I gather up enough courage to look and so I place myself in full view.

I blink a few times as I am taken aback. I wasn't aware I had any expectation about what my new physicality would resemble but I was not expecting this. The dyed black hair is styled and all over the place. The rings in my nose and all the way up my ears may be confronting to some. Make up from the night before is smudged around my eyes and I am very pale indeed. I now understand why Joe has rejected me. I must make my new form resemble my own style and appearance. Then I may stand a chance.

I sound the buzzer and the nurse comes to my aid. I explain my dilemma about Joe not accepting my appearance the way it is by saying he hasn't seen me for some time.

"I never used to be this radical, so I would be grateful for any help," I say.

"Ah." She smiles and nods. "Leave it with me."

Later that day, Nurse Gail comes to visit me.

"Now young lady, this is my sister Francis. She will sort out your hair. And here is a bag of clothes that I hope will fit you."

Tears of gratitude fill my eyes. "Thank you so much. How can I repay you?"

"You can get that guy to recognise you, fall madly in love and name your babies after me," she says, giggling her way out of the room.

She has a big kind heart I think as she departs.

CHAPTER THIRTY-TWO
New Life

The next day I stand in front of the same mirror. I see a new me. A new me that I feel more comfortable with. The jet-black locks have been replaced with a light brown bob style. The nose rings and ear rings have been taken out and I have a little colour in my cheeks, courtesy of the makeup Gail provided. The clothes are perfect: black trousers and a purple camisole and blouse set. Even the shoes are spot on. I decide not to wait any longer and visit Joe again.

When I arrive at his room I take a moment to peer through the window in the door. He is sitting upright in the bed reading a newspaper. I am relieved that he has made a full recovery. When I open the door and walk in, he turns his head and acknowledges me.

"Hello," he says and then gets back to reading his paper.

"Hello," I reply.

I am disappointed that he has no instant reaction to my presence.

A thought comes to me. *Finalise your wish, you are the Wish Giver.* At this moment I realise that my wish has been coming true all along, but I hadn't realised it. I have not opened myself up to the possibility of receiving and that's why it is not happening easily. I catch a glimpse of a twinkle and so I find the courage to approach Joe. I am ready to be happy forever.

"Joe, it's me, Claire," I say, awaiting a reaction.

He lifts his head from the paper and looks at me. He stares deep into my eyes which are the gateway to my soul in the hope that I am telling the truth. I put my hands in my pockets as I feel slightly nervous. I feel something and so I take it out. It is the envelope with the beautiful letters Joe left for me. *How did they get there?* I feel a presence, and, in the corner, I see Syd with baby Arianna, swaying to and fro in a rocking action to soothe her. She makes a sign for me to give them to Joe and so I comply.

"Can I give you these?" I ask and then hand him the envelope.

He smiles and hugs me.

"Claire, I always knew you would find a way to come back to me."

I am filled with relief and love. I watch as the twinkle rises and shines its beautiful energy on us as we lie in sheer bliss on the hospital bed. I watch Syd retrieve the twinkle. She blows me a kiss and then disappears. In this moment I am in Heaven.

Suddenly Joe jumps off the bed. He disconnects the monitor that is attached to him.

"Joe, what's wrong?"

Grabbing me in his arms he replies, "My gorgeous Claire, there is nothing wrong at all. I am now complete. It is time for us to go make my house our home."

It is really happening!

"Oh, and we have a ring to choose along the way. Do you like diamonds or sapphires?"

I go weak at the knees and heat rushes to my cheeks.

"Oh, don't be shy, my princess. I will take care of you forever more." He lifts me up and swings me around.

Just at that moment the door opens and in walks Nurse Gail with Irene.

"Isn't it a sight to behold?" Nurse Gail says.

"Joe, what are you doing? Are you okay?" Irene asks in concern.

"Never been happier, Sis." He puts me down and brings me closer to Irene. I feel our instant connection.

"Hello, I am Irene, nice to meet you," she says warmly, holding out her hand.

"Hello, I am Claire, nice to meet you too," I say in response.

She then proceeds to give me a welcoming hug. "Welcome to our family. We have heard so much about you over the years and I am so glad to finally meet you. Are you here to stay?"

I look at Joe and we hold hands and stand side by side.

"Yes, I am here to stay."

Joe hugs me and we all leave the hospital together, never to be apart again.

EPILOGUE

The true magic is when it all comes together

Well nobody ever said that being an Earth angel would be easy but oh goodness, it is fulfilling. I have it all. I assist the Waiting Zone with the distribution of twinkles whenever there is need. The rest of my precious time is spent with my husband who by the way does have his moments but is still perfect in my eyes.

I know that because of my past experiences, both good and bad, I am now living true to myself. I know that I will always have life's challenges ahead of me to endure but I also know I am strong enough to endure them. I now have the ability to approach these challenges from a place of love and wisdom that I have gifted to myself simply because I now live my life in love, forgiveness and peace for the best for me and for those whose lives I touch. I cannot be truer to myself than that.

My future is glorious. I have never planned for my future before; this is new to me as I have always resided in the pain of the past. I am now aware that I have the potential to make my future anything I want it to be and with Joe by my side and sharing in my aspirations, I feel invincible. I know I can truly love and be loved in return. I am looking forward to children in the not so distant future, something I never allowed myself to hope for previously.

My first mission as the *Wish Giver* will always be in my heart; it changed my life and now I live my life connected to all of the ladies whose twinkles I delivered. They are now my family. Heaven on Earth is possible if you believe it is possible. It will find its way to you. Never lose faith.

ABOUT THE AUTHOR

Karen McDermott currently resides in Perth, Western Australia, with her husband and six children, after emigrating from Ireland in September 2008. Her children are the most important things in her life. Writing and publishing come a close second.

She came from Ireland—a place of magical beauty—and she now resides in Australia—a place of inspiration and opportunity; these two special, but very different places, together, give her the passion and determination necessary to incorporate positive writing in her life daily.

Karen successfully completed a diploma in humanities, which instilled in her a desire for learning new things; this, combined with the experience of a miscarriage, led her to write this book in order to give hope and a degree of understanding to women who suffer such pain.

Karen has had many successes in life and writing is one she is proud of.

Find out more about Karen at
www.makingmagichappenacademy.com
www.karenmcdermott.com.au

MORE BOOKS IN
THE ENLIGHTENMENT SERIES

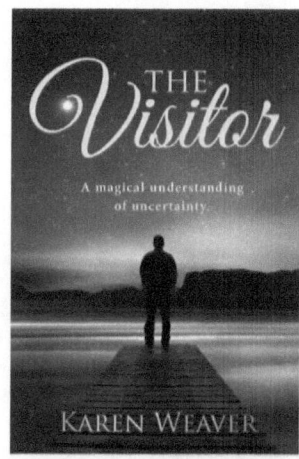

Check out all of Karen's books at
www.makingmagichappenacademy.com